Only
the
Dead
Within

Kensington Books by Lisa Childs

The Bane Island Series

The Runaway

The Hunted

The Missing

The Buried

The Grave Diggers Series

The House by the Cemetery

Only the Dead Within

Novellas

Afraid: Three Riveting Stories of Suspense

Published by Kensington Publishing Corp.

Only the Dead Within

LISA CHILDS

KENSINGTON
PUBLISHING CORP.

kensingtonbooks.com

KENSINGTON BOOKS are published by

Kensington Publishing Corp.
900 Third Avenue
New York, NY 10022

Special book excerpts or customized printings can also be created to fit specific needs. For details, write or phone the office of the Kensington Sales Manager: Kensington Publishing Corp., 900 Third Avenue, New York, NY 10022. Attn. Sales Department. Phone: 1–800–221–2647.

The K with book logo Reg. U.S. Pat. & TM Off.

ISBN: 978-1-4967-4901-7

ISBN: 978-1-4967-4902-4 (ebook)

First Kensington Trade Paperback Printing: August 2025

10 9 8 7 6 5 4 3 2 1

Printed in the United States of America

The authorized representative in the EU for product safety and compliance is eucomply OU, Parnu mnt 139b-14, Apt 123 Tallinn, Berlin 11317, hello@eucompliancepartner.com.

Only
the
Dead
Within

Chapter 1

The wind whistled through the cemetery, hurtling leaves across the grass and the graves and even into the mouths of the swans that gurgled out water into the fountains. Tyler Hicks pulled up his hood and hunched his shoulders, bracing himself against the cold slap of that breeze. Bracing himself like he had to for other slaps.

Other blows.

He didn't want to go back. But how much longer could he stay here before someone found him? His time was running out.

Mom kept leaving him voicemails and messages.

"You need to come home, Ty. You need to talk to that CPS investigator. Tell her what you told the other one."

That everything was fine at home. The bruises were from a stupid fight at school. Or he fell down.

Or . . .

Anything but the truth.

He never told anyone the truth. Not even Noah, and he'd

really wanted to. But he was so used to lying that he hadn't been able to do it. Then Noah had fired him.

God, he wanted to talk to Noah, to tell him what he'd been too afraid to tell him before. Maybe that was why he was hiding here, sleeping in the equipment building that Noah didn't know he still had the key for, and hanging out in the cemetery where he'd worked over the past summer.

Because he wanted Noah to find him. Not that CPS investigator. Claire Underwood. She'd left him a voicemail, too. "Tyler, I really need to talk to you as soon as possible. We can speak at your school with a counselor present or with another adult."

Because he wasn't an adult yet. He was only sixteen. That was why . . .

That was why he was trapped.

But what if Noah could be that adult? Maybe then Tyler would be able to tell the truth, finally, to him and to CPS investigator Claire Underwood. On the voicemail she sounded older than the last one he'd talked to, who must have been fresh out of college because she'd been young, like just a few years older than he was. She hadn't realized he was lying, but maybe this one would if he agreed to talk to her.

Or maybe he would just stay here in Gold Memorial Gardens. He'd found enough places to hide. And at night, which it was now, he walked the grounds like the grave digger was rumored to walk them. Using the light of the full moon as his guide, Tyler continued through the cemetery toward the edge of the woods and lowlands where the cheaper plots were located, which was where the grave digger was buried. Years ago, before they had the special equipment they had now, some old man used to dig the graves by hand the night before funerals.

Tyler used the toe of his sneaker to clear the fallen leaves from a flat tombstone and revealed the words and numbers chiseled into the granite: *Lyle McGinty 1899–1990*. Despite all the time Tyler spent in the cemetery, he'd never seen the ghost of the old man other people claimed they saw here at night. He had seen a light a couple of times, something wavering in the distance in the cemetery that encompassed acres and acres of land in Gold Creek, Michigan. The light was supposed to be the old man's lantern.

Tyler might have also heard a scrape or two, which was supposed to be the sound of the old man's shovel hitting rocks and stones as he dug a grave.

The wind kicked up again, hurtling the leaves so hard that they stung his face. Tyler flinched like he did when that hand swung toward him, and he shivered, too, from the cold and the sudden fear. Thick clouds moved over the moon, blocking it from his sight, plunging him into darkness. Hell, he couldn't see a damn thing.

Blindly, he fumbled in his pocket for his cell. When he pulled it out, the screen lit up with notifications of missed calls and texts. But he had no interest in returning any of those. Instead he intended to make a call, or maybe just send a text.

He scrolled through his contact to the Golds. Gigi. She was in his class at school, but they never talked. Either she was shy or a snob. Her brother, Toby, was probably in his contacts, too, and also that new girl, Sarah. She actually seemed pretty cool, especially for a kid who'd been homeschooled before moving here. But he couldn't dump his problems on her; she'd been through a lot since she showed up in Gold Creek with her mom. The whole Gold family had been through hell since the old man had died a few weeks ago, so he really shouldn't bother them. But Noah was the only adult Tyler wanted with him if he actually agreed to meet this new CPS lady. So he stopped scrolling at Noah. His fingers shook a little when he texted: *I know you hate me, but I need to talk to you. Please.*

He hoped Noah didn't hate him, but Tyler knew that he'd really, really disappointed him. And that sucked. For both of them.

Noah didn't have to give him a second chance. He didn't even have to answer him.

Tyler let out a sigh and slid his cell back into his pocket. It didn't matter. Nothing mattered anymore. Even if Noah answered him back, Tyler was still trapped.

He wished he could just disappear like the ghost of the grave digger. Because while Tyler had seen that wavering light before and heard the scrape of the shovel, he had never seen him before. Well, he'd never seen anything other than some mist around that light. But that was just mist, fog, whatever. It hadn't been a ghost. He hadn't actually seen the ghost.

Until now. Until the clouds shifted away from the moon and Tyler saw what was standing right in front of him. But was this a ghost or a real person or something even worse?

The shovel swung toward him, the moonlight glinting off the metal blade. He didn't even have time to flinch before it connected. Pain radiated through his skull, and there was a loud ringing in his ears. His knees buckled, and he dropped to the ground. But he was conscious, and he reached for his cell to call for help.

But before he could even pull the phone completely out of his pocket, the shovel swung toward him again and everything went black.

Gold Creek, Michigan, was a nightmare Claire Underwood had vowed to never relive. Yet she was driving through that nightmare right now, the headlights of her state vehicle barely penetrating the thick darkness of the night. The darkness made it hard for her to see the numbers on the mailboxes along the road. But she had to be close.

She'd actually been back in town a few weeks already. But nineteen years ago, when she'd made that vow at fifteen, she'd still been young and naive enough to think she could make a fresh start and leave the past in the past. And whenever she thought of it, she liked to pretend it was just a memory of a grim fairy tale. Just a bad story someone had made up. Fiction. Nothing that had actually happened, in a place that never existed.

But now she was finally where she needed to be, as the headlights illuminated the correct numbers on the side of a dinged up and rusted mailbox. She braked in front of it, but she didn't turn into the driveway.

Not yet. She had to wait for backup. She had to abide by the rules, or she wouldn't just be relocated, she might lose her job entirely. She snorted at the thought, though. Child Protective Services was always understaffed; they couldn't afford to fire anyone unless that investigator wasn't doing their job. Claire did her job, sometimes too well. So maybe she could have refused the relocation to Gold Creek without repercussions. But she hadn't been willing to risk it.

And maybe some of the issues she'd been having were about this place, and she needed to come back to figure out what was real and what wasn't. Or if *she* was even real anymore. As lights illuminated her back window, she glanced into the rearview mirror and noticed her own reflection first. While she was pale, she wasn't a ghost. Her eyes were big, staring back at her through the lenses of her black framed glasses. And she'd bound her curly hair back with a clip. She looked real.

On the outside.

On the inside . . .

Red and blue lights flashed in her rearview. Just once, before the SUV that had pulled up behind her went dark. This was what she'd been waiting for. But instead of turning into the driveway, she pushed open her door and stepped out onto the crumbling asphalt of the street. This area wasn't like other parts of Gold Creek, with the big houses on large lots where the roads were often repaved and well-maintained. She'd grown up around here where the long dirt driveways led back to small houses or manufactured homes sitting in the middle of un-kempt acres. When she'd lived in this part of Gold Creek, the main road used to be dirt, too, like the driveways, with enor-mous potholes.

When she started toward the SUV, the driver side door opened, and she saw the emblem on the door. Gold Creek Sheriff's De-partment. She'd been waiting for a deputy to show up before approaching this family again, but the person who closed the door and started toward her wasn't a deputy. Luke Sebastian was the sheriff now, but he'd once been a kid like her who'd needed someplace safe to live.

"Claire, is that really you?" he asked, and he extended his arms as if he intended to hug her.

But Claire stepped back and held out her hand instead. "Sheriff Sebastian," she said. "I'm surprised you even remem-ber me."

"Of course I remember you," he said.

"I didn't expect you to," she admitted. But she had an idea why he had, because it was real. That nightmare. It had hap-pened, and she wasn't the only one who couldn't forget it. "A lot of kids went through your parents' house, and I was just there for a couple of months. I think you might have even been gone to the army or navy or whatever when I was staying there." She remembered him, though, because he was one of the Sebastians' success stories. He'd always stayed out of trou-ble and had devoted his life to service, first in the military and now in law enforcement.

"Marines," Luke replied. "And I was gone for most of your stay, but my parents talked about you a lot back then—"

"I can imagine why," she muttered. She shouldn't have come

back; it was clear too many people remembered what she'd spent the last nearly twenty years trying to forget.

"They still talk about you, Claire," he said. "They're really proud of you."

She wasn't a success story like Luke; she was just a survivor. She shrugged. "I'm surprised *they* remember me, with all the kids they had going through their house."

"They remember every one of them," he said with affection.

Clearly he believed that. After over a decade as a child protective services investigator, she wasn't sure she did. The Sebastians might not have had as many short-term fosters as some families did, where kids stayed only until other family members could be located. The kids, who were just someplace for a few hours or days, were probably forgotten. Like she should have been, since she'd only stayed with the Sebastians a couple months. She wasn't the only one who'd stayed for a short time, though; she'd had a friend who'd passed through that house quickly, too. And she still wondered where he'd ended up.

"That's kind of them," she remarked, then reminded him of why they were there. "I have been trying to track down Tyler Hicks. His school counselor reported seeing bruises on him. Not the first time."

"You think it's abuse?" He pointed toward the driveway. "Parents?"

"I don't know what to think," she said. "I haven't been able to interview him."

For some reason her new supervisor had ranked the case a priority two, which allowed seventy-two hours before initial contact and the interview. Claire had been trying to find him from the minute she'd been assigned the case forty-eight hours ago. The bruises, along with not being able to locate him, had Claire feeling like it should have been a priority one case, which allowed only twenty-four hours to make contact and ensure the child was safe. But her supervisor had, with great irritation, pointed out that the prior case had been closed on the family because there were no concerns of abuse. That investigator, who was no longer with CPS, had believed the kid's story about a fight at school.

But Claire had been doing this a long time, so long that she didn't really believe anyone anymore.

"So the parents aren't letting you talk to him?" Luke asked.

"Mom and stepdad," she said. "Dad skipped out a while ago. Mom insists that the kid, like his dad, has run off, probably crashing with friends, because he doesn't want to rat out one of those friends over the bruises." She snorted slightly, doubting that it was a friend he didn't want to rat out.

"You don't believe her?" Luke asked.

She shrugged. "I have often had parents try to hide their kids with other family members so that I can't interview them."

Luke sucked in a breath. "Oh, I didn't realize that. I haven't been the sheriff very long and have only gone out a couple of times with CPS before this. And in the Marines, as an MP, I had a few domestic situations I needed to investigate, but I guess there wouldn't have been many places for them to hide their kids on the base."

"I wouldn't have thought there would be many places in Gold Creek, either," she said. But she'd had a friend disappear never to be seen again. Had Peyton run away, or was he just *gone*?

Luke let out a shaky sigh now. "You'd be surprised."

"Probably not," Claire said. "Not after nearly a dozen years of doing this job."

Luke whistled. "That's impressive. From what I understood from other CPS investigators, people usually don't last long in your career."

She shrugged again. But what she really wanted to say was, "It helps when you're already dead inside." Because that was how she felt, how she'd felt for so damn long.

"Hello? Is there someone out here?" a female voice emanated from the darkness.

Claire recognized it from their calls. "Mrs. Buczynski, it's Claire Underwood."

"I saw police lights," the woman said as she stepped out of the shadows into the light of the state vehicle Claire had left running on the street. Mrs. Buczynski's home didn't sit as far off the road as some of the others, but still she would have had to be staring outside to see that brief flash of lights before Luke had shut them off again. Mrs. Buczynski turned toward the sheriff. "Did you find Tyler? Is he in trouble?" She glanced toward the dark SUV then, as if trying to see inside it.

"Why would he be in trouble?" Luke asked.

The woman wrapped her arms around her thin body. Maybe she was cold since she wore only a flannel shirt over a tank top and jeans. Or maybe she was nervous. "I don't know. I don't know why he hasn't been home, either, since the school started this whole misunderstanding."

Claire held in her snort of derision. Misunderstanding. God, she'd heard that word so many times. *This is just a misunderstanding.* So you didn't molest your child?

You didn't strike them?

You didn't treat someone dependent on you, someone you're supposed to love, so horribly?

Sure, it was just a misunderstanding.

"You haven't reported Tyler as missing," Luke said. "Ms. Underwood is the one who came to me. Why haven't you contacted me about your son?"

"I . . . I . . ." the woman stammered. "I thought he had to be missing seventy-two hours to report him."

"Tyler is under eighteen," Luke said. "You should have reported him missing immediately."

The woman shrugged. "But he does this sometimes. Skips school, hangs out with his friends, crashes with them. If I called every time I didn't know where he was, I'd be calling you all the time." She glanced nervously at Claire then. "That doesn't make me a bad mother. That's just how it is with teenagers, Ms. Underwood. Do you have kids of your own?"

God, no. She wanted to say that, but she just shook her head and ignored where Mrs. Buczynski was going with that, where all parents went to—her being unable to understand parents since she wasn't one. She didn't have to have kids in order to know when they were being abused or neglected. She knew because she'd once been one of those kids herself. "So you haven't heard from or seen Tyler since the school called CPS?"

The woman shook her head. "No. I think that spooked him. He didn't like all the unnecessary attention and questions from . . ."

"The last investigation," Claire finished for her.

The woman shrugged. "That was stupid then, too. The school overreacts."

And this mother underreacted. Or maybe that was just because she knew exactly where he was and how he'd been hurt.

"Do you have anything on his phone?" Luke asked. "Any tracking devices?"

The woman's eyes widened as she stared at the sheriff. Her eyes were dark while her hair was nearly white it was so bleached. "I . . . I don't know."

"Do you pay for his phone?" Luke asked.

She nodded. "Yeah, the only job he had was this past summer and it didn't last long before that prick Gold fired him." She gasped. "Guess I shouldn't say bad stuff about that family in this town. But . . ."

Everybody always said bad stuff about the Golds, even back when Claire had lived here. They just never dared to say it to their faces, at least not to the older Golds. The younger ones had been taunted and called ghouls at school. But the older

Golds had too much power in this town, definitely over the old sheriff and probably over this one, too.

"The Gold family has been through a lot," Luke remarked softly and sympathetically.

Claire hadn't been back long enough and didn't care enough to listen to town gossip, but she faintly recalled something making the national news about the Golds. Even though she couldn't remember exactly what it was, she didn't ask. She wasn't here about the Golds.

"We need to find Tyler," she reminded his mother and the sheriff.

"Yes," Luke agreed. "Mrs. Buczynski, if you pay for his cell phone, you can give me permission to have the company locate where it is, if you don't have the app on your phone. Sometimes the app is installed and you might not know it. Can I see your phone, Mrs. Buczynski?"

The woman stiffened and her arms tightened around herself. "I . . . I . . ."

"Don't you want to find your son?" Claire asked.

"Of course I do," the woman replied, her thin body bristling with defensiveness.

She just didn't want the sheriff to find whatever else she might have on her phone, Claire concluded.

"I will look only for the app," Luke assured her. He must have drawn the same conclusion Claire had. "I won't open your texts or any other private communications."

The woman stood there, almost as if she hadn't heard him, for a long moment. Then she finally pulled her phone from the back pocket of her jeans. "It's not like I have anything to hide," she said. "It's just awkward having someone look through your stuff."

Claire thought about the messages on her phone. There was nothing on it that was awkward or embarrassing. No sexting.

Not even flirty texts. Mostly just work conversations, except for the coworkers who talked about TV shows and documentaries they'd watched.

"I promise, just the app," Luke said.

She held up the cell to her face, probably to unlock it, and handed it to him.

"You do have the app," Luke said. "And Tyler's phone is on it."

Had his mother lied about it then?

"I . . . I didn't know that," she said. "Could someone else have put it on there?"

"If your phone was unlocked," Luke said. He touched the screen, pulling open the map that pinpointed the teenager's location.

Claire didn't need to read the address to know the location from all the little tombstones and crosses on the screen. "He's at the cemetery." There was only one in Gold Creek, because the Gold family had had the monopoly on death in this county for generations. Then that monopoly had extended to other areas in other states. Their local family business had gone national, maybe even international for all she knew or cared.

"What the hell would he be doing there?" his mother asked.

"Kids hang out there a lot," Luke said.

So not much had changed in Gold Creek since Claire had lived here nearly two decades ago. Hopefully they didn't also still disappear from the cemetery like they had nearly two decades ago. That was where Peyton had been heading the last time she'd seen him.

"Other kids, yeah, but not Tyler, not after that prick fired him," his mother insisted.

Claire couldn't help but wonder which prick she was talking about. Thanks to the old patriarch's multiple marriages, there were a lot of Golds. "Who, specifically, fired him?" she asked.

"Noah," Mrs. Buczynski replied. "He's the one who takes care of the cemetery, the modern-day grave digger. Tyler was helping him with lawn maintenance and stuff. But for some reason the prick fired him and threatened that if he ever found Tyler on the property again, he would have him arrested for trespassing."

"You don't know what that *some* reason for his getting fired was?" Luke asked. "Because that seems like a pretty extreme reaction from Noah."

Noah was a few years older than Claire was, but she remembered him as a high school senior to her freshman. And she remembered something else about him that unsettled her, too. So she wasn't a bit surprised at how extreme he or any of the Golds had been. All of them were as odd as they were entitled.

Mrs. Buczynski lowered her head and stared down at the ground as if she couldn't hold the sheriff's gaze any longer. "I don't know. But we should go get him, shouldn't we?"

"I do need to speak with Tyler as soon as possible," Claire said. She should have already interviewed him.

"Don't I have to be there when you talk to him, like last time?" his mother asked.

The fact that she'd been present when he'd been interviewed last time might have affected what the kid had actually felt comfortable telling the previous CPS investigator.

"No, he just needs to have an adult with him," Claire said. And she glanced at Luke. "I think the sheriff will qualify for that, as long as Tyler consents."

"But I'm his mom," Mrs. Buczynski said. "I should be the one protecting him."

"He doesn't need protection from me," Claire assured her. "I just need to ask him a few questions and make sure he's safe."

"That's all we all want, right?" Luke pressed the woman as he handed her phone back to her. "To make sure he's safe. Ms. Underwood and I will find him and talk to him."

"Bring him home," Mrs. Buczynski said, her voice so sharp that it was an order, not a request.

But that wasn't an order she could give. Claire needed to interview the kid, and then she would assess whether he would be returned to his home or removed from it. That was the job of a child protective services investigator, to make sure the child was safe.

The woman didn't give her or Luke a chance to reply; she just turned around and headed back down her driveway toward the house with lights aglow in the windows except for where the silhouette of a man blocked the light. He was tall and broad. Maybe the stepfather.

"I'll meet you at the cemetery," Claire told Luke. It wasn't a place she particularly wanted to go, especially at night. The only time she'd gone after dark had been another one of the many nightmare experiences she'd had while growing up in Gold Creek.

"Follow me there," Luke told her.

"I remember where it is," she assured him. Despite her efforts, she'd never been able to forget.

"I'd still like you to follow me," Luke said.

She shrugged. It didn't matter who got there first, just that they found Tyler and made sure he was all right.

Maybe Luke thought he'd offended her because he added, "It's just that a lot of bad things have happened in that cemetery."

"Lately?" She narrowed her eyes. "Something that isn't just more of the grave digger lore?" She'd grown up with people sharing the legend of the grave digger at slumber parties and around campfires. And in the very cemetery itself. Kids had hung out there to catch a glimpse of the ghost. But then some of those kids had never been seen again.

They'd run away. That was what the police at the time had determined. And her friend had had reason to run, just like she had. She hadn't run fast enough, though.

"The things happening in the cemetery lately had nothing to do with the grave digger," he said. "But I spent enough time there that I don't know anymore how much of that legend is lore and how much is true."

"The new sheriff believes in ghosts?" Claire asked, her lips twitching with a slight smile.

"The *new sheriff* believes in being careful," he said. "I already made the mistake of thinking that Gold Creek was safe. I didn't realize how dangerous it could be until it was too late. And, tragically, some people lost their lives."

So Gold Creek was still exactly how Claire remembered it: dangerous.

Then she remembered the story that had made the national news recently. "Some Golds died," she said. "Gregory Gold the first." His death, or rather his murder, had dominated all the headlines for a bit.

"Some other people died, too," Luke said. "A young woman he was involved with, a private investigator, his first ex-wife, his oldest son, and his oldest daughter."

A gasp slipped out of Claire. "That is a lot of deaths. But *I* would never make the mistake of thinking that anywhere is safe," Claire said, "especially not Gold Creek."

"I'm sorry, Claire," he said. "I didn't forget what happened to—"

"Stop," she said, and used one hand to wave off his apology while she used the other to open the driver's door of the state vehicle. "It's fine. Let's go find Tyler." And then because she could see how uncomfortable she'd made Luke, she tried to lighten up and teased, "Before the grave digger gets him."

But Luke didn't laugh. He didn't even smile. Maybe he actually believed in ghosts.

She didn't. But then she didn't believe in much of anything anymore.

Despite all the deaths last month, there were still too many people in that house by the cemetery for Noah Gold. The "house" was much more than that, though, with four levels of stone and brick. There was a funeral parlor on the main level, preparation rooms, crematorium, and cold storage in the basement with living quarters on the second and third floors above ground. Even with all that space, Noah couldn't escape from the madness inside the house. There were too many personalities, too much arguing even now that the old man was gone. Just like when he was alive, his family was still fighting for his favor, for control, for money.

Gregory Gold I had to be loving it . . . wherever he was.

As Noah walked through the cemetery, he passed the Gold family mausoleum where his father's ashes were interred. The wind picked up, howling around Noah almost like a banshee cry over the dead. But nobody was really mourning Gregory Gold I. Maybe he was the one howling, in protest of his death and the way his body had been dispensed. Gregory Gold I hadn't wanted to be cremated; he'd always said it would feel too much like hell. Was that where he was now?

Or was he just like the grave digger, wandering around here somewhere in the gardens, hiding among the graves? Someone else *was* hiding around here. And Noah had a pretty good idea who it was.

He'd found a duffel bag in the office off the maintenance building. It had been stashed behind the couch where Noah slept sometimes when he wanted to escape from the madness and chaos of the house. He'd intended to crash there tonight and had found that bag when he'd dropped his phone behind the couch and had to move it. And when he'd picked up his phone, he'd seen the text: *I know you hate me, but I need to talk to you. Please.*

That text was from Tyler. Noah didn't hate the kid; in fact, he'd been hating himself since he'd fired him. Something else was going on with the teenager. Noah had suspected that even before he'd caught him selling drugs in the cemetery. But once he'd caught him, he'd had no choice but to terminate him and threaten him to never return. Because if Tyler came back and someone else caught him dealing, they would have him arrested.

Noah hadn't wanted the kid to get into legal trouble. He'd figured Tyler already had enough personal problems with his family. Noah knew his mom and stepdad, and he wouldn't have trusted them to raise a kid. But CPS had already investigated and left Tyler in their household. So what did he know?

He didn't have kids, and he tried as much as he could to keep his distance from the ones in the house, even though they were his nieces and nephews. He'd kept his distance from Tyler since firing him, too. But it sounded like the kid needed his help.

"Tyler?" he called out into the darkness, raising his voice to be heard over that ominous howl of the wind and the crack of branches moving, the rustle of leaves being swept along with the sharp breeze. "Tyler!"

Noah started across the cemetery toward the grave digger's grave. That was where he'd caught Tyler dealing, which made sense because it was where a lot of teenagers hung out, hoping to catch a glimpse of the grave digger's ghost. Based on the money he'd found in that duffel bag, he figured the kid had to be dealing again, so this was probably where he was, where the other kids from town would show up.

At least the kids from the house knew not to come out here anymore, especially after dark. They'd been through a lot over the past month.

Maybe Noah should try to be supportive of his nephew and nieces, too, instead of avoiding them. But first he had to stop avoiding *this* kid.

"Tyler!" he yelled again, but the wind picked up, as if trying to drown him out. And branches moved, as if trying to slap at him or catch him as he walked around and under the massive, old trees.

When the boy had texted him, Noah had assumed he'd wanted to meet, but Tyler hadn't said where or when. Maybe he expected Noah just to text back. He drew out his cell, but instead of texting, he called the teenager. That was easier than all this damn texting and Snapchatting everybody else did.

First he heard music in his ear from his cell speaker, and then the music echoed from somewhere in the darkness. It was just barely loud enough for him to hear above the wind, but too distant for him to figure out exactly where it was.

"Tyler, I don't hate you," he assured the kid. "You don't have to be afraid."

But Tyler did need to explain some things. About the money. About crashing in the equipment building. Noah wanted to know why Tyler was staying here most of all, and he also wanted to see the teenager, to make sure he didn't have more bruises that he explained away too quickly, as if he'd rehearsed the explanation. But the music just continued to peal out as his call went unanswered.

"Tyler, I can hear your phone," he said. "I know you're here." But he couldn't see him in the darkness. He could see only the shadows of swaying trees and branches.

He should have grabbed a damn flashlight before he'd left the maintenance building, but he knew the cemetery so well, despite its size, that he blindly and instinctively knew his way around it. He knew where he was by the sound of the water gurgling in the fountains and the scent of the flowers planted all around the grave sites. Each area of the cemetery had different smells: roses near the house and around the fountains; lilies near the mausoleums; lavender toward the back, where the cemetery ended and the woods and marshy swamp began.

Also, when there was some light, he could see the monuments, statues, and tombstones. He knew where he was.

But where the hell was Tyler?

Using the sound of that music, like he used the gurgle of the fountains, he kept hitting redial, making it play again and again, so that he could pinpoint where it was coming from. In order to follow it, he stepped off the paved road that ran through the cemetery and onto the soft grass. He walked toward the musky smell of the marshland. This portion of the cemetery had actually once been part of the swamp long ago, but then it had been drained to provide more burial space for cheaper plots. The drained water had been routed into ponds behind the marshland or scattered around the memorial gardens.

Leaves and fallen twigs crackled beneath the soles of his hiking boots. Hopefully they'd just fallen in this wind, because Noah wanted this area as carefully maintained as the rest of the cemetery. His crew, however, didn't like to be around the grave digger's grave. Tyler hadn't minded, though.

He hadn't minded at all.

"Tyler?" he called out. He took another step, but something besides leaves crunched beneath the sole of his boot. Plastic and glass snapped and shattered, and the music stopped. He'd found Tyler's phone. And he'd broken it.

Alarm shot through him. Not over a cell. But over the teenager who would never willingly have been separated from it. Even when Tyler had been working for Noah, he'd always had it on him. "Tyler!" he yelled with urgency now.

When he'd found that bag in his office, he'd suspected the teenager was caught up in something messy. Maybe even dangerous.

He swiped the flashlight feature on his screen and stepped

back to shine his light onto Tyler's phone. Even in the dim glow from his cell, he could see the blood on it. Bright red and fresh. It wasn't Noah's. Only his work boot had touched it. The blood had to belong to someone else.

Tyler?

It had to be his; he probably wouldn't have given up his cell without a fight. The kid was definitely involved in something very dangerous.

But was Noah too late to help him?

Chapter 2

The wrought iron gates of Gold Memorial Gardens stood open, as they always did. If they didn't want trespassers inside at night, why didn't they close them?

Maybe they didn't want to limit anyone's time to mourn and visit their loved ones' graves. But the only people she'd known who visited after dark were the teenagers who'd visited the grave digger, and they had always parked on a dirt road near the swamp at the back of the cemetery and walked to the grave digger's grave from there. So maybe the Golds had realized that closing the gates wouldn't keep out trespassers anyway, and there was really no point at all.

Despite having enough ghosts of her own, teenaged Claire had once accepted a challenge to seek out the grave digger's grave. She'd also been looking for her friend. She hadn't found Peyton or seen the ghost that night, but she'd seen other unsettling things. Hopefully that would not be the case tonight.

The police SUV stopped at the funeral home, its brake lights shining in the dark. Maybe the paved roads that wound through the cemetery weren't wide enough for the four-wheel-drive vehicle, but they were wide enough for her state car, so she drove past the sheriff. The low beams of the headlights barely penetrated the darkness, so she flipped them to high. The brighter light bounced off headstones and monuments and statues, casting shadows over the manicured grass.

Shadows. Not ghosts. Ghosts weren't real, not even the ones Claire had; they were just memories she wished she didn't have. Now was not the time for her to dwell on the past, though; she had a kid to find, one she instinctively knew was in trouble.

Because he was here.

Somewhere.

Luke should have kept the mother's phone, so he could keep tracking Tyler's. But they'd been lucky she'd let him look at it at all. The cemetery wasn't that far from Tyler's house, so he should still be here. But where?

Her headlights didn't glint off any metal; there were no other vehicles in the cemetery. Maybe because the drive was so narrow, the trees crowded it, the branches of the ones on either side stretched out to each other to form a canopy over the drive, blocking out the stars and the faint moonlight. Moss hung down from those tree branches, dangling down nearly to the windshield, like hands grasping for her out of the darkness.

"I hate this place." Even now, as an adult, as much as she had as a teenager. She was here for the same reason that had brought her here all those years ago . . . to find a missing kid.

Why would Tyler want to hang out here, especially after being fired? Why would anyone want to hang out in a cemetery? Unless they were ghoulish like the Gold family, or the *ghoul* family, as everyone in town had always called them.

One of those swaying tendrils of moss dipped low and

swiped across her windshield like the bristles of a carwash, blocking her vision. Then the vehicle shook, and metal clanged as something struck the hood. She stomped on the brakes, and whatever it was scraped across the metal and dropped down onto the lane in front of her. With a shaking hand, she shifted into park, threw open the driver's door, and stepped out. A long strand of moss brushed across her cheek and over her shoulder, leaving a wet and cold trail on her skin. She shuddered and swiped at it.

Then, with breath held, she walked around the side of the car toward the front. She wasn't sure what had fallen, what she'd hit, and she was so damn afraid that it was a living being. She nearly closed her eyes, but instead forced herself to look. Seeing a tree branch lying in the beam of the headlights, she released her breath in a ragged sigh of relief. The branch was long and thick and so heavy that it had dented the hood of the state vehicle. She wasn't sure she could move it. And even if she did, she wasn't going to try to drive any farther down that path under that canopy of branches and moss. The car was the least of her worries right now. She had to find the teenager.

"Tyler!" she yelled. "Tyler? Where are you?"

She was pretty sure he was still here, and if he was, he was probably by the grave digger's grave. Although she'd been gone a long time, she still remembered where it was. But it wasn't the only grave she knew that was way out there on the edge of the grounds, toward where the land turned to marsh and swamp. The cheap area.

Despite all the years Lyle McGinty had worked for the Golds digging graves by hand throughout the night, they hadn't given him a better plot or a monument. He only had a flat tombstone marking his grave. For Claire, that said it all about the Gold family: all they cared about was money, not people, not loyalty. Perhaps not even the law.

Where was the sheriff? Why had he stopped at the house and not continued into the cemetery? If it was because his SUV was too big for the lane, where was he? Why wasn't he walking out here? He must have gone into the house. Was he warning the Golds about their search?

Maybe that was the right thing to do—get permission to be on the property since it was so late at night. But if they didn't want trespassers this late, they needed to close their damn gates.

Standing on the lane, under the canopy of branches and moss, she peered around, but the only light in the cemetery came from her vehicle. There was no light behind her; the sheriff wasn't coming.

Technically she should wait for him, but she had this sudden urgency to find the teenager, to make sure that he was safe. Because she had a horrible feeling that he wasn't.

Ducking low beneath those tendrils of moss, she hurried down the lane toward that area of the cemetery where she would find the grave digger's grave. Hopefully not his ghost or anyone else's, though. Just the teenager, alive and well.

"Tyler!" she called again, making sure to pitch her voice loud enough to be heard over the wind.

Was he not responding because he didn't know who she was? Or because he did?

"Tyler, I'm Claire Underwood from Child Protective Services," she identified herself. "Please come out. I need to talk to you."

She needed to make sure that he was safe and unharmed. Because that horrible feeling was gripping her, chilling her more than the autumn wind that whipped across the grounds, that whipped those strands of moss at her as the trees swayed. Another branch cracked, so close that Claire gasped and ducked like she would have in Detroit, suspecting that it was a gunshot.

But the only shots usually fired around Gold Creek were hunters shooting at deer or small game. But that was a long time ago, and based on what the sheriff said, things had apparently changed. The place was even more dangerous than it had been.

She stepped off the paved lane onto the grass, trying to get out from beneath that canopy of branches. It was as if the trees had come alive in this wind, trying to hurt her.

"Tyler!" she yelled.

Had a tree limb struck him like it had her vehicle? Was he lying out there somewhere? Hurt?

Or was he just ignoring her like so many of the other kids she'd tried to help? She knew why; they didn't trust her. They didn't trust anyone. And she could so relate to that.

"Tyler!" Her voice cracked, her throat straining from yelling for him. But she had to find him. She was so worried he was in danger.

Finally she saw light, but it wasn't coming from the direction of the house where the sheriff had stopped. It was a wavering light moving through the trees across the grounds from her. The grave digger's lantern?

That was what that was supposed to be. She'd seen it that night she'd come here, but she hadn't admitted it. She'd figured it was just another teenager, or one of the Golds, trying to scare her. She'd already been used to fear by then; she'd felt it so often in the first fifteen years of her life.

And now even though she'd thought she was over all that, that she wasn't even capable of feeling much of anything anymore. That was actually a good thing, especially in her line of work. She didn't care enough that it was crippling. She could stay objective. Uninvolved. And just do her damn job.

Which was all she wanted to do now.

Find a missing kid.

Not the damn grave digger's ghost.

But then a sound reached her ears while she was straining to hear Tyler. This sound wasn't a kid though. It was the scraping noise of metal hitting rocks or stones.

The sound of the grave digger's shovel.

What the hell?

Maybe it was just the kid messing with her, trying to scare her off so that she didn't bother him. Or bring him back home?

"Tyler," she called out. "Talk to me and I'll do whatever I can to help you." She would have promised that she would make sure that he stayed safe, but she knew better than to do that. There were only so many promises she could keep when judges and families were involved.

From her own experience, she knew that judges liked to keep families together, sometimes even when that wasn't in the best interest of the child. She always tried to do what was in the best interest of the child, which was the reason she'd been forced to leave the last county she'd worked for and take another open position.

Every county in Michigan had open jobs for CPS investigators. She hadn't really had to come back here. And right now she was wishing like hell that she hadn't, because it was as if that light was moving toward her, as if the grave digger was coming for her.

"Tyler!" Maybe it was him messing with her, trying to scare her away.

She wished now that she'd waited for the sheriff. Where the hell was Luke?

She turned around to head back toward the house, but it was so damn dark. She couldn't even see the lights from her car anymore. Had the battery already died? Because she'd thought she'd left it running.

She reached into her pocket for her cell to call Luke and to use it as a flashlight, like she should have once she'd stepped outside the range of her headlights. She fumbled with it now until the screen lit up, which cast enough of a glow to illuminate the man standing before her.

His face was in shadows; she couldn't see it, just the width of his broad shoulders. He was tall, too, towering over her. And the way he stood there so silently scared her.

He wasn't a ghost. There was nothing wispy or insubstantial about him. But she would almost have rather found the ghost. She opened her mouth, but instead of yelling for Tyler, she just screamed.

And she hoped that Luke or Tyler or somebody heard her, somebody besides the person standing so intimidatingly in front of her.

Noah flinched at the scream, which was so loud and so close that it struck him like a slap across the face. Instinctively he reached out to stop her, but she smacked his hands before he could even touch her.

"Get off me! Stay away!"

"I'm not trying to hurt you," he said, his voice gruff. He was trying to figure out who the hell she was and why she was here. She'd been yelling for Tyler. Trying to find him to finish him off? Had she hurt the boy? Was that why there was blood on his phone? He clutched that phone more tightly in his hand and asked, "Who the hell are you?"

"Who the hell are *you*?" she shot back at him, her body tense.

"Noah Gold," he said.

She released a breath that sounded like the hiss of a pissed-off cat.

"And now tell me who you are and what you're doing here this late," he demanded. She was no teenager partying at the cemetery on the pretext of looking for the grave digger's ghost.

"I'm Claire Underwood," she said, and then waited as if expecting him to recognize her name.

A lot of people in Gold Creek did that, expected you to know who they were because they were rich and influential. Most of those people were his family, though.

He shrugged. "And?"

"I'm a child protective services investigator," she continued. "What did you do with him?"

"Who?" he asked, but he had a feeling he knew. He'd wanted CPS involved, but he hoped it wasn't too late.

"Tyler, the kid who used to work for you. What did you do with him?" she asked.

"I didn't do anything with him," he said, but admitted, "I'm out here looking for him. He texted me and wanted to talk." Noah wished he'd tried harder to do that this summer when the kid had been working for him, that he'd tried harder to find out what was going on at the kid's home.

"So you haven't seen him?"

He shook his head. But then he opened his hand and showed her the phone he clasped against his palm. "I found this."

She lifted her phone and shone her flashlight on it. And she made that hissing sound with her breath again. "There's blood on it."

He nodded.

"And it's not yours?"

He shook his head. "No." The cracked screen hadn't even scratched his skin because his hands were callused and rough from working outside all the time.

"It's Tyler's?"

He nodded. "I called him and heard it ringing."

"It's his blood, too?" she asked, and she looked at Noah like she was afraid of him, exactly the way she'd looked at him when he'd first walked up to her and she'd screamed.

"I don't know for sure," he said. He hoped like hell it wasn't Tyler's. "But I found it with the blood on it."

"Where did you find it?" she asked.

He drew in a breath before releasing it on a ragged sigh. "Near the grave digger's grave."

"And Tyler?"

He shook his head. "No sign of the kid, just his phone."

"I saw a light," she said, then turned slightly away from him and pointed in the other direction. "Moving that way."

"He's walking back toward the grave, then," Noah muttered. "Maybe he's looking for his phone." Or for Noah. And since Tyler was bleeding, he was probably hurt. Not wanting to let the kid down again, Noah started off in the direction where she was pointing.

She walked beside him and then quickened her pace, almost as if she was trying to get ahead of him and like she knew where she was going. But probably most of the people in Gold Creek knew where the grave digger's grave was located within the cemetery, in one of the plots that had once been part of the swamp. Lyle had been the one who'd drained it to make those, just as he was responsible for so much of the beauty in the gardens, not just for digging the graves.

Noah preferred being out here, in the cemetery, rather than in that house with the rest of his family. Maybe he should have moved away like his half sister, River, had. Hell, she'd run away, but she was back now. He'd never been able to imagine himself living anywhere else, though. Gold Memorial Gardens wasn't just his home; it was his life.

"Be careful," Noah said just as the woman stumbled over the edge of a flat grave marker. He reached for her again, but she jerked away. "I'm not going to hurt you," he said.

"You didn't hurt Tyler?"

"I haven't even *seen* Tyler," Noah said, raising his voice over the renewed roar of the wind. "And I wouldn't have hurt him if I had."

"That's not what his mother thinks," the CPS investigator said.

Noah snorted. "I wouldn't believe much of what she tells you."

"You know her?"

He sighed. "I know of her and her husband. And I wouldn't trust either of them." Of course that was what most people said about the Golds, too, especially after the recent rash of murders starting with his father. Even now he wasn't sure that it was all over, that everyone responsible for the murders was gone even though his dad's first wife and her son had claimed responsibility before they'd died, too. But now that Tyler was missing . . .

"I don't trust anyone," the woman replied, her tone as cold as the night breeze that whipped around them, hurling leaves across the grass as it sent tree branches swaying.

He and his crew would have a hell of a mess to clean up to-morrow, and the mercurial Michigan weather had already been keeping them busy. But he didn't care about that. He was wor-ried about Tyler and about this woman.

Along with leaves, branches were falling. The wind was so high that it tugged her dark hair out of the clip on her head and tangled it around her face.

"Be careful," he advised, but he knew better than to reach for her again, even just to steady her. "You could go wait in your vehicle or at the house and let me search for Tyler. I know this cemetery well."

"I'm sure you do," she said. "But I need to talk to Tyler as soon as possible."

"Someone made another report about Tyler," he surmised. "Will CPS do something this time?"

"Do what?" she asked. "We can only act on the information

we have. If you know something about the kid's situation, you should have come forward then and now."

"I don't know anything for sure," Noah admitted. "He told me probably the same thing that he told CPS last time. I was hoping, when he texted that he wanted to talk, that he was going to finally tell me the truth, but then I came out here to find him and found that phone instead." And that scared the hell out of him.

"Teenagers are obsessive about their phones," she said, her voice a bit shaky. Or maybe that was just the wind making her sound like that, whipping her words around them.

"Tyler especially so," Noah said. "I don't think he would have left that area until he found it."

"The light I saw must be him walking back to find it."

"He would have had to go get a flashlight out of the equipment shed," Noah said, and then his steps slowed. "But I would have been walking out to meet him then, and he would have passed me on his way. I would have seen him."

"Did you see the light?" she asked.

"No. I heard you yelling for him," he said. "That's how I found you."

"You crept up on me," she said, her tone accusatory now.

"I didn't know who you were," he said, "and what you wanted with Tyler." So he'd intended to check her out before making his presence known and to see if Tyler responded to her and showed up. God, he hoped the kid was okay.

"I also yelled my name and who I am and that I want to help him," she said.

"With this wind, I could only hear some of what you were saying, but I did hear you wanted to help him." But he was worried that she was too late, just like he was. He'd had a chance to help Tyler; he should have pushed him harder for the truth.

"Maybe he can't hear me, either, because of this wind," she said. And she yelled, "Tyler!"

Noah was afraid that the wind wasn't the reason the teenager couldn't hear her. "Where did you see this light?" he asked, peering into the darkness beyond the glow from his cell phone.

"Going toward the grave digger's grave," she said. "If it's not Tyler, it might be the sheriff."

"Luke's here?"

"He stopped at the house," she said. "But that's probably just because his SUV is too big for the paths."

"Most vehicles are," he said. "Did you drive?"

"Until a tree limb fell on my car."

He flinched at her words. "Are you all right?"

"Yes, it hit the car, not me," she said. "It rolled off the hood when I stopped, and it's blocking the path. So I started walking."

She obviously felt that same urgency he did to find Tyler. Maybe a tree limb had hit the kid, too, and that was the reason for the blood on his cell phone.

"I'm glad you didn't get hurt," Noah said.

However, the damage to her vehicle was going to help his half brother win the argument that Noah had been having with him since Lawrence had taken over running the business after the death of their father. Noah needed patience to deal with Lawrence being in charge. Lawrence wanted a lot of the trees cut down and the paths widened. But Noah was all about preserving as much of nature as he could. He wanted to also preserve the vision of the cemetery as memorial gardens, not make it a drive-through where you dropped off your dead and then your flowers on your next trip out on Memorial Day or the deceased's birthday or something, without ever having to leave your vehicle. He wanted visitors to walk through the gardens and appreciate and find peace in the beauty.

"We don't recommend anyone drive out here anymore," he said. "There's a sign posted on the gate and another at the house." She must have blown past both of them without reading the warning. "We have golf carts that we use to escort guests who can't walk to their loved ones' grave sites."

She flinched now and shivered. But maybe she was just cold. "No one's visiting the grave digger's grave because he was their loved one."

"He does have a daughter," Noah said.

His half sister, River, had pointed the elderly woman out to him at the last funeral. Lyle McGinty's daughter was one of the groupies who showed up for every funeral whether they knew the deceased or not. But despite how much she was here, he had never seen her visit her father's grave.

"I meant that the people who go out there don't even know him," she said. "They just know *of* him."

"Of the grave digger's ghost, you mean," he said. "He was dead before most of those people were born."

"You, too?" she asked.

"I was three or four years old when he died." He knew this because there was a picture of the old man holding him. It had been taken just a year or so before Lyle McGinty died. According to Noah's mother, even as a toddler he'd been fascinated with flowers and grass and so had enjoyed her walking him in the memorial gardens. However, one day he'd been awake before everyone else and had slipped out of the house on his own. She'd been terrified when she woke up and found him missing. While Lyle hadn't been working for the Golds anymore, he had been walking around the cemetery that morning, and he'd found Noah.

That might have been one of Noah's earliest memories, wandering around, heading toward the swamp. And if he'd made it through there, he might have drowned in one of the ponds on the other side of it. But he'd been saved when gnarled hands caught him and lifted him up. Noah had turned toward the man who'd grabbed him. Even before he'd died, Lyle McGinty had looked more like a skeleton than a living being. He'd been so thin that his skull had shown through his wrinkled skin, and his eyes had been sunken into their sockets, one of them gleaming like the glass that it was.

Other children might have screamed when such a specter picked them up, but Noah had somehow instinctively known that he was safe. Or so the story went.

Maybe he wasn't remembering anything at all but what had been repeated over the years. Or maybe he remembered so well what the grave digger looked like because he had seen him since that day, since Lyle McGinty died. Noah had seen the grave digger's ghost.

And he wondered about that light that Claire had seen moving toward the grave . . .

If it had been Tyler, Noah would have crossed paths with him. So had that been the grave digger again?

Luke shouldn't have been surprised that Claire hadn't stopped at the house like he had. Her supervisor had already warned him about her, and he remembered what his parents had said about her as well as the time he'd met her when he was home on leave.

She'd been quiet and had kept to herself. She'd also been very independent.

But then she'd had to be. He understood all too well how that felt when the only person you could really trust was yourself. He had learned to give the Sebastians a chance, though, and they hadn't let him down.

They wouldn't have let her down, either, and she probably would have realized that if she'd been allowed to stay with them. But CPS had found a biological relative who'd agreed to guardianship of her.

And so she'd moved away from Gold Creek. While she'd been away, she had gotten more than independent. According to her supervisor, she had a reckless disregard for authority and procedure. Not that it was procedure to stop at the house instead of just entering the cemetery. Not if the kid was really in trouble.

But hanging out in the cemetery wasn't something kids did alone; he was no doubt with some friends. Luke had to make sure one of those friends wasn't his niece. He was just getting to know her, and he didn't want to lose her like so many teenagers had been lost in the cemetery. Sarah was the one link to his brother who'd gone missing so long ago. The fifteen-year-old was even more important to her mother, River, who was also becoming very important to Luke.

River unlocked the door and gestured for him to come into the lobby. A lamp cast a soft glow across the patterned carpet. "Hey," she said softly, and her green eyes glowed brighter than the light.

He smiled for a second because he couldn't help it. But then his smile slipped away.

"Oh," she said as her gaze moved over his uniform. "You're not here on a personal visit."

He sighed and shook his head. "No. I'm here with CPS—"

She gasped. "What? Why? For Sarah or Gigi and Toby? I know a lot of horrible things have happened around here, but I don't think . . . God, I can't even say it. Of course my daughter was in danger."

His stomach pitched as he remembered just how much danger Sarah and River had both been in, and she was right. CPS could have been here for Sarah or visiting him about Jackson.

River peered around him and out the door he'd left open behind him. "Where is the CPS investigator?"

He sighed. "I don't know. She kept going. She's not here for Sarah or Toby or Gigi," he assured her. "She's looking for a kid that worked here this past summer, for Noah."

River let out a shaky breath. "I hope this kid is okay."

Luke nodded. "Me too. Apparently, CPS was called about him before. And also, Noah fired him."

River's forehead furrowed. "Really? Then why would the kid be here?"

Luke sighed. "Why are any kids in the cemetery?"

"Looking for the grave digger."

He nodded. "Yeah, I was able to track his phone from his mom's. He's here."

"Do you want me to get Noah for you?" she asked, glancing over her shoulder at the double staircase that led to the second story.

"No. I just wanted you, and Lawrence, to know that we were on the property. And also . . ." He'd wanted to check on Sarah. But before he could finish that thought she bounded down the staircase. She wasn't alone; the cousin who looked so much like her that they could have been twins was with her. They both had dark eyes and sleek dark hair, but while Gigi's hung past her shoulders, Sarah's was cut to her chin. And that chin . . . it was Michael's, with the dimple in the middle of it. She also had the same dimple in her left cheek that he'd had when he smiled.

"Oh, good, you're here," Sarah said.

His heart lifted. That was the first time she'd been really happy to see him.

Then she continued. "Gigi and I heard a scream a little bit ago."

"Where were you?" River asked, her tone full of dread.

"Not in the cemetery," Sarah assured her mom. "We were in our room, but we had the window open; we were listening to the wind howling."

"We didn't know if the scream came from outside or if it was inside the house," Gigi said, and she shuddered.

Sarah nodded. "I thought it might be Grandma Fiona."

"Why would she be screaming?" River asked.

"Uh, sometimes she does when that family lawyer is with her," Sarah said, her face flushing.

"Ew," Gigi said with a grimace. "Old people sex. Gross."

Luke barely suppressed the urge to laugh.

"But Grandma Fiona isn't even home," Sarah said. "We checked in her room."

Gigi shuddered. "I'm so glad it was empty."

Luke wasn't. He still didn't completely trust River's mother. While Gregory Gold's first wife, Caroline, had eventually confessed in her suicide letter to killing him and the others, Fiona, his third wife and River's mother, had been Luke's prime suspect. He would rather know where she was if the girls had really heard a scream and not because he was worried she was the victim. But Claire . . .

Claire had not stopped with him at the house. She'd gone into the cemetery on her own.

"I have to get out there," he said, already reaching for his holster. He had to make sure that nothing had happened to Claire. Again.

But Tyler hadn't sounded dangerous. Unless that was why Noah had fired him. "Uh, girls, do either of you know a Tyler Hicks?"

Sarah nodded. "He's in one of my classes. I've talked to him a couple of times, but he's kind of quiet."

"Probably because he's stoned," Gigi said. "The kid's big into weed and stuff."

Which was probably why Noah had fired him. Operating grounds-keeping equipment in the cemetery while stoned was beyond dangerous for the kid and for anyone else around him.

Gigi's face flushed. "I just know that because of what people say. I haven't . . ."

Luke smiled at her. "I know, Gigi. I want you all to stay in the house and lock the door behind me," he said.

"Luke?" River asked, her voice a bit shaky. "Do you think they really heard someone scream? It could have been the wind."

He nodded. "It probably was," he agreed. "But I have to check it out." He had to find Claire.

And Tyler.

"It wasn't the wind, Mom," Sarah said, and she sounded very certain and almost resigned. Since coming to Gold Creek with her mom several weeks ago, the girl had seen too much.

Too much death.

Luke had hoped the murders were over, that the danger was past. But he realized now that he'd been naive to think that. There was always danger. He turned toward the door he'd left open behind him and walked toward it. River followed him.

"Lock it," he told her again.

She nodded. Then she rose up on tiptoe and pressed her mouth to his. "Be careful," she told him.

Pleasure shot through him at the sensation of her smooth lips against his, and he wanted to *really* kiss her. But he heard another "ew" from behind her. He smiled and stepped back, through that open door. He waited until River closed and locked it before he turned away from the house. Even under the long portico that stretched to the parking lot, the wind whipped around him, howling just like the girls had said.

But he heard only that howl and the creak of branches and rustle of leaves. He heard no scream.

He stopped at his vehicle for a flashlight. It wasn't as powerful as the searchlight that was connected to the battery of the SUV, but the sheriff department SUV was too wide to fit through the trees on either side of the lane. He was surprised that Claire's car had. He directed his flashlight down the lane as he started toward where the grave digger's grave was. If the kid was still in the cemetery, that was where he would be.

But Luke didn't make it far before he saw the taillights of the vehicle stopped on the lane. The driver's door stood open, the motor running. But when he neared it, he found the front seat empty.

Claire was gone. She must have been whom the girls heard scream. What the hell had happened to the CPS investigator?

Chapter 3

Claire had made a serious mistake, just like she had all those years ago when she'd come here to seek out the grave digger's ghost. She wasn't looking for a ghost now, though, any more than she had really been looking for one then.

She'd wanted to find her missing friend. And now she wanted to find a missing kid. Tyler Hicks.

Both times she'd had to accompany a Gold for her search. Years ago, she hadn't found Peyton. Just another nightmare that had haunted her.

And now . . .

What would she find with Noah Gold? More of his secrets? They weren't heading toward the equipment shed, though, like she'd been shown the last time. How had she, after what she'd been through, still been naive enough to trust anyone back then, let alone a Gold?

She certainly didn't trust Noah Gold. As Mrs. Buczynski had said, he was the modern-day grave digger. But after seeing that blood on the phone, finding Tyler Hicks had taken on even more urgency. Still, she should have waited for the sheriff.

She glanced back over her shoulder, but they were so far from the house now that she couldn't see any lights from it or from the sheriff's SUV. Or even the state vehicle that she'd abandoned after the tree limb fell on it.

If only CPS investigators were allowed to carry weapons . . .

But the sheriff was here. Somewhere. So if she needed him and she screamed . . .

But she had screamed, and nobody had come to her rescue then. Fortunately, she hadn't really needed rescuing. Tyler might, though, if that blood on the cell was his. Who else would it belong to, if not him?

She glanced at the man walking beside her. His broad shoulders were hunched against the wind that had grown even stronger so that it plastered their clothes against their bodies and blasted bits of leaves and moss against them. Her skin stinging as if she'd been slapped, she flinched.

"Why would Tyler be out in this?" she asked. "Why would he be out at the cemetery at all? You *fired* him." That wasn't all he'd done, but she wasn't going to bring up the threat while they were out here alone.

Where was the sheriff?

Was that light she'd seen heading this way his? Or had that been the legendary grave digger himself?

"I think he's been staying in the maintenance building," Noah said, his voice gruff. "I found his duffel bag in it tonight just before he texted me to meet him out here." He stopped walking and stared almost reverently at the grave digger's grave. While everyone else had feared the ghost, Noah seemed to respect his predecessor. The light from his cell illuminated the engraving in the flat granite marker: *Lyle McGinty 1899– 1990.* But there weren't just those words written on the stone, there were also drops of something. It wasn't rain, although there was a faint mist in the wind now as it continued to whip around them.

Claire raised her cell so the beam of light could illuminate the area around the grave. Thin branches from the willow trees of the nearby marsh were strewn around the grass and over some of the nearby graves.

The grave she never took the time to visit was close to this, just a few yards to the right. She wasn't here to visit that grave, though. She was here for Tyler.

She called out for him now.

Then Noah joined in, his deep voice a loud rumble like thunder. "Tyler? Come out. I'm here. I don't hate you. I want to help you."

I don't hate you.

But obviously the kid thought he did. Why?

"Tyler, I'm Claire Underwood from CPS. Please come out so I can talk to you."

Their only reply was another howl from the wind and more cracking branches.

"He's not out here," Noah said.

"Where did you find the phone?"

He moved the beam of light from his phone around the grass near her feet. "It was around here."

She stepped back and trained her light on the ground as well. "Where?" And then she saw some droplets of blood sprayed across the grass. She directed the beam back toward the gravestone. Those drops weren't rain or mud; they were also blood. A wide blood spatter meant a serious wound. She'd learned that a long time ago.

She sucked in a breath. "We need to call the sheriff."

"Luke!" Noah shouted.

"Do you have his direct line?" she asked. "Or call the house where he stopped." If she called, she would have to go through police dispatch. And she was worried that there wasn't enough time. "We have to find Tyler right away."

While they could still help him.

If they weren't already too late.

The "grave digger" stood in darkness, watching the lights flickering around "his" grave. There were often flickering lights in the cemetery. Sometimes it was kids messing around, partying. Sometimes it was "this" grave digger, and sometimes it might even be the *real* one.

But now it was a woman out there, the one who'd been calling for Tyler, calling herself Claire Underwood. There was a blast from the past. A name that nobody in Gold Creek had probably ever expected to hear again.

Why was she back?

And what did she want with Tyler?

She was too late to help him.

Just as Noah Gold had showed up too late to help. But had he been early enough to see something he shouldn't have?

Early enough to see "him"?

Just in case he might have, Noah would have to go the same way that Tyler had.

Away.

Forever.

"What the hell?" Noah muttered as his phone suddenly went black, as did the space around him.

The only light came from Claire's cell as she swung it around the area, studying those droplets they'd found in the grass and on the grave. What the hell had happened here? To Tyler?

"Aren't you going to call Luke?" she asked. "You said you have his cell number."

He had told her that just moments ago, but he hadn't had enough time to follow through and make that call.

"My phone died," he said. Using the flashlight for as long as he had must have drained the battery. "You'll need to call Luke."

"What's his cell number?" she asked.

"Damn. I don't know. Once I put him in my contacts, I only use that to call him." And he hadn't had to look at the actual number since he initially put him in his contacts.

"What about the phone number for the house?" she asked. "Luke might still be there."

Since Luke hadn't heard Noah yell for him, he probably was still at the house, maybe with River. But the sheriff was too good at his job to be distracted when a kid was possibly in trouble. So he probably just hadn't been able to hear Noah shouting for him over the roar of the wind.

"I don't call the house number, either," he said.

"But you lived there all your life," she said. "You don't remember it?" She sounded skeptical, as if she suspected he was lying to her.

And he knew it sounded suspicious.

He could remember nearly every plot number in the acres and acres of cemetery, but he couldn't remember the number for the business or the house where he'd grown up and spent all his life but for the years he'd gone to college. But even when he'd been gone, Noah hadn't called home. He wasn't much of a talker on the phone—or in person, if he could help it.

But they were wasting time, time that Tyler might not have. "Just call the emergency number." Because he had a bad feeling this was an emergency.

"Can you find the house in the dark?" she asked.

"Of course." Just as he'd found the grave digger's grave earlier in the dark, he would use the scent of flowers and the gurgle of fountains to guide him, if he could smell or hear over the roar of the unrelenting wind. "But you can use your phone to light the way," he pointed out.

"No," she said. "I'm staying here in case Tyler is around here somewhere."

He didn't think that was her only reason. She was clearly suspicious of Noah. Did she think he'd hurt the boy and that was why Tyler wasn't coming out of wherever he was hiding? He hoped the kid was hiding and not hurt as badly as all that blood indicated he was.

"If somebody hurt Tyler, it's not safe for you to be out here alone," he said. "You need to walk back to the house with me."

"I don't want this area, and whatever evidence might be here, disturbed anymore," she said. "I'm going to stand here until the sheriff can get some crime techs out."

He gestured with his arms out wide even though she probably couldn't see him in the dark. "There's nobody else out here," he said, but as he did, a chill raced down his spine, raising goose bumps on his skin underneath his flannel shirt. Because he didn't feel like they were actually alone out here. He felt as if someone was watching them. Was it Tyler? Or someone else? The person who might have hurt Tyler? Or had a tree limb just fallen on him like it had on her vehicle? And maybe he'd stumbled back to the maintenance building, and they'd just missed each other in the dark.

God, he hoped that was the case. But that chill shot through him again, and he didn't think it was because of the unrelenting wind. "You need to come with me back to the house," he said. Because he did not want to leave her here alone. "Nobody's going to disturb anything."

"You already stepped on his phone," she said. "We need to preserve this area."

"Are you a cop or a CPS investigator?" he asked.

"Sometimes the jobs are very similar," she said.

"But do you carry a gun like police officers do?" he asked. Because he was worried that she might need one if they truly weren't alone out here.

She sighed. "CPS investigators aren't allowed to carry. Not even pepper spray or a taser."

He wasn't sure if that answered the question, though, because he had a feeling that Claire Underwood might do things she wasn't allowed to do. He didn't know her; he barely remembered her from school. He just remembered a little about the scandal around her, but that had been because of her family more than her. However, she hadn't stopped at the house with Luke. She'd driven into the cemetery alone, intent to find Tyler.

He was, too. And they were wasting time.

"I'm not going to convince you to walk up to the house with me, am I?" he asked.

"No," she said, her voice sharp with decisiveness and something else.

Maybe more of that suspicion.

"I didn't hurt Tyler," he said. "I want to help him, too."

"Then go find Luke," she said.

He had no choice but to leave her standing where she was by the grave digger's grave. But he couldn't help but think that Tyler had been standing there earlier tonight and something had happened to him, something that had sent blood spattering across the grass, his phone, and the grave digger's tombstone.

"Be careful," he said.

"I'm not the one walking up to the house," she said.

As if he was the one who needed to be careful.

And maybe he did need to.

Just weeks ago, so many horrible things had happened in that house and around it. Members of his family had died. His dad had been poisoned. His sister had been pushed down the concrete steps to the basement. And behind it all had been the man Noah had believed was his older brother, and that man's mother. But Gregory Gold II hadn't actually been Gregory Gold I's son; he'd been his stepson. And that man's mother,

Caroline, had killed to keep that secret. She'd even taken other lives, like Noah's sister Honora and the private investigator that Honora had hired who'd found out the truth. And a young girl who'd gotten romantically involved with Noah's father.

It wasn't just members of his family who'd been in danger then, but the people around them as well. It was all supposed to be over, the people responsible for those deaths dead, too. But Noah's dad's will had created more problems and more potential for bad things to happen.

Was that why Tyler had been hurt? Because he'd been here?

And now Claire was here.

But even though he was worried about her, he couldn't convince her to come with him. So he started off alone, in the dark, moving in the direction where he knew the house was. The grave digger's grave was so far from it that he couldn't see any lights from the house.

He couldn't even see any lights from where she'd left her car running on the lane. But he didn't need light to hear, and from the sounds around him, he wasn't alone.

Maybe it was just the wind snapping twigs and rustling leaves behind him. But he doubted it, because he could feel that stare on him like he'd felt back at the grave site. The creepy sensation chilled him, unnerved him.

But he was also a little relieved, too.

It was better that whoever had been back there, watching him and Claire, had followed him instead of staying near her. He whirled around, trying to catch a glimpse.

Trying to see who was lurking in the darkness.

Was it the grave digger's ghost?

Maybe he'd let the legend get to him over the years, but he swore that he'd seen, more than once, Lyle McGinty walking the grounds like he always had. It was as if, even in death, the man was unable to quit working. He took care of the cemetery; that was his job. But that was all he was doing.

Not hurting people.

If someone had hurt Tyler, it wasn't a ghost.

And that was not a ghost following Noah. At least not the grave digger's ghost, because Noah couldn't see that shimmer of light, that glint of an old glass eye.

"Hello?" he called out into the darkness. "Tyler? Is that you?"

The howl of the wind was his only reply, so he turned around again and started walking. But the feeling persisted that he wasn't alone. That someone was out there watching him.

Stalking him?

"Tyler?" he called out again.

The kid had to be alive. He had to be, because Noah couldn't stand seeing any other ghosts like he saw the grave digger's. Noah had been so young the first time he'd seen him that he hadn't even realized that the grave digger had already died by then. That he wasn't seeing the actual man through a fine sheen of fog.

His older half-siblings had set him straight, though, that he couldn't have seen the real Lyle McGinty because the man had died. And they'd teased him about seeing things that weren't there.

But he knew what he'd seen then, just as he knew what he heard now. And it wasn't the wind snapping the twigs behind him. It wasn't the wind whose stare he could feel boring into him.

Somebody was out there.

And the person didn't want to talk to him like Tyler had claimed he'd wanted to talk to Noah. Was that why he'd been hurt?

Because somebody hadn't wanted him to talk? What had Tyler been going to tell him?

About the drugs? About his family?

"Tyler?" Noah called out again like he had so many times before. And like so many other times before, nobody answered him. Was it because Tyler wasn't able to answer him anymore?

The blood proved he was injured. How badly?

Bad enough that he needed help. Noah increased his pace so that he was nearly jogging across the cemetery in the direction of the house. But he was blinded by the darkness, so blind that he couldn't see the ground beneath his feet.

The steel toe of his work boot hit something hard, and he lurched forward, stumbling over what must have been another tree limb. He put his arms out to catch himself and his fingers sunk into the grass that was damp from the mist of rain riding on the high wind. Mud oozed between his fingers as he tried to push himself back up.

But his hand slipped in the mud, and he fell back onto the ground, his face now in the damp grass. The rain continued to fall on him, dampening his shirt even more until it stuck to his clammy skin. And his hair was so wet, a drop trailed from it down his face.

He needed to get up, to run to the house, and not just for Tyler. He had a bad feeling that he was going to need help, too.

More twigs snapped. Whoever had been watching him, following him, was getting closer now.

He rolled over onto his back, then squinted against a sudden flash of light in his eyes. It blinded him like the darkness. He couldn't see who held that light.

He could see only a shadow looming over him. He'd been worried that it was too late for Tyler.

Now he was worried that it was too late for him as well. That he was going to be the next one of his family whose funeral would be held in the house by the cemetery.

Chapter 4

Claire expected to feel a rush of relief when Noah Gold finally left her alone. But instead she felt a rush of cold, so sharp that it bit into her skin and dug into her flesh, making her shiver. She didn't trust Noah; that was why she'd tried so hard to get rid of him.

But was he really gone?

Sure, he'd walked away from her, and he seemed to be heading toward the house. But once he was out of the beam of the flashlight on her cell, he could double back and come up behind her. Was that what had happened to Tyler?

He'd been waiting for Noah and someone had come up behind him, striking him? Or had it just been a tree branch like the one that had fallen on the roof of the state vehicle? She moved the light from her phone across the ground. There were twigs and leaves littered all around but nothing big enough that could have caused that spray of blood across the grass and Tyler's phone and the grave digger's grave.

"Tyler?" she called out. She needed to find him, needed to make sure that he was all right. If he was hurt, and she had a horrible feeling that he was, he couldn't have gone far. She and Noah hadn't come across him when they'd walked out here. So had he gone off in the other direction?

She swung around, flashing her cell light behind her where the cemetery ended and slipped off into the woods and the marsh. The long branches of the willow trees danced in the high wind, brushing across the tops of the cattails that rose up from the wet ground. There was no sign that anyone had walked through them. Wouldn't they have been trampled or at least broken if someone had?

But he could have stumbled off to the left or the right instead of straight ahead or behind him. She knew what was off to the left even though she hadn't gone there for many years. So she shone her light first to the right. There were only flat grave markers and leaves and twigs. There weren't big monuments or fountains in this cheap area of the cemetery. There was nothing for someone to be hiding behind, so she knew Tyler wasn't there.

And neither was Noah. He hadn't circled back to attack her like she was worried he might have attacked Tyler. But why would he have done anything to the teenager?

He'd already fired the kid. Why hurt him?

Then she remembered what she'd seen the last time she'd come out to Gold Memorial Gardens. While it hadn't been the grave digger, it had haunted her. Before she'd thought that people had reasons even for the horrible things they did, but then she'd learned that people could be evil for no reason at all. Just because they were.

Was Noah Gold one of those people? Or had one of the other Golds been responsible for what she'd seen that day?

It didn't matter. It had already been too late then. Was she too late now?

She'd known this case should have been a priority one, and that other case that had been closed on Tyler should have been investigated more thoroughly. Obviously, something had been going on with the kid, something that had put his life in danger.

"Where are you?" she muttered just to herself. She'd been yelling his name since she'd gotten out of the state vehicle, and he hadn't responded to her. After finding that blood, she didn't really expect him to respond now.

But she had to find him.

So she shone her light to the left now. There were more twigs, some willow branches, and many leaves littered across the ground and strewn over the grave markers.

Where was *it*? The grave she'd made a point not to visit after the funeral during which Mary Sebastian had held her hand while Pastor Sebastian had done the graveside service. Her temporary foster parents, the Sebastians, had restored her faith that there was good in the world as well as evil.

She found herself drawn to the area where that particular grave was. Claire suspected that nobody visited it, unlike the grave digger's. Nobody was left now except for her. And she'd been away from Gold Creek for so long. But even if she'd lived here, she wouldn't have visited. She felt no connection to a granite stone lying on the ground or even to the bones that lay six feet beneath the grass covering that grave.

Which grave was it, though? Where was *she*?

With the light rain streaking down her glasses and wetting her hair, she struggled to see anything at all. But she used the toe of her hiking boot to push aside some of those willow branches and leaves.

Melissa Underwood Barton, loving mother, daughter, and wife.

And Claire found a snort slipping out.

Loving? Maybe.

But she'd loved someone else more than she'd loved Claire. And in the end that love had killed her.

Was Tyler dead?

She had to focus on him. She had to find him like she should have found him days ago. Or at least hours.

Within the past few hours, he'd been well enough to send that text to Noah. Why Noah? What had he wanted to talk to him about?

She turned away from the grave, from the past, and called out, "Tyler?" When she turned, the light from her cell illuminated a wider circle, and something loomed just on the outside of that circle. Something big and dark. She gasped and raised her phone higher so she could see better. The light reflected back at her from the wet canvas of a tent. Beneath the tent were other canvases covering mounds of something.

Her heart began to pound fast and hard. Because she had a horrible feeling that she might have found Tyler Hicks.

Was this why Noah hadn't wanted her to stay out here? He hadn't wanted her to find this?

This wasn't some grave that the ghost of a grave digger had crudely dug with an old shovel. Equipment had been used for this, equipment that Noah had to know how to operate.

Had he buried the boy here?

Had he made sure that there was no way that the kid could talk to Claire or anyone else?

Noah flinched and braced himself for a blow, but he moved, rolling to his side as he tried to get out of the way of the shadow looming over him. Behind that light.

Who the hell had been following him?

He managed to scramble to his feet, but the light continued to blind him. This wasn't a small glow from a cell phone, but a high-powered flashlight.

"Noah, are you all right?" a familiar voice asked him.

"Luke?"

"Yeah, what the hell's going on?" the sheriff asked.

"I wish I knew," Noah said. "Were you following me?"

"Following you? I just started out here from the house. The girls, Sarah and Gigi, said they heard someone scream."

"It was Claire," he said. "Claire Underwood."

"You heard her scream, too?" Luke asked with concern.

"She screamed because of me. It was my fault," Noah said. "I surprised her when she was walking through the cemetery. Apparently, a tree limb fell on her car and then blocked her way."

"So that's why she left it running with the driver's door open. Where is she now? Is she all right?"

"Yeah, she didn't get hurt." Yet. But he was uneasy over leaving her where someone's blood had already been shed.

"She's a CPS investigator now," Luke said. "She's out here looking for Tyler Hicks. His phone showed that he was here."

"He was. I think he was sleeping in the maintenance building." But Noah had no idea where the kid was now. "I left Claire alone. We should get back to her. She's waiting for you by the grave digger's grave."

"Why? Did she find Tyler?"

"No. But I found his phone earlier, and we found some blood in the grass and on the grave marker." He hoped like hell that it wasn't Tyler's. But who else could it belong to?

Luke's breath was loud and shuddery. "Damn. And you thought someone was following you? You asked if it was me."

Noah shrugged. "I don't know. I didn't see anyone." Not even a ghost this time.

Luke swung his flashlight around the area; the beam glanced off monuments and statues but no person. "You shouldn't have left her out there alone."

"I didn't want to, but she didn't give me a choice," Noah said. "She wanted to protect what she considers a crime scene, and she wanted me to find you. I didn't argue with her because if Tyler is hurt, we need to find him right away."

"Yeah," Luke said. Then repeated, "Damn."

"This way," Noah said as he headed back from where he'd come.

"I know," Luke said. "I've been out here entirely too much lately."

A body had been found near that grave not long ago.

Were they about to find another one?

And what about Claire?

If someone had been following Noah, they were not anywhere around him now. So, had they gone back already to the grave digger's grave?

To Claire?

She didn't have a gun or even pepper spray if she followed the rules of her job. He hoped like hell that she didn't, that she was armed, because he had a feeling that she was going to need protection.

And then, over the howl of the wind, a scream rang out.

Because he'd already heard it once tonight, Noah recognized it as hers. Claire was screaming. He shouldn't have left her alone. And even though he started running, he wasn't sure that he and Luke would make it back to her in time to help her.

Or if he was too late again, just as he'd probably been too late to help Tyler.

Luke had told them to lock the door behind him. And River had. But she knew her daughter and niece too well to suspect that they would go back to bed without knowing who had screamed and what was going on in the cemetery. So instead of trying to coax them back upstairs and worrying about them sneaking out, she opened the French doors onto the courtyard off the lobby. The wind howled around them, sending leaves and twigs rolling across the brick pavers and into the fountain in the middle of it.

Some leaves rustled as they tumbled into the lobby and stuck to the thick patterned carpeting. Lawrence would probably be pissed. He was taking his new role as CEO of Gold Memorial Gardens and Funeral Services a little too seriously, in that he stressed over every detail. But then he'd always been the one handling the details while their father had handled the big picture. Lawrence wasn't a big picture guy, but now someone else was: River's mother, Fiona. And since she had controlling interest of the business, she'd put Lawrence in charge.

"You're sure Grandma Fiona wasn't in her room?" River asked her daughter.

Sarah nodded. "Yeah, when I first opened her door, I had my eyes closed, just in case she wasn't alone, but when I opened them, I could see that her bed was neatly made yet and the suite was empty."

Was Fiona somewhere else inside the building? Maybe in the basement prep room redoing the makeup that River had done for the recently deceased Susan Hughes who was being interred tomorrow. But Fiona hadn't seemed to care about that client since the service wasn't going to be a big one. At ninety-two, Susan didn't have any friends or much family left to mourn her. Nor had she had much money, so she was being buried in the cheap plots near the grave digger's grave.

"I really think the scream came from outside," Gigi said. "It would have been louder if it was inside the house."

With its thick walls and extra insulation, the house was pretty soundproof, so it was possible that someone had screamed inside, like that night not so long ago when Sarah had found her aunt Honora's body lying at the bottom of the concrete steps to the basement. But Sarah hadn't screamed over finding the woman with her head smashed against the ground; she'd screamed when Honora's son, Garrett, had fired the weapon he'd been pointing at Sarah and at River.

River shuddered, shaking off the memory of that gruesome death and how close she'd come to also losing her daughter and her own life. Thankfully Garrett had missed, and Luke had arrested him. River's nephew was in rehab now and after completing it, he would return to jail for a while. He hadn't killed anyone, but he could have.

"We can close the doors if you're cold, Aunt River," Gigi said.

But Sarah stepped farther out onto the patio. Reflexively, protectively, River followed her. The wind whipped her long hair around her shoulders and her face, slapping it against her while a fine mist of rain dropped over her like a wet curtain. "We should go back inside," River said. "It's cold out."

But River wasn't sure if she felt cold on the outside or on the inside, from all that had happened, from being back here in Gold Creek, Michigan. If not for Sarah and for Luke, she wouldn't have stayed after her father's funeral. But she'd needed to find out the truth about how her father died, and now she needed to find out the truth about what had happened to Sarah's dad.

Sixteen years ago, he was supposed to meet her at the grave digger's grave so they could run away together. But he'd never shown up, or so she'd believed. And she'd run away alone. She'd always believed he'd stayed behind in Gold Creek, while his brother, Luke, had always believed Michael had run away with her.

Luke had looked for him for the past sixteen years, but he hadn't been able to find a trace of him online or through searches of documents like deeds or vehicle titles or driver's licenses. So what had happened to Michael? Had he ever left Gold Creek?

Now Luke and a CPS investigator were looking for another lost teenager in the cemetery.

Besides Michael and now this Tyler Hicks, there had been a few others over the years. She and Luke had already discovered that while trying to find out what had happened to Michael.

Those kids had been written off as runaways, like River had been. But she had really run away, taking a cross-country bus trip to her grandmother's house in Santa Monica.

While there was no trace of Michael anywhere. He hadn't left with her. Had he left at all?

"There are lights out there," Sarah murmured. "I can see lights in the darkness."

River shivered. Years ago, she had seen one particular light out there, the wavering glow from a lantern. She'd also heard the scrape of a shovel hitting rocks and gravel. And, while she struggled to admit it even to herself, she was pretty sure she'd seen the grave digger's ghost. That strange collection of mist and light and movement. She shivered again.

"We really should come back in and shut the doors," Gigi said, her voice shaky with nerves. She was nearly sixteen, like Sarah, but unlike Sarah she had lived here her whole life, in the house by the cemetery. Had she seen him, too?

River considered asking her niece about the ghost, but then she heard what the girls had heard earlier. A woman's sharp scream full of terror or horror or . . .

"That's it," Sarah said, and she reached out and grasped River's arm. "Mom, that's what we heard—"

"But worse this time," Gigi cut in. "It sounds worse. Like the person's getting murder—"

"No!" River interjected. "Nobody else can die around here." They'd already lost too damn many people.

"That would be bad for business and unrealistic," a familiar female voice remarked. "People are always going to die. Even your father discovered that he wasn't immortal after all."

River turned to find her mother standing in the open doorway behind them. She was dressed all in black, as if she was actually mourning her late husband. But River wasn't sure yet that her mother hadn't been somewhat responsible for his death. Other people had confessed to killing him, but still River wondered about the truth of those confessions. Maybe they were real. Or maybe . . . The black dress Fiona wore was a little too short and a little too tight to be widow's weeds, as the funeral groupies called the clothes wives were supposed to wear when their husbands died. This outfit looked more like a cocktail dress, like Fiona had been out on the town. But she wore no shoes with the outfit.

"Why are you barefoot, Grandma Fiona?" Sarah asked. River's daughter was even more observant than she was.

Fiona Gold didn't look old enough to be a grandmother of a teenager, and she barely was, still just in her early fifties. Her hair was like River's: long and thick and streaked with lighter blond strands among the golden brown, and maybe a few silver strands, too. Her face, as always, was artfully made up. Except maybe her lipstick was a bit smudged.

"They were stilettos, and I accidentally snapped a heel," she said, and shrugged. "What's going on here? Why are you all standing out in the rain?" Even though she stood just inside those open doors, her hair looked a bit damp around her face with some curling tendrils, like she had been out in the rain, too. Maybe she'd been wearing a trench coat with a hood that had covered her head and protected her dress. And she could have gotten rid of that like she had her shoes.

"Didn't you hear the scream?" Gigi asked. "There was one earlier, and we just heard another one."

Fiona shook her head. "Who would be screaming besides my mother?" she asked. And then almost hopefully added, "Was it Mabel?"

"No," Sarah said. "After I checked your room, I checked hers. She was snoring away."

Which was probably why Mabel hadn't heard anything. But she also needed hearing aids and was too vain to admit it, like her daughter. Fiona and Mabel were very alike, which was probably why they didn't get along. But they were both loving and supportive of River and Sarah. So River felt a twinge of guilt for not completely trusting her mother.

But maybe that was partially why she couldn't trust her, because she didn't know how far her mother would go to protect her. What would she have done to Michael, all those years ago, for getting River pregnant and then planning to run away with her? Was Fiona the reason nobody had seen him again after that night? She'd lied to Luke when he'd asked her about his brother over the years; she had claimed that Michael and River were happily raising their daughter together and that Michael wanted nothing to do with him. When River had found out about her lying, Fiona had claimed that she'd only lied out of pride, that she hadn't wanted to admit River had run off alone and pregnant. But was pride the real reason she'd lied?

"So who is screaming?" Fiona asked.

"Someone out there," Sarah replied as she gestured beyond the light spilling out from the lobby. "In the cemetery."

Fiona sighed. "When are these kids going to learn that if you keep looking for the ghost, that eventually you're going to see him?"

"Have you seen him, Grandma?" Sarah asked.

There was an intensity in her daughter's voice that had River wondering if Sarah had seen the grave digger. Since they'd come to Gold Creek, she'd been out in the cemetery quite a few times. Probably more than River was even aware of; when River was a teenager, she'd snuck out to the cemetery so many times to meet Michael.

Fiona shrugged. "It's hard to say sometimes what's real and what's just a trick of the light"—she turned from her granddaughter to her daughter—"or your own mind."

River shivered again, wondering if her mother was aware that she still had suspicions about her.

Sarah shook her head, as if trying to clear it, maybe from that trick of her mind, of the grave digger. "We should call my uncle Luke," she said. "And tell him that we heard the scream again."

But sirens wailed in the distance, growing louder as they drew nearer, and then lights flashed as emergency vehicles pulled through the gates. That scream hadn't been because someone had seen a ghost.

That scream had been because something horrible had happened, yet again.

Chapter 5

Claire had found Tyler Hicks. But she wouldn't be able to interview him now. She wouldn't be able to remove him from his home if he'd been in danger there. She couldn't even remove him from where she'd found him.

In an open grave.

When she'd seen that tent over the mounds of dirt, she'd moved closer and shone the light from her cell into the hole. At first she hadn't seen him. He hadn't been in the concrete vault into which the coffin would be lowered and sealed. He'd been wedged between it and the ground next to it, on his side. Thinking he might have fallen and gotten trapped, she lowered herself into the grave next to him and tried to pull him up by his arm. Dirt had fallen from his face, and his eyes, open and wide with shock, had stared blindly at her. Blood had matted his blond hair, turning it dark, but his hair wasn't thick enough to hide his misshapen and broken skull.

Someone had smashed in Tyler Hicks's head, murdering the teenager. It hadn't happened where Susan Hughes, according to the marker, was going to be buried. It had happened at the grave digger's grave, where blood had spattered the grass and the granite marker.

"We don't know for sure yet what happened," Luke said.

Claire glanced across the console in the sheriff's SUV at her former foster brother sitting in the driver's seat. Her car was blocked in at the cemetery by the crime scene techs' and coroner's vans. The vehicle could potentially have engine damage from the tree limb falling on the hood, so towing it back to the Department of Health Services parking lot was smarter than her driving it there. Not that she intended to go right there, where her personal vehicle was parked.

She'd insisted on going with Luke for the death notification. "We won't give the parents a cause of death," she agreed.

"You don't have to go with me to do this," Luke said.

"There are other kids in that house," she said. They were young, four and six. Tyler's half-siblings. His mom's children with his stepfather. She'd read the file from the previous case. Those kids had had no marks on them, had appeared well taken care of, whereas Tyler had had bruises, and now he was dead.

That first case never should have been closed.

The system had failed Tyler; she was going to make sure that it did not fail his siblings, too. And she wanted to make sure that someone was held accountable for Tyler's death.

"He could have been hit by a branch like the one that fell on your car," Luke said. "It could have been an accident."

"Did you see a branch around?" she asked.

"I saw a lot of branches."

"Around the grave digger's grave where Noah found his phone and I saw the blood, there were only twigs and leaves. Nothing that would have done that damage to his skull." The image of his head flashed through her mind, but she was ready for it now. It wasn't like when she'd first noticed him lying in the dirt, and she had screamed. It wasn't a surprise, like Noah popping up out of the darkness had been.

She wasn't a screamer. And her throat was raw from the ones she'd uncharacteristically uttered. That was so not like her. But then she wasn't herself here in Gold Creek, which was ironic given that she'd agreed to come back here to find herself. Or at least answers.

"The techs will search the area more thoroughly," he said. "They have floodlights."

"Good," she said. "Maybe they will find evidence to lead you to whoever murdered that kid."

Noah Gold?

He'd found the cell. He'd had been so upset with the kid that he'd fired and threatened him to never return to the cemetery. But Tyler had returned.

"Or they'll find the tree branch that hit him," Luke said.

"He was hit hard," Claire said. She'd seen that up close and personally. "He didn't get hit by the grave digger's grave and then walk over to that open one. There was no way he was capable of walking with that head wound. Someone had to have dragged him there."

"You seem to want it to be a murder," Luke said.

"I don't want it to be," she said. "I just know that it is. And why are you so certain that it isn't?"

"I'm not certain of anything," Luke said. "I'm just keeping an open mind until the coroner and crime scene techs confirm what happened to Tyler Hicks."

"So your open mind will consider all suspects when you have confirmation that he was murdered?" she asked.

He glanced over at her. "I take it you have a suspect you want me to consider."

"Noah Gold," she said. "He was first at the scene. He had Tyler's phone. He might have deliberately broken it, and he would have known where that open grave was. And he tried really hard to get me away from that area."

"If he killed Tyler, why didn't he just kill you, too?" Luke asked.

"He knew you were in the area," she said. "I made certain that he knew that."

Luke sighed. "Noah had no reason to kill that kid—"

"You heard what Tyler's mother said about Noah. That he fired Tyler and threatened him to never come back to the cemetery," she reminded him. "But he came back, so that might be the reason he had to kill him." Maybe Tyler had seen what Claire had that night so long ago.

"If Noah killed every kid that trespassed in the cemetery, there would be no kids left in this town," Luke said.

"I know that some kids have gone missing from there."

Luke gasped. "You heard about Michael?"

"Michael?"

"My brother," he said. "He was a couple years younger than you, but he didn't come to live with the Sebastians until in his mid-teens. You might have already been gone then."

"He could have been there when I lived there," she said. "But I don't remember much about when I stayed with them. I wasn't there long. And when I moved in with my maternal grandmother, I left a lot behind me in Gold Creek. A lot of memories." Or so she'd thought, but for those awful dreams.

Luke sighed again. "I have a lot of things I'd like to forget, too," he said.

"From when you were in the military?" She remembered how proud his adoptive parents had been of him. "How long did you serve?"

He nodded. "I served until a year ago when I took early retirement."

"That bad?" she asked.

"My godson Jackson's last parent died, and I needed to be there for him," he said. "And I thought moving back here, to

Gold Creek, would be good for both of us. That he would be safer here."

She snorted. "Nobody's safe anywhere."

"I know. While Jackson's dad died on a deployment, his mother was just shopping with him at the mall when a gunman killed her."

She felt a twinge of sympathy for the kid, like she'd felt one for Tyler when she'd found him earlier. Maybe she wasn't as dead inside as she'd thought she was, as she needed to be in order to do this damn job.

"How is he doing?" she found herself asking, despite the fact that she already had too many other kids she needed to worry about. Her old cases, this one, her upcoming case.

Because there would always be more cases, more kids getting hurt, in danger, dying.

She'd failed Tyler Hicks. She should have found him before whoever killed him.

"Jackson is doing well," Luke said. "We're staying with my parents, who are great with him."

"They're still taking in fosters?" she asked.

He chuckled. "Nope. Just me and Jackson. I think Dad would still take them, but Mom insists that they need to retire and take life easier. He's not even preaching anymore."

"Really?" she asked. She remembered that being a pastor was the older man's whole identity, even more so than being a foster father, though he'd been good at both.

He nodded. "He does deliver a lot of sermons, though, and still presides over many funerals and weddings."

She smiled. "Of course."

"You should drop by their house," he said. "They would love to see you."

She shrugged. "I'll try to, but I think I'm going to be busy for a while, though."

"Will you get in trouble over this?" Luke asked.

"For a kid dying after a case was opened on him?" She nodded. "Possibly. It depends on the parents right now." Luke turned the sheriff department SUV into that driveway she'd nearly passed earlier in the night.

Lights still glowed in the house at the end of it. Shadows moved across the light. "They're up yet," Luke said, his voice gruff. "Probably waiting for us to bring Tyler back home."

Or maybe they'd already known what Claire and the sheriff would find in the cemetery: Tyler's dead body. She and Luke had no idea yet how long he'd been lying in that open grave. Like the sheriff had said, they would need more information from the coroner and the crime techs to determine exactly when and how the kid had died.

But Tyler wasn't Claire's main concern at the moment. Right now, she had to determine if the other children were safe in this home, with these people.

Luke shut off the engine and uttered a faint groan. "You sure you want to do this?"

"It won't be my first notification," she assured him, and unfortunately, it probably wouldn't be her last, either.

"I forget, you've been doing this a long time," Luke said. "Too long?"

He must have sensed what other people had, that something had died inside her. But that had happened long before she'd become a CPS investigator. And maybe that was why she was good at what she did. Usually.

"My supervisor talked to you," she guessed.

He nodded and his mouth curved into a slight smile. "Warned me."

She shrugged. "She's not used to dealing with what I have, because, like you said, Gold Creek seems safe." But she knew better than that, and after the recent murders Luke had told her about, her former foster brother knew better, too.

She opened the passenger door and stepped out onto the gravel driveway. And as she did, the front door opened.

Mrs. Buczynski rushed out. "Did you find him? Is he with you?" she asked, and she peered into the back of the SUV as if she could see through the tinted windows.

"We should go inside," Luke told her.

Mrs. Buczynski shook her head. "No. I just got the littles to bed. I don't want them to hear unfamiliar voices and wake up."

"I need to see them," Claire said. "To make sure that they're safe."

"What are you talking about? My babies don't have a mark on them," the woman replied, her voice shrill with defensiveness. "They're fine. They don't get into trouble like Tyler. They don't fight. They're good kids."

"Do you think Tyler is bad?" she asked the mother before Luke could interrupt her.

The woman sighed. "He's just a teenager. Does stupid stuff, you know, like teenagers do. Like I did. Like you probably did."

The only stupid thing Claire had ever done as a teenager was go out to the Gold Memorial Gardens all those years ago.

"Mrs. Buczynski," Luke said. "We need to talk to you about Tyler."

"Did you find him?" she asked. "Is he all right?" Something about the seriousness of the sheriff's tone must have given away what had happened because tears began to roll down her face. "Where is he?"

She knew he wasn't in the back of the SUV now.

"I'm sorry, Mrs. Buczynski," Luke said. "We found Tyler in the cemetery, but he had already passed away."

"That son of a bitch!" she screamed. "That son of a bitch!"

"Who?" Claire asked her. Was she talking about her son? Or Noah Gold? Or . . .

"What's going on?" a man asked as he stepped outside the house and pulled the door shut behind him. "I can hear you screaming. You're going to wake up the kids." He was in his thirties. Tall. With greasy long hair, worn and dirty jeans, and boots with mud caked on them.

Where the hell had he been? And was he the son of a bitch? The one who might have been hurting Tyler? The one who might have killed him?

Claire wanted to ask more questions, but the woman dropped onto the gravel driveway, screaming and sobbing incoherently.

"I'm sorry," Luke said. "We found your son dead."

She had found Tyler dead, but she didn't bother correcting him. She was studying Mr. Buczynski instead.

His eyes widened for a moment before he turned away to stare down at the woman crumpled on the gravel. "My son's in the house," he said. "He's sleeping. So's his sister."

"Tyler," Claire said. "We found Tyler dead."

"Fuck," the guy said, and brushed his hands through his greasy hair. His hands looked swollen and scraped. From a fight? From his job?

Claire needed more information about Vernon "Buzz" Buczynski—about both of the Buczynskis—because neither of them was asking how Tyler died. Granted, the mother could hardly speak at all, but the stepfather just kept shaking his head.

Were they in denial?

Shock?

Or trying not to give away their guilt?

"I need to see your other children," she said. "Make sure that they're all right."

"I told you. They're sleeping."

But that door opened again, and two kids stood in the opening staring out at them. "There they are," she said. She started forward, but the man reached out and grabbed her arm, his grasp tight as he held her back.

"Don't," he said. "They love Tyler."

They. Not him.

She noted all the little things that the parents were giving away. "The kids obviously know that something has happened, and I need to make sure that they're safe here."

He gasped. "What? You think I would hurt them? They're *my* kids. And they're good kids. Quiet. They do what they're told."

"Didn't Tyler?" she asked.

"Stop!" the woman shouted now. "Stop! Go away! Leave us alone! We have to deal with this as a family."

"We'll leave," the sheriff agreed. "After Miss Underwood talks to the children."

The man held her arm yet so tightly that he would probably leave a bruise. But she didn't so much as flinch. She recognized a bully when she saw one. She'd lived with one once herself. But the CPS investigator and judge hadn't believed her. And she might have wound up like Tyler, if not for . . .

"Let go of her," Luke said. "Or I will bring you down to the holding cells, Mr. Buczynski, and book you for assault of a state official."

"God, we just lost a kid," the woman said. "What are you doing? Buzz had nothing to do with it. He was here with me all night. It had to be that creepy ass Noah Gold." She was able to talk clearly now, the sobs gone even though her face was still wet.

Was she more worried about losing her husband than she was upset over losing her son?

Claire's stomach churned with how familiar that scenario was.

"I need to make sure that your other kids are safe," Claire said, and she jerked her arm free of the man's grasp and headed toward the house. Nobody tried to stop her.

But as she approached, the kids stepped back into the house. And she half expected them to slam the door in her face. She'd had that happen before, parents who coached their kids not to talk to her, who'd threatened and berated them into denying they needed help. "Hey," she said. "I'm Claire. I'm here about your brother."

The kids' pajamas looked clean, and their light blond hair was damp either from recent baths or from getting sweaty when they slept. Claire could feel the warmth emanating from the house through that open door.

"Tyler?" the little girl whispered. She was the younger one.

Claire nodded.

"Where's Tyler?" the boy asked. "Isn't he coming home this time?"

She shook her head. "I'm sorry. No. He won't, but I'm sure that he would want me to make sure that you're safe."

Tears pooled in the boy's eyes, and as he nodded one slipped out and rolled down his chubby cheek. "Yeah . . ."

"You're sure?" she asked. "Nobody has ever hit you? Hurt you?"

The boy glanced over her shoulder. She knew the others could hear her and them, could see them, too. But Luke was back there; he would notice if either parent tried to coach or threaten them behind her back.

The little girl shook her head. Then she glanced at the boy standing next to her. "Bubba hit me."

"I don't hit you," he said, and the way he said it chilled Claire. It was almost as if he was repeating something he'd heard someone else say like a practiced denial. Or gaslighting.

"She was playing with his Xbox," the dad said. "And he grabbed the controller out of her hand. He didn't hit her. They have no bruises."

Not like Tyler.

But Tyler had more than bruises now. He had a smashed skull. Who had done that to him?

And would they hurt anyone else?

* * *

Cold and tired and damp from the rain, Noah stepped inside the lobby with the intention of heading right up to his bed. Hell, he would have slept in his office in the maintenance building, but the crime techs intended to process that, too, once they were done in the cemetery. The funeral parlor lobby wasn't empty and dark like he'd hoped it would be.

Obviously, everyone else had heard the sirens and had seen the lights because they were standing around, talking among themselves. But when he walked in, all conversation ceased, and they stared expectantly at him. Or suspiciously?

That was how Claire Underwood had looked at him a few times tonight. First over Tyler's phone, then over the blood they'd found, and finally over the kid's dead body; she had looked at him with disgust and condemnation, like he was a killer.

His half sister, River, walked up to him. "Are you all right? Luke told us that he and a CPS investigator were here to look for a kid named Tyler Hicks."

He nodded.

"Did they find him, Uncle Noah?" Gigi asked. "Is that why all the police are here?"

He nodded again.

"What happened to him?" Lawrence asked now. "Why are the police all over the cemetery?"

"He's dead. It looks like someone, or something, hit him in the head." He really hoped that it had been an accident, but clearly Claire Underwood didn't think it was. And Noah really didn't, either, not after the text he'd received from the kid.

Tyler had needed help. Noah's help. But he'd been too late. Too damn late.

"That poor kid," River murmured.

"What are you saying?" Fiona asked now, her tone impatient. "Was he murdered or not?"

He shrugged. "The wind is wicked right now. There are a lot of fallen tree limbs—"

"I told you that we needed trees cut down or at least cut back," Lawrence said. "We could be liable—"

"The kid was trespassing after dark," Fiona said. "He was bound to get hurt, especially on a night like this."

"Mother," River said. "He didn't deserve this."

Noah's stepmother, Fiona, shrugged. "I didn't say that he did, just that we are not liable for him getting hurt here when he had no business being on the property after dark."

"But still, liability is a bigger concern than the aesthetics of the *memorial gardens*," Lawrence persisted, trying to win the argument he'd been having with Noah since he'd taken over as CEO.

Unlike the rest of his family, Noah hadn't wanted that job. All he wanted was to manage and maintain the cemetery. To be outside with the grass and the flowers and the trees.

And the dead.

They didn't argue with him or with each other like his family did.

He couldn't argue right now, not with his head pounding with exhaustion and with grief. He'd liked Tyler because the kid had liked working in the cemetery like Noah. He hadn't seen it as creepy and sad; he'd seen it as beautiful and safe. But it hadn't been safe for Tyler. He'd died here, like so many other people recently had.

"I'm tired," Noah said. "We can talk about this in the morning. I'm sure Luke will know more about what happened then."

"Of course, you must be exhausted," River said. "Go up to bed." His half sister showed more concern and compassion for him than his mother did.

Linda Gold stood next to Holly Gold, who was the recent widow of the second Gregory Gold. But he hadn't really been a Gold, and he'd killed some people so that information wouldn't come out. Noah's mom and Holly were nearly the same age, but Linda looked older, her hair going nearly all white since the murders began, and her eyes had a blank stare to them, almost like Tyler's. Linda had been in a daze since the death of her ex-husband and her daughter, and her grandson was in rehab. And once Garrett was done with that, he would probably have to serve some prison time for what he'd done, for his part in the madness of the Golds' fight for control of the empire of death. Noah didn't want control of the family business, just of this one cemetery. And of his own life.

"I'm going upstairs," he said as he walked past Lawrence, who wore a robe like Noah's mom and Holly did.

Gregory Gold III and his wife, Karen, were also in robes. But Fiona was still dressed, all in black, like she was actually mourning her dead husband even though everybody knew better now. The teenagers, Sarah, Gigi, and Toby were all dressed yet, or maybe they slept in the sweats and leggings they were wearing. River was dressed, too. Lawrence's kids, who were nearly as old as Noah, weren't present. Taylor and Wynn might have left again; they were in and out of the house and seemed uninterested in anything that happened in it. So maybe they were here and just hadn't cared enough to find out why there were emergency and police vehicles on the property. Mabel, Fiona's mother, wasn't present, either, but he'd figured out pretty quickly that she couldn't hear very well.

Noah wished he hadn't heard Claire's scream. That he hadn't wanted to release one of his own when he saw what she'd found. That poor kid.

If only Noah had found him first before whoever had hurt him . . .

Because even though he'd implied to his family that it could have been an accident, he was nearly as certain as Claire Underwood that it wasn't. That Tyler had been murdered.

* * *

In his dark SUV, Luke sat in the driveway of the house that had been his first real home. He'd stayed inside the parked vehicle to make a few calls and send a few texts, but nobody had answers for him yet. The coroner wasn't going to start his autopsy on Tyler until the morning. Morning didn't seem that far off right now. It was probably closer to dawn than to midnight.

That was why he'd stayed in his vehicle to make the calls, so he wouldn't wake anyone up. But when he stepped out and walked up the porch steps, he could see lights glowing within the house. Maybe Mom, Mary Sebastian, had left some on for him. Probably with a note on the table that would tell him what leftovers were in the fridge.

She loved taking care of him and Jackson. She'd loved being a mother to all the kids who'd needed mothering so badly, like him. Like Michael. Like Claire Underwood.

He opened the door as quietly as he could and pushed it softly closed behind himself.

"You're home!" Jackson exclaimed, and he jumped up from where he'd been sitting on the stairs in the dark. The lights were on in the kitchen.

"I hope you didn't stay up on my account," Luke said. "You have school tomorrow."

Tyler Hicks had skipped a few days, but now he had no option of going back. Of ever growing up.

"Sarah and Toby FaceTimed me about what happened out there." Jackson shuddered. "That you were looking for Tyler. And that you found him."

"Claire Underwood found him."

"Claire?" a female voice asked.

And he turned to find Mary Sebastian standing in the doorway to the kitchen, aglow with light.

"You're up, too?" he asked. "I'm sorry."

She sighed and touched her hair. "I have trouble sleeping sometimes. I got up to make some hot chocolate." She glanced over at Jackson who stood next to him now. "There is more than enough for all of us. And some cookies and muffins, too."

Maybe she'd overheard Jackson talking to his friends, and that was why she hadn't been able to sleep.

"Claire Underwood is back in town?" she asked.

Luke nodded. "I thought I told you that she came back home, that she's a CPS investigator now." Maybe he'd meant to tell her but hadn't, but he was pretty sure he'd mentioned it.

"Ah, that's right. Someone said something," she murmured. "Why hasn't she been by to visit?"

"She's been busy," Luke said. But he had a feeling that there were parts of Claire's life she didn't want to revisit, like the time she'd spent in this house because of the horrific reason she hadn't been able to live with her mother and stepfather anymore.

"She's been busy finding a dead kid in a cemetery," Jackson remarked. "Where was he? By the grave digger's grave?"

Luke shook his head. He hadn't been found there, but that was where Claire thought he'd been killed. Had he been killed?

"So who's this Claire?" Jackson asked. "I thought you liked River."

Luke smiled. "I do." Hell, he more than liked her, but he was still struggling with the fact that she'd been Michael's girl. That they might have been together all this time, if Michael had run away with her like Luke had believed all these years. Like Fiona Gold had told him whenever he'd asked her about Michael, but she'd lied. So where was his younger brother?

Had he wound up like Tyler Hicks nearly had? Buried with someone else?

"Claire is like Luke's sister," Mary replied. "She was one of our foster children."

"I wasn't really around much when Claire was here," Luke said. "I just know that she had some bad breaks in life."

"Haven't we all," Jackson murmured.

This kid had definitely had some.

"She lost both her parents, too," Mary told him, and tears of sympathy glistened in her blue eyes.

"I know how much that sucks," Jackson said.

"Murder-suicide," Mary said with a slight catch in her voice. "So very sad, and poor Claire found their bodies."

"That really sucks," Jackson said. "She must have been a mess when she came here."

Mary shook her head. "I remember her being very quiet and very stoic about it all, even at their funerals. They're buried there in Gold Memorial Gardens."

"Well, she's back," Luke said. And he wasn't certain he was happy about it. If she was right that Tyler had been murdered, then she'd put herself in danger because the killer could have still been in the cemetery when she'd been running around it on her own. Luke turned toward his handsome young godson who was slurping down the hot chocolate. "What do you know about Tyler Hicks?"

Jackson shrugged. "Not much."

Luke smiled. "Which means you know *something*."

"Just that if you wanted something, he was your go-to guy," Jackson said.

"Go-to guy? For what?" Mary asked.

Despite all her years of being a foster parent, she was still naive in some ways. Or maybe she just refused to let all the bad things she'd learned about affect her, unlike Claire Underwood.

Jackson glanced at Luke who nodded at him. "Drugs, Miss Mary. Like weed and some stronger stuff. But I never went to him. And because everybody knew what he was into,

I stayed away from him. I'm one of the only Black kids in this school, so the principal and teachers are already watching me extra hard."

"Jackson!" Luke exclaimed. "Why didn't you tell me that?"

Jackson shrugged. "It happens. I'm new. I'm different. I just know not to give them another reason to watch me, and eventually they back off. And it helps that my guardian is the sheriff and I'm living with saints like Mary and Pastor Sebastian."

It helped. Luke really hoped that it did, that Jackson felt safe and happy in Gold Creek. Like Luke once had.

"Somebody say my name?" Peter Sebastian asked as he walked into the kitchen wiping sleep from his bleary eyes. His white hair was mussed and a little damp as if he sweated when he slept, like Luke sometimes did. But that was because of the things that sometimes went through Luke's head when he closed his eyes. Like losing Jackson's dad, his best friend . . .

"Yeah," Jackson said. "I was saying how living with you two helps my street cred in Gold Creek."

Mary blinked and asked, "What?" She probably just didn't understand the term, but sometimes she acted a little confused. She blinked and focused on her husband, too, as if she hadn't realized he'd joined them.

Pastor Sebastian laughed. "Street cred? I'm not sure that two old fogies like me and Mary give you much street cred."

No. They gave much more than that. They'd given Luke a sense of security he'd never known.

Then Mary laughed, too. "Who are you calling an old fogey?"

"Not you, my beautiful wife," Pastor Sebastian said, and he slid his arm around her thin shoulders.

Jackson grinned at the older couple, affection lighting up his dark eyes. He loved them just like Luke did. That was why Luke had wanted to bring Jackson here.

He'd thought he was doing a good thing moving his best friend's son to Gold Creek, but there were so many things Luke hadn't considered. Like racism. And the politics that came with being sheriff. And his attraction to his brother's former girlfriend.

And murder—he hadn't considered that happening at all. But it had, many times since he'd moved himself and Jackson to Gold Creek.

Chapter 6

Last night, every time Claire had closed her eyes, she'd seen those wide eyes blankly staring up at her. Tyler's.

Then her mother's.

And even his, the man who'd killed her mother and then himself. He'd done it, so why had he looked so damn wide-eyed and surprised, too? It wasn't as if he hadn't known what was going to happen when he pulled the trigger, that his brains and blood would blow through the back of his skull and embed in the wall behind him. That crime scene had definitely been one of the goriest that Claire had ever stumbled across, worse by far than Tyler's battered skull.

Tyler.

She'd failed him, just like the system and her mother had failed her. Tyler wasn't the only teenager she might have failed. Had she failed Peyton, too?

He had been her closest friend in school and in the Sebastians' house. Last night, or actually this morning, she'd even seen his face when she closed her eyes. He had been staring up at her from an open grave just like Tyler had. Was that why she hadn't been able to find out what happened to him?

Because he'd been buried before anyone could find him?

She stood up and peered around her. The other cubicles were empty in the big open area that had once been the gym of a school that was now the Department of Health Services building. Some of the cubicles were empty because they couldn't get enough workers, and some were empty just because it was early yet this morning.

So she dropped back into her chair and closed her eyes and tried to bring up Peyton's face. He'd had delicate features and big eyes that he'd highlighted even more with eyeliner, and sometimes he'd worn lipstick and blush, too. He'd bleached his long hair blond with peroxide, and he had a slightly crooked grin that showed off a chipped tooth. His stepfather had done that; he'd been abusive just like Claire's. Maybe that was why they'd bonded as quickly as they'd had.

But then, just like everyone else Claire had cared about, he was gone. The Sebastians had said that he'd run off with a friend because he'd taken his things with him when he'd left that night. She knew he had been meeting someone in the cemetery, someone he'd been secretly seeing. He hadn't told her who it was, though, and he hadn't told her that he would leave with that person. But she could understand why he would have; Gold Creek wasn't known for being particularly open-minded.

But why had he left her, too?

"You're asleep at your desk," someone said.

And she opened her eyes to see her boss leaning over the half wall of her cubicle.

Mallory Owens was not much older than Claire, and by her own admission had not been working in CPS as long as Claire had. Mallory had been a social worker at a retirement home before this, which she'd also admitted had been a much easier job. Maybe that was why even though she was older, she looked younger than Claire did. There weren't any lines on her face or bags under her eyes, unlike the crease between Claire's brows and the dark circles around her dark eyes. Claire had even noticed a few silver hairs threading through her black hair while Mallory's hair was thick and fully brown.

"I didn't expect you to come in this early," Mallory said. "You were out late and then you must have stayed up to write that report you submitted to me."

"It's not complete yet," Claire said. "I just wanted to let you know what had happened. That Tyler Hicks is dead. His case should have been a priority one. And that previous investigator dropped the ball. She'd had no business closing that case."

Mallory closed her eyes for a moment, maybe over Tyler's death or maybe she was just searching for patience with Claire. "This probably isn't your first dead kid, not with twelve years on the job."

"Not even close," Claire admitted. There had been babies who'd died in hot cars and in their sleep. Kids who'd died in drunken driving accidents with a parent behind the wheel. Kids who'd been mowed down by mowers and four-wheelers. Kids who'd been stabbed, shot, and beaten to death. "I've had quite a few over the years." But she'd been assigned those cases when it was already too late for her to save them.

She might have had a chance with Tyler, if only she'd gotten to him sooner.

"So why is it affecting you so much?" Mallory asked.

Affecting her? She wanted to deny that, but she had lost sleep over it, over Tyler. Or maybe it was just being back here with all those old memories resurfacing that had made it impossible for her to keep her eyes closed, let alone sleep.

"I'm frustrated that this happened," she admitted. "This case should have been a priority one, and I should have tracked him down sooner." So she felt responsible. But not as responsible as whoever had killed the poor kid. Or even as responsible as her supervisor should have felt. "And I'm worried about Tyler's half-siblings still being in that house."

"Why?" Mallory asked, her tone sharp as she ignored Claire's condemnation of how this case hadn't been prioritized. "We don't even have any proof that Tyler was abused by anyone. And no matter what you think, the prior CPS investigator did her job. She talked to those little kids and to their teachers and their doctor. There was no evidence of abuse."

Claire had reread the previous report, and she intended to follow up and make sure that the investigator had actually met with the people she'd claimed to have interviewed. She'd worked with other investigators who'd been so desperate to close cases that they'd falsified records. "I need to confirm for myself that those kids are safe."

"Then once you do, we will be able to close this," Mallory said.

Claire shook her head. "We need to know what happened to Tyler before we can close anything." She wouldn't let him slip through the system again.

"The sheriff will figure that out and let us know," Mallory said.

"He shouldn't be investigating this," Claire said. "He is obviously close to the Golds."

"They helped get him elected," Mallory admitted. "And I've heard that he's personally involved with the one who recently moved back here from California. River."

"That proves my point," Claire said. "He should turn this investigation over to the state police."

Mallory shook her head. "No. Despite his involvement with River, he still did his job with Gregory Gold's murder. He brought River's mother in for questioning as his prime witness right in the middle of her husband's funeral. He thought she was responsible for his death, and for the death of her husband's pregnant mistress who was murdered during his funeral."

Claire sucked in a breath. "Wow. A lot has happened here recently."

Mallory nodded now. "Yes, several other people died, and all over the old man's money and control of the company. But Sheriff Sebastian figured it out. He even had to kill one of the murderers who pulled a gun on him."

"One of the murderers?"

"Yes. Gregory Gold II was trying to get control of the estate and the business before it could be proven that he wasn't really a Gold. Apparently, his mother conned the old man all those years ago. Caroline, the first wife, was behind everything, apparently, and she killed herself at her son's funeral."

"That sounds like quite the mess . . ." Claire had lived through tragedies herself, but this family had certainly endured a lot. And for some reason she thought of Noah Gold, of how all of it must have affected him.

"So Sheriff Sebastian can be counted on to be impartial," Mallory said. "He will do his job. And we don't even know what happened to Tyler. His death could have been an accident."

Claire didn't believe that any more than she trusted Luke Sebastian and any of the Golds. She knew better than to trust anyone.

So in order for her to close this case, she was going to have to keep investigating; she was going to have to find out what had really happened to Tyler and who was responsible. Even if she had to go back to the cemetery, to the grave digger's grave and maybe someone else's . . .

*   *   *

Noah always woke up before everyone else in the house. He liked to watch the sunrise over the gardens, the colors reflecting off the water in the fountains. But after staying up late to fill in his family on the little he knew about what had happened to Tyler Hicks, he hadn't gotten much sleep. That wasn't just because he'd been up late but because even when he'd been in bed, he hadn't been able to get any rest.

He couldn't get Tyler out of his mind. That poor kid.

Guilt gripped him, making him feel sick. So he walked right past the dining room. Even though the rest of the house wasn't awake yet, the cook was. There would be a carafe of coffee in there, but he couldn't stomach that right now.

All he needed was to be outside. In the fresh air. Away from this house and people. Then maybe he could recharge and re-center himself.

According to all the stories Noah had heard about Lyle McGinty, he'd been like that, too. That was why McGinty had liked working nights digging the graves, because he hadn't liked being around people. And he'd enjoyed the outdoors and the solitude. Even after he'd retired, he'd walked the cemetery in the early morning hours like the day he'd found Noah. Or after dark, like he was rumored to still be doing now.

Sometimes Noah thought he saw the grave digger's ghost in the morning, in the mist rising from the grass as the sky began to lighten. He didn't have his shovel or lantern then; he wasn't working, he was just walking and enjoying the peace and quiet.

Peace and quiet.

Noah craved it, too, so he quickly slipped down the double staircase to the lobby and then out the French doors onto the brick pavers of the patio. He'd just stepped out of the courtyard onto the asphalt walkway when he noticed something, or somebody, coming toward the house through the mist rising from the grass.

Lyle?

But this image was solid, not filmy, and familiar. "Luke?"

"Noah?" Luke said. "You're up early."

He shook his head. "This is a late start for me," he said. He was usually outside before the sun rose, but it was already up, a yellow orb rising higher into the sky as the pink receded.

"Well, it's early for me," Luke said, and he rubbed a hand over the stubble on his dimpled chin.

Sarah had that same chin. So had her father, Luke's brother, Michael. Noah didn't remember him that well, not even as well as he remembered the grave digger.

"I make you meet me earlier than this when we're fishing, but I don't think you're here today to go fishing with me," Noah said. They either fished Gold Creek, which was more like a river, or they fished in the ponds behind the marsh. After what had happened last night, Noah wouldn't mind shutting off his mind and just dropping a line in some calm water. The wind wasn't blowing today like it had last night, but because it had been so fierce last night, he had a lot of cleaning up today.

Luke sighed. "No, I'm not here to fish," he said, and he sounded wistful and regretful, too. "I was checking out the grave site and the building, making sure that the techs were done processing both scenes."

"Lawrence and Fiona are going to want to know about the grave site. There is a funeral today," Noah said. But that wasn't his concern. He would cover the grave and spread the grass sod whenever the deceased was interred in the vault. "Can I get back into my maintenance building?"

Luke nodded. "Yeah. It was pretty clear that nothing happened in it except for the kid staying there. You really had no idea he'd been crashing in your office?"

Noah noted how the sheriff, a man he'd considered a friend, was looking at him, with narrowed eyes, as if checking for any tells that he was lying. But they weren't playing poker. This was serious. "I had no idea he'd been staying there until I found his duffel bag behind the couch."

Luke gave the most imperceptible nod.

"So am I your prime suspect, too?" Noah asked. "Or just Ms. Underwood's?"

"I'm not even sure what happened yet," Luke said, and he was rubbing his chin again. "There are tree limbs down all over the place from that wind."

"Yeah, that's why I need to get back into my building. I'm going to need all the equipment to clean up the gardens. But I also need the truth, Luke. You don't really think a tree limb hit Tyler."

Luke shrugged. "I'm not thinking anything right now. I'm keeping an open mind since the investigation is just starting."

"Don't bullshit me, Luke," Noah said. "I found that phone with blood on it near Lyle McGinty's grave. And there was blood spattered in the grass and on the marker, too."

"So what are saying? You think the grave digger is responsible?" Luke asked, his lips curving into the slightest smile.

Noah shook his head. "I know the legend has it that Lyle McGinty is some bloodthirsty ghost killing off kids in the cemetery, but there is no fact to that legend." The man he remembered had rescued a runaway toddler from death; he wouldn't have killed teenagers or anyone else. Lyle just wanted to keep watching over the memorial gardens that he loved. But Noah wasn't about to share his opinion of McGinty with anyone else, or they would think he was unhinged from reality.

He suspected Claire Underwood already thought he was some kind of monster from the way she'd screamed when she'd first seen him last night and how she'd continued to look at him with such suspicion.

"The CPS investigator thinks I'm responsible," Noah said.

He hated that she thought he could be evil enough to kill a kid. But he couldn't deny that there had been evil in this house, in his family. People who hadn't cared at all about life. Just about money and power. His worst fear was that there were still some evil people in this house.

They hadn't all been laid to rest in the cemetery.

Would one of them have hurt Tyler, though?

He wasn't in Noah's dad's will. The old man had set it up so that even after he was dead, he was still manipulating his family, pitting them against each other. Only those who survived the probate period would inherit, leaving a bigger percentage to the ones who managed to stay alive until the estate was settled. But nobody had anything to gain from killing Tyler. Just a young life lost way too soon.

"I can't arrest a bloodthirsty ghost," Luke said. "So I hope that legend is just fiction, not fact. If Tyler's death wasn't an accident, I want to put away the person who killed him. And I want to do it before anyone else gets hurt."

"Let me know what I can do to help," Noah said. He didn't want the same thing to happen that had when his dad died. Gregory Gold I's death had been the first of a chain event of others dying until there had been six dead.

Was Tyler's death going to be just the first of many more?

Luke nodded. "I'm going to need to follow up with you later, once I know where this investigation is headed."

"Toward an accident or murder," Noah muttered. But Luke had to know what Noah and Claire Underwood already suspected: Tyler had definitely been murdered.

And the person who'd killed him needed to be caught.

The rumble of deep voices outside her bedroom window awakened River. She'd left that window slightly open for air and to stay vigilant. If anyone else screamed in the cemetery, she wanted to hear it even if just to call the police. To call Luke.

One of those deep voices was his. So she got up and hurriedly dressed, and by the time she got down to the lobby he was alone. "Hey," she greeted him, and suddenly she felt shy with him.

Uncertain.

Had he realized what she had last night? That Michael might have wound up the same way that Tyler Hicks had, buried in someone else's grave?

"Hey," he said, and he stepped close enough to brush his mouth over hers. Then he lifted his head and asked, "Are you okay?"

She nodded. "Yes, I feel horrible about Tyler, though."

He flinched, as if remembering how they'd found the kid caused him physical pain.

She was glad that she hadn't been there this time. Seeing a kid's life cut too short was so hard, no matter how they passed away. "Are you okay?" she asked.

He nodded. "Yes, I wanted to see you though. I'm sorry I didn't stop last night, but I had to notify the parents."

She touched his hand, entwining their fingers. "I'm sorry. That must have been horrible."

"Claire went with me," he said.

"I'm surprised she would want to do that," she said. "It must have been horrific."

"It was . . . strange," he said. "The mother was upset, but Claire just wanted to make sure the other kids in that house were safe. That was her focus."

"It's her job," River said. "And it must be a tough one."

He nodded. "But it's more than a job to her. Claire didn't have an easy childhood. After her stepfather killed her mother and himself, she lived with my parents for a couple of months until her maternal grandmother agreed to be her legal guardian."

River sucked in a breath of shock and sympathy and remembrance. Claire was a couple of years older than she was, so she'd been ahead of River in school. By the time River got into high school Claire had already moved away, and the gossip about her had died down. But River remembered that tragedy now, and that Claire had been the one to find the bodies of her mother and stepfather. "Wow. A life like hers, like Jackson's, like yours, really puts mine in perspective. I was privileged."

"I wouldn't call growing up in this house privileged," Luke said. "And you ran away and raised a child on your own."

She smiled at his defense of her. He hadn't done that years ago; back then he'd voiced his disapproval of her and his brother becoming such young parents. "I didn't raise her alone. I lived with my maternal grandmother." Like Claire, whom she wanted to meet. Since moving back to Gold Creek weeks ago, she had yet to make friends. Except for Noah and Toby and Gigi, none of her family had even made much of an effort to be friendly with her.

Sarah was making more friends here in Gold Creek than the teenager had in Santa Monica. So being here was a good thing for her daughter; River had to keep reminding herself of that.

"Who were you talking to earlier?" River asked. "I heard you and someone else on the patio."

"Noah," Luke replied.

"He was up already?" she asked. "He came in late last night, and he looked exhausted."

"He didn't look much more rested this morning," Luke said. "But he wanted to get back to work."

"Is that why you're here?" she asked. "You were checking the crime scene?"

"It's Susan Hughes's grave," Lawrence said, and he walked downstairs. He was already dressed in a dark suit and tie.

She'd once thought that he was so quiet and unremarkable with his average build and average looks that he was nearly invisible. But since the death of his father and his half brother and his mother, he'd stepped out of the shadows. No. Her mother had brought him out of the shadows and into the light.

Because she respected him? Or because she was manipulating him?

River had no idea, and she wasn't sure she wanted to know what her mother was really up to. Fiona had controlling interest now of the estate of Gregory Gold I. Or she would once probate was settled.

"Are we going to be able to bury her today?" Lawrence asked.

Luke sighed and shook his head. "I need another day or two."

"But I heard you tell Noah that he could go back into the maintenance building," Lawrence said.

And Luke narrowed his eyes. "You were around when I was talking to Noah? I didn't see you."

So maybe Lawrence was still capable of being invisible, or he'd eavesdropped through his window like River had.

"Nobody died in the maintenance building," Luke said. "So it doesn't have to be sealed off. But that area of the cemetery where the open grave is and where the grave digger's grave is has been cordoned off. You'll have to postpone her funeral."

"I think it will be fine," River assured her half brother. "She only has a great-niece left. I can call her if you'd like."

He shook his head. "No. I will call her. But you might want to reach out to the funeral groupies and let them know that there won't be one for them to crash today."

River smiled as she thought of the trio of blue-haired ladies who showed up at every funeral. She didn't know if it was curiosity to see how the deceased looked; her mother got a lot of compliments from them. Or if they wanted the free luncheon food. Or if it was Luke's dad, Pastor Sebastian, that they were hoping to see. It wasn't for Gregory Gold I anymore.

"I can do that," she said. She had the phone number for Estelle McGinty, the daughter of the grave digger. The woman had never married, which she'd told River she blamed on her father for chasing off every suitor she'd had with his orneriness and the glass eye he'd gotten after losing his in one of the wars. He might have fought in both the first and second World Wars.

Lawrence nodded at her and Luke, then turned and headed across the lobby to the hallway that led back to the business's private offices.

"Are you sure that you and Sarah should live here?" Luke asked. "In this house?"

"I work here now," she said. "And Sarah loves living with Gigi and Toby. She's never really had friends or any family her own age before."

"But is it safe?" Luke asked. "I thought it was all over but then . . ." He gestured out the French doors toward the cemetery.

"Tyler Hicks died," she said. "Do you think it's murder then?"

"I've been telling everyone that I'm keeping an open mind until I hear back from the coroner and the crime techs."

But she knew he wouldn't lie or deflect with her.

And he nodded. "Yeah, I think so."

Her pulse quickened with fear. "So there's another murderer on the loose?"

"It would seem so . . ." The way he trailed off left so much unsaid.

But River had to say it; she'd spent too many years wondering what was true and what was a lie. She hadn't even believed that she was really her father's daughter until a DNA test had confirmed it.

"Or maybe this murderer has been around a long time," she said. "Maybe they killed Michael and his body is lying in someone else's grave just like Tyler Hicks was."

"That thought occurred to me, too," Luke said.

From the dark circles beneath his green eyes, it was clear that those thoughts had probably kept him awake just like they had her. Maybe that was why he was up so early, too.

"Can you look through old records and find out who was buried around the time he was supposed to run away with you?" he asked.

She remembered that date well, the one for which Michael stood her up. All these years she'd thought that he'd changed his mind about running away with her to raise their baby together. Maybe he had still run away, but he'd run away from her as well as from everyone else.

But yet she had this feeling . . .

That Michael was still in Gold Creek. They just had to figure out where, and who killed him. Was it the same person who'd killed Tyler Hicks?

Chapter 7

Claire's supervisor had sent her home. She was probably lucky that Mallory hadn't fired her instead. But Gold County already had too few CPS investigators. Maybe if they'd had more, Tyler's first case wouldn't have been closed so quickly and without a thorough investigation.

Claire was going to make damn certain this one stayed open until there was justice for Tyler and that she was convinced his younger siblings were safe. She'd had a couple short conversations with their teachers and a call in to their doctor, but she'd made appointments for more in-depth interviews with them. While she'd had a lot of dead kids during the dozen years she'd done this job, she didn't want any more.

That was why she didn't go home despite her supervisor sending her there to get some rest. Mallory had probably just wanted a break from Claire complaining that she hadn't prioritized the case right. But she hadn't. And Claire wasn't like the investigators who sucked up to the supervisor so they would get less on-call hours. Claire cared only about doing what was best for the kids, not about her career.

Career.

She nearly snorted over even thinking that her job was a career. It felt more like a penance or a prison sentence. So it was probably fitting that sentence had brought her back to Gold Creek.

And now she was in the cemetery again. This time she'd left her personal car in the big parking lot next to the house. But she didn't go up to the house like the sheriff had the night before. She didn't need a golf cart ride or directions to where she was going.

She knew where the grave was that she intended to visit. And she didn't need a ride there. She enjoyed the walk, the sun on her face, and the scent of flowers wafting in the air. Even the soft trickle of the water through the fountains was restful.

It was not the same place it had been last night in the all-encompassing darkness with the wind whipping branches and moss at her like a knife thrower chucking blades at her while she'd spun around in a circle. Last night she'd been disoriented and unsettled. Even scared.

And she hadn't been scared for herself for many years. Despite the dangerous situations she'd encountered in her job—the death threats, even a few physical assaults—she hadn't been as scared as she'd been last night. Once she'd left Gold Creek all those years ago it was as if she'd been numb, and since her return all the feelings were coming back.

So maybe she'd been right to think she had unsettled business here, and that wasn't just finding out who'd killed Tyler Hicks and what had really happened to Peyton. Now she also wanted to find out what had happened to *her*, the Claire Underwood she'd been before the nightmare began.

As she walked through the cemetery, she clutched the small pot of mums she'd purchased from a roadside stand just a short distance from the Gold Memorial Gardens. But she wasn't sure yet on which grave she would leave them. Or if she would leave them at all. Her sad little rental house could use some color, and the mums were purple.

Her mother's favorite color.

She stopped walking when she reached the area of the cemetery between the grave digger's grave and the open grave where she'd found Tyler in the dirt beside the concrete vault. Then she ducked under the yellow tape that cordoned off the area and walked over to one of the graves between those two. And she stared down at that cheap marker for her mother. Melissa Underwood Barton. But the rest of it, the loving mother, daughter, wife, was covered with a bouquet of lilacs and irises. Both purple like the mums.

Those flowers hadn't been there last night. And it was still early. Who'd been out already this morning?

She spun around and surveyed the area. The crime scene tape was stretched taut around the tent poles of the canvas that acted as a canopy over the open grave. Nobody had messed with that. On the other side of her mother's grave, tape had been strung around a willow tree and some stakes to cordon off the grave digger's grave. But the tape had come loose from one of the poles, and it fluttered in the slight breeze.

But it was quiet. No howling wind like last night. No creaking of trees and snapping of branches and twigs. In fact, this area was free of the branches and twigs and even the leaves that had covered so much of the grass the night before. Had the crime techs collected it all to try to figure out if any of them had killed Tyler?

She didn't remember seeing any that would have been big enough to do the damage to Tyler's skull that had been done. Except for the one that had fallen on the hood of her car. But she suspected Tyler had already been dead before that had fallen.

She and Noah had both been calling for him, and he hadn't

answered. Had Noah already known then that the boy wouldn't be able to reply? Had he already known that the kid was dead? Had he killed him?

He'd seemed concerned about him, maybe even more frantic to find Tyler than she had been. But some liars were so accomplished that nobody would ever guess they weren't telling the truth. She'd dealt with that more than once, starting when she was young, which had her turning back toward her mother's grave.

Who had left the flowers?

Since Grandma died, there was no family left. And Claire doubted her biological father, whoever he was, had left the flowers. He'd wanted nothing to do with her mother after she'd gotten pregnant. He'd wanted nothing to do with Claire even though CPS had tracked him down after her mother died. Thankfully, they'd found her grandmother.

Because if they hadn't, Claire wouldn't have gotten away from Gold Creek until she left for college. And without Peyton here, she wouldn't have survived. Pity and shame would have suffocated her.

She drew in a deep breath now that smelled of freshly mowed grass and rain and flowers. In the daylight the cemetery was actually beautiful, like the gardens it claimed to be. Then she caught a glimpse of that crime scene tape and remembered that not only were the dead within this garden but that a teenager had also died here.

"You came back," a deep voice murmured.

He'd snuck up on her again like last night. But this time she didn't scream. She didn't even turn around to face him. Was this how he'd killed Tyler, sneaking up on him? Hitting him over the head with something? He could do the same thing to her right now.

But yet . . .

She didn't think he would.

"I don't have the answers I need to close Tyler's case," she said.

"You brought flowers," he said. "Why do that if you're just looking for answers?" His voice was louder now, and his shadow fell across her mother's tombstone as he walked up beside Claire. He must have ducked under the tape like she had and whoever had left that other sprig of flowers. "Oh, your mother?"

She nodded.

He bent down and moved the flowers off the words and the date. "You were young when she died."

"Fifteen."

"Is that when you went to live with Luke's parents, the Sebastians?"

"I was just there for a little while," she said.

"I don't really remember you."

"You never lived with the Sebastians," she said. "You always had family."

He chuckled. "Sometimes too much family." Then he sighed. "But I find myself missing the ones who've died recently."

"I'm sorry for your loss. Your father just died," she said. "I saw that on the national news." And she'd learned a lot more about it now from her supervisor just that morning.

"Murdered," he corrected her. "He and some others who lost their lives too soon, like my sister."

"Your sister died, too?" she asked.

"Six people," he said. "Including the ones who apparently were behind it all."

That was what Mallory had shared, that Luke had killed one of the murderers and the other one had killed herself.

"You say that like you're not sure," she said, and she turned to look at him now. With his intense dark eyes and overly long dark hair and sharp features, he was really good-looking. She'd thought so all those years ago, too, but he'd been one of the ghoul family that the town had both ridiculed and feared. Now she felt a twinge of pity for him and for the rest of his family.

He sighed. "I'm not sure of anything anymore." Then he shook his head and said, "But I meant that I don't remember you from school. You must have been just a few years behind me."

"I was a freshman when you were a senior," she said.

"So you were in my nephew Wynn's class," he said.

Even though the sun shone brightly on her, she felt a chill. "Yes."

"He was here for the funerals," Noah said. "I'm not sure if he and his sister, Taylor, are still here, or if they've left again."

"You're not close?"

"I'm not really close to anyone," he said.

With the size of his family, he still managed to be a loner? Like the grave digger was rumored to have been. Tyler's mother had been right about him being the modern-day grave digger.

"You live in a house full of people," she said.

He gestured around the cemetery. "But this is where I spend most of my time."

"With the dead."

"Yeah, they're quieter than my family," he said with a slight grin.

He was good-looking. But she had to remind herself what else he was. If the grave digger was the bloodthirsty ghost that his legend claimed he was, was Noah also like him in that respect?

"What about the animals?" she asked.

"What animals?" he asked. "There are some squirrels and chipmunks running around, but I don't have a dog or cat."

"You used to have animal skeletons in the maintenance building," she said. "I saw them one night." And that image—of the tiny skulls and bones and the couple of animals that had been carcasses yet as he'd waited for the flesh to rot off their bodies—had haunted her.

"What?"

"Wynn showed me your collection." And she hadn't intended to bring it up, but she was compelled now to see his reaction, his guilt, his remorse, if he was capable of feeling those things. True psychopaths weren't, though.

"I've never collected skeletons of anything," he said. "I don't even keep the fish I catch. You can ask Luke."

"I saw them that one night I came here," she said. "Did Tyler see them, too, when he was staying in the building? Is that why you fired him? Why you killed him?"

"What the fuck..." Noah said, his dark eyes wide with shock. "Are you crazy? No. You think *I* am. That I'm some kind of psychopathic killer."

"Serial killers start with animals," she said. Maybe that was why seeing Noah's collection had scared her so much. Even back then she'd known enough psychology from the books she'd read to know that was how serial killers worked. And she'd been worried that one was on the loose, waiting to kill something bigger than animals. Something human.

"Now you're calling me a serial killer?" Noah asked, again with shock and indignation.

But that could have all been an act. Psychopaths were very good at lying.

"More than one kid has gone missing from the cemetery," she said. "Tyler wasn't the first. My friend Peyton came here one night to meet someone, and I never saw him again. That was why I came here with Wynn that night, to look for him." Wynn had showed her a lot of bones that night, but those had been from animals, not humans. The skeletons had been small and maybe even more tragic because they'd had no way to defend themselves, to protect themselves.

"Luke's brother, Michael, disappeared from here, too,"

Noah said, and his forehead was furrowed. "My sister, River, was supposed to meet him out at the grave digger's grave. They planned to run away together. But when he didn't show, she ran away on her own."

"River . . ." She remembered the only Gold with the light-colored hair and the bright personality. River had been a couple of years behind her, but Claire had never hung out with her. Nor had she protected River from the kids who'd teased her for being one of the "ghoul" family. She felt bad now as she realized that she'd done nothing to stop the bullies, but she'd been focused on the bully of her own that she hadn't been able to stop.

"River's back now," Noah said. "And she and Luke are determined to find out what happened to Michael."

Claire needed to talk to Luke and have him look for Peyton as well. She turned away from the grave with the potted mum still in her hands. Someone else had already left flowers here, probably by accident. Maybe they'd been intended for the woman who was supposed to be buried today but hadn't wanted to leave them on an empty grave so they'd left them at Melissa's. Claire would bring the mum back to her rental house, but she'd stop at the sheriff's office on her way.

Noah reached out and clasped her elbow as she started to walk away from him. "Don't go," he said.

Of course he wouldn't want her to share her suspicions with anyone. That was probably why he'd killed Tyler. But yet she couldn't imagine him doing that; she couldn't imagine him hurting animals, either.

"Let go of me," she said. "Or I will scream again."

He jerked his hand off her elbow. "I'm not going to hurt you," he said. "I just want to show you that I'm not some weirdo, that there's nothing in the maintenance building."

"I'm not going back there with you," she said. "I'm going to talk to Luke."

"He'll tell you that there's nothing in there, too," he said. "His crime techs went all over the building."

"They were in a back room, where the gas and oil cans were stored." Even all these years later, she could remember the smell of gas and oil and decay burning in her nostrils.

"I'll show you that room," he said. "But I'm sure that the techs searched it already."

"Maybe you removed what Tyler had seen once he'd seen it, to protect yourself," she said.

"I have nothing to protect myself from," he said.

She cocked her head and studied his handsome face. "Everybody has something they need protecting from." But that didn't mean they got it. She knew that all too well. "Just look at your own family."

He shook his head. "I was never part of it, part of the fight for control in my family."

"A fight for control is why six people lost their lives?"

He nodded. "For money, for power. I don't want any of that. I just want to take care of this place."

"Like the grave digger did?"

He nodded. "Yes."

"So you're admitting you're like him?"

"Lyle McGinty wasn't a bad man. He worked hard, and he loved nature. So yeah, I guess I am like him. And I haven't killed anyone or anything, especially not Tyler. I wouldn't have hurt him or any other living thing. My only regret is that I didn't help him when I should have."

Should she trust the sincerity she heard in his deep voice? Should she trust him?

No. She'd learned long ago to trust no one.

Noah wished now that he'd never approached Claire Underwood when he'd found her staring down at the grave with the flowers on it. But there'd been something so tragic about her, so vulnerable and fragile. But that must have been a trick of his mind.

Because there was nothing vulnerable or tragic about Claire Underwood despite her past. Or maybe because of it, she'd hardened her heart and sharpened her tongue.

And what the hell was she saying about him having a collection of dead animals?

His stomach churned at the thought. Sure, he found some dead in the cemetery, but he either buried them or tossed their bodies into the marsh beyond the cemetery, which was rumored to be like a bottomless pit. He didn't save them.

What the hell had Wynn shown her? And why?

Wynn and Taylor had always been a bit odd to him. They were like their dad, Lawrence, who you didn't realize was lurking around until he just popped up somewhere. People probably thought Noah was odd, too, because he wasn't an extrovert. He didn't put himself out there for anyone. But he had for Claire.

And that had been a mistake.

He walked off and left her alone at her mother's grave. He left her alone with her accusations and suspicions. He had to finish cleaning up the cemetery from the wind damage the night before. And he would have to cut back and cut down some of the trees that were as vulnerable and fragile as he'd thought Claire was.

He would cut off the weak branches and cut down the trees with the dead leaves. He had a team of maintenance staff, but he didn't like sitting back and managing them. He preferred to work beside them. For one, they respected him more for doing that, and for another, he liked to work hard. It got his mind off things, off his family, off the future he wasn't quite able to envision. Would he just stay here the rest of his life?

Get buried here one day like Lyle McGinty? And even in death, would he walk the grounds, keeping watch over the gardens and over the graves, like Lyle did?

Maybe he was a freak like Claire thought he was because he'd never imagined more for himself. He'd never imagined a wife or family of his own, just his job.

Just the cemetery.

But he remembered that nobody visited the grave digger's grave who'd actually known him except for Noah. And Noah had been too young to really have known him. Lyle's daughter didn't come visit him even though she was often at the house and on the grounds, standing around while other people were buried.

Maybe there was no point in having a family when they either deserted you or turned against you.

Why the hell had Wynn told Claire that collection was his? Maybe it had belonged to one of the maintenance staff who'd worked here at that time and Wynn had just assumed it was his. Even when he was still in high school, Noah had worked with the grounds crew. He'd loved being outside and working with the heavy equipment.

He headed back to the maintenance building now for some of that equipment. He needed chainsaws and safety equipment. "Hello?" he called out when he stepped inside the enormous metal building. His voice echoing back at him was his only reply.

The staff must have been out cleaning up the branches and leaves yet. Or maybe they'd taken off early for lunch. A lot of the equipment, the tractors and mowers and a couple of trucks were all still in the shed.

"Hello?" he called as he noticed a shadow between the trucks. He wasn't alone in the building like he'd thought.

Even though he'd invited Claire to come back with him, it couldn't be her. She wouldn't have been able to beat him back here when he'd left her standing beside her mother's grave.

It had to be someone else.

"Luke?" he asked.

Again, there was no reply.

But Noah felt a sudden chill, and the side door he'd walked through blew closed behind him. That happened sometimes around here, strange things like that. He figured it was Lyle's ghost, that just as he hadn't been able to leave the cemetery, that he spent time around here, too, looking after the equipment. But with that door shut, he realized now that the overhead lights weren't on. The building was dark.

He headed around the equipment toward the light switches on the wall next to his office. There was another panel just inside the door to the outside, but after how the door had slammed shut, he didn't necessarily want to walk over there.

As he flipped on the lights, he noticed the paper stuck to his door next to the computer everyone used to enter their time at work. *Police shut down cemetery. No work today.*

That wasn't his handwriting. But his staff might have figured someone else wrote it. Like Lawrence who was in charge now. Or Fiona who was probably really running things. He peered closer at the note, trying to determine who'd written it. And then that shadow loomed over him, blocking out the light, so that he couldn't read. He started to turn, but before he could see anything, something struck his head.

Hard.

His knees gave out, and he dropped down to the ground. And blackness fell over him like the night. He couldn't see anything. But then he heard engines starting up, one after another.

He had to get up, had to shut them off, because he could smell the fumes. The exhaust. And then he was suddenly too exhausted to fight, and his consciousness slipped away from him.

It had been too easy to get rid of the maintenance crew with that crude note, the one wadded up in the killer's pocket now. No sense in letting anyone else see it and maybe identify the handwriting. But another note probably should have been left next to Noah's body. A suicide note professing his guilt over Tyler Hicks's murder. Since Noah had messed up the plan the night before when he'd showed up suddenly at the grave digger's grave, he deserved to die. His sudden appearance meant he might have seen something and also that Tyler couldn't be disposed of like the others.

So his body had been found. And people would know he hadn't run away like the others. He was dead. Murdered.

And someone had to be held responsible.

Noah Gold was going to be a good scapegoat. That was why the blow hadn't been hard, just enough to knock him out, and so that it would look like he'd hit his head on the ground when he succumbed to the monoxide poisoning. The killer slipped out of the building that was already filling with fumes, then locked the door and pulled it shut, enclosing Noah in that makeshift tomb. If the blow to the head hadn't killed him, the fumes would.

Soon.

Chapter 8

So much of Claire's job involved figuring out what was true and what was a lie. She'd had kids accuse their parents of horrific things just because they'd had their phone or video games taken away. And she'd had parents do horrific things to their kids and then lie and pretend it never happened despite the medical evidence and, in some cases like Tyler's, despite the death. For some reason, though, she was beginning to believe Noah.

That the grotesque collection Wynn had shown her all those years ago wasn't his. And that he'd had nothing to do with Tyler's death.

She suspected she hadn't just offended him with her accusations, but that he was hurt, too. Of course she'd been wrong in the past. She'd trusted the wrong person, had believed a lie.

So she wasn't entirely sure about Noah Gold yet.

But if she checked out the maintenance building like he'd offered, maybe she would be less suspicious of him. The police had already thoroughly searched the place, so it wasn't as if they would have missed all those little skeletons that had been there so long ago. They had to be gone now, just like Noah claimed. So she wasn't sure why she was compelled to search it now. Just as they wouldn't have missed that collection of bones, they wouldn't have missed anything Tyler had left behind, either.

Noah had already told her that he'd found the kid's duffel bag. That had to be with the police now. So there was nothing for her to find in the maintenance building.

But Noah.

She was drawn to him for some reason and wanted to talk to him some more without the accusations. She wanted to talk to him about Tyler and Peyton and Michael. He was the one who spent the most time in the cemetery, so if he wasn't responsible for their deaths or disappearances, maybe he had some idea who was.

So she found herself walking in the direction Noah had gone a short while ago, in the direction she remembered Wynn taking her all those years ago. She'd met him at the grave digger's grave where he'd been asking her to meet him for a few weeks at school. But she'd always refused. She didn't want to see a ghost.

But after Peyton disappeared, she'd wanted to see him, so she'd agreed to meet Wynn at that grave. He'd told her that he had a crush on her, that he thought she was beautiful. But he'd just been messing with her; he'd laughed when he'd shown her that collection and she'd screamed. Then when she'd called him sick, he'd insisted it was Noah's.

It had probably been Wynn's. But he and his sister, Taylor, had always been popular despite being Golds. They'd had friends, or maybe they'd just bought them with the big allowances their parents had given them. Wynn had had a group of kids around the grave that night she'd joined; they'd all been drinking and doing drugs. And she'd wanted no part of that; she'd already seen too much of that in her life.

So he'd taken her away from everyone else. To this big metal building. She spied it through the trees now. The metal had a fresh coat of charcoal paint on it and a new black metal roof. Engines rumbled inside it, and exhaust seeped out from beneath the many overhead doors. Why were they all shut?

Why would someone be running engines with no ventilation?

Unless . . .

She jerked on each handle of the overhead doors, but they didn't budge. Then she ran around to the side where a normal entry door was. It was steel, painted charcoal like the metal walls. She grabbed the handle and tried to turn it, but it held tight. It was locked.

She pounded on it. "Noah! Noah!"

Was he in there?

If he was, he wouldn't last much longer with those fumes. Had he done this on purpose?

Was he trying to kill himself? Maybe all her accusations had been true. That he was a psychopath, a killer.

But a true psychopath never felt remorse, let alone guilt. A psychopath wouldn't kill himself, but he would kill anyone who got in his way. Was Noah in his way?

Or was she just overreacting, and nobody was even in the building?

She had to know for certain. She had to make sure that another person didn't die because she was too late to help them.

River wished school had been canceled due to Tyler Hicks's death. She would feel better if Sarah was home with her, where she knew she would be safe. But maybe Sarah and Gigi and Toby were safer at school than here in this house or on the property.

This was where Tyler had died. Where so many other people had died as well.

What about Michael?

Was he dead like Tyler?

She'd promised Luke she would check the records for funerals around the time he'd disappeared. But she hadn't wanted anyone else to know what she was looking for, so she'd waited until nobody was around before going into the business offices.

She would never forget the month, day, and year, and even the time that Michael was supposed to meet her so they could run away together. Midnight. But he hadn't shown up.

And so she'd left on her own, taking the bus out west to her grandmother. To get away from Gold Creek, to make sure she was allowed to keep her baby.

But she wasn't sure how to even log onto the computer, let alone pull up records that were sixteen years old. So she sat in Lawrence's chair with her fingers hovering over the keyboard. The screen was locked with the login box the only thing showing.

How many attempts would she have before she got locked out?

How many tries to get into the records?

For some reason she was reluctant to just ask Lawrence to pull them up for her. Maybe because he reported to her mother. And there was no way she was asking Fiona to show her the records because she had a horrible feeling they might disappear if she did.

Maybe Fiona would hide them just because she wouldn't want any more scandal around Gold Memorial Gardens and Funeral Services. Or maybe she would hide them because she didn't want River and Luke to know what had really happened to Michael.

A twinge of guilt had her wincing a bit. She didn't want to believe her mother could be duplicitous in murder or a cover-up, but she couldn't quite bring herself to trust the woman. Her mother was able to lie so convincingly that River was never sure what was the truth and what was some story she'd concocted. Mabel, Fiona's mother, claimed that she was always that way, making up tall tales to make herself more interesting.

Mabel would know because the apple hadn't fallen very far off the tree. Whereas River hated drama and conflict. Maybe that was why she didn't want to ask her mother for those records; she didn't want to deal with the drama her request would cause.

"Hello! Help! I need help!" a woman frantically yelled from somewhere down the hall.

Her voice was vaguely familiar to River, but it wasn't a family member or employee calling out. Was it someone from the school where she'd sent Sarah that morning despite her qualms?

River jumped up from the desk and rushed down the hall to the lobby. "I'm here. What's wrong?"

The woman had dark hair that was tumbling wildly around her shoulders and her damp face. And she wore glasses that were slightly smudged or maybe misted from her physical exertion. She was breathing hard as if she'd been running.

"Are you okay?" River asked while the woman hesitated to answer her. Maybe she was just struggling to breathe.

"I . . . I don't know," she replied.

"You don't know if you're okay?" River asked. "What happened?"

The woman shook her head and drew in a breath. Then she replied, "I don't know if anything's wrong for sure, but I could hear a bunch of engines running in the maintenance building and the door's locked."

River didn't know anything about the maintenance of the grounds, and she didn't want to. She had enough on her plate with learning from her mother how to use makeup and other materials on the deceased so that there could be open casket showings at their funerals.

"My brother Noah is in charge of the cemetery," she said. And she pulled out her cell phone. "He'll know why things are running with the doors shut." She also wanted to know why this woman had clearly run from the building to the house. But her call to Noah went directly to his voicemail. "He didn't answer."

"Nobody answered when I knocked either," the woman said. "And I'm pretty sure that Noah is in there. That was where he was heading after he talked to me in the cemetery."

"And you are?" River asked.

"Claire Underwood. I'm a CPS investigator. I was here—"

"Last night," River finished for her. She'd been looking for Tyler Hicks, and unfortunately, she had found the poor teenager too late to help him. "Luke told me. I'm River Gold."

The woman nodded. "I know. You're the only one who doesn't look like the others."

Her family had played upon that, making her feel like she wasn't a real Gold, that she wasn't one of them. And she'd actually been more relieved than upset about it. But she had DNA proof now that she was a Gold for better or worse. And lately it had been worse. Except for Noah and Gigi and Toby and, of course, her daughter, too. She loved them.

"Do you have keys to that building?" Claire asked. "We need to make sure that nobody's in there." From the urgency in her voice, she was obviously pretty worried that someone was.

River ran back down the hall to the office. There was a cabinet with keys dangling from hooks. Some belonged to the vehicles, like the van she'd borrowed one night and had nearly been killed in. And there was a hook with a label above it that said MAINTENANCE; it held a ring with several keys on it. She snatched it off the hook and ran back into the lobby. But she didn't stop. She pushed open the doors and ran out under the portico.

"My car is here," Claire said, and she jerked open the driver's door of a hybrid vehicle.

There was a service road between the maintenance building

and the parking lot for the home, so her car would get them back to the building faster than their feet and even faster than a golf cart. So River opened the passenger's side door and dropped onto the seat. "We should call Luke," she said. "Just in case . . ."

In case Claire was right, and Noah was trapped in that building with engines pumping exhaust into it. But Luke had left some time ago. Would he make it back from town in time to help them?

In time to help Noah?

"I called the sheriff," Claire said, "when I was running here. I figured he had Noah's number. He was going to try to call him, too, so I let him go. He didn't call back."

"Probably because his call went to Noah's voicemail like mine did," River said. "So Luke knows that he might be in trouble. They're friends. He should be on his way." Some of the pressure on her chest eased. "And we don't even know that Noah is in the building. You said nobody answered when you knocked."

"That doesn't mean that he wasn't inside," Claire said, "just that he either didn't want to answer me or he couldn't."

"Why wouldn't he want to answer you?"

"I accused him of killing Tyler," Claire replied almost matter-of-factly.

Which made River gasp. Obviously, this woman didn't mind conflict at all, unlike River who avoided it at all costs. Like even running away from it. She'd hoped that she might have enough in common with Claire Underwood to become friends, but clearly they weren't anything alike.

"Noah wouldn't have done that," River said. "He's a good man." Unfortunately, probably one of the few in the Gold family. "He would never hurt anyone."

"Not even himself?"

A jolt of alarm shot through River when she remembered how her father's first wife had died, how she'd taken her own life. Or at least it had looked that way. "You think Noah's trying to kill himself? Why?"

"Because I was right," Claire said. "Because he did kill Tyler."

River shook her head. "No. That's not possible. Noah is quiet, but he's sweet. He's funny. He's kindhearted. He could never hurt anyone."

"Surely you know now that people are capable of anything," Claire replied.

Unfortunately, the cynical CPS investigator was right; after all the murders several weeks ago, all the manipulations and power moves, River knew all too well that anyone was capable of anything.

A light burned behind Noah's closed lids. Just a single beam, like from a lantern that wavered and moved.

He had to follow it like he'd followed it before through the cemetery. Lyle was here, trying to guide him away from danger, just like he had when Noah was a toddler.

When he'd kept him out of that bottomless marsh.

When he'd kept Noah from disappearing forever.

Metal scraped across metal or rock, and he flinched at the sound. His head hurt. So badly.

Something had hit him. Something hard. A shovel?

But the grave digger wouldn't hurt him; he'd saved him. And he'd guided him.

That had to be what he was doing now. Noah tried to open his eyes, tried to see that light.

Where was Lyle?

Where was he going?

A cough bubbled up his throat that felt dry and raw. And then he heard the engines running. Where was he?

What was happening?

He finally dragged his lids open all the way, but he couldn't see through the smoke, it hovered on the concrete like mist on the fountains and the marsh. A cough burned his throat again, and his lungs were burning, too, aching in his chest. Diesel fumes filled the building and his pounding head.

Why was everything running? The tractors, the mowers, the trucks.

He had to get up. Had to shut off the stuff . . .

Or get the hell out of the building.

So he pressed his palms against the concrete floor and pushed himself up. And his head pounded harder as black spots danced across his vision. He needed fresh air.

But he kept coughing, and the movement to his head sent pain crashing through it. Was this what Tyler had felt last night?

Someone had struck him, too.

When he and Luke had rushed out to where Claire had screamed, they'd seen what had made her scream. The teenager with the open eyes and the damaged skull. Hopefully, the kid had died instantly. Hopefully, he'd felt no pain.

"Tyler . . ." Noah whispered, and now his heart ached like his lungs. That poor kid had had his whole life ahead of him. And it had been cut short.

And now Noah . . .

He was more than twenty years older than Tyler, but he was still too young to die. And too determined. He had to get up. He crawled over to one of the trucks and grabbed the running board. Using it, he levered himself up to his knees. Then he reached for the handle and tried to open the door. But it was locked. Someone had locked the keys inside with the vehicle running. He wouldn't be able to shut off the trucks.

But the tractors and the lawn mowers . . .

Maybe he could shut off those.

But it was already too late. The building was nearly full of exhaust fumes. He had to get out. But when he let go of the door handle, he dropped back to the concrete.

And he couldn't push himself up. He was too weak.

But he could hear that sound again, of metal against concrete. And the light wavered behind his eyes.

"Lyle . . ."

Would he save him this time like he had when he was a kid? But Lyle was dead now. And Tyler was dead. And so many of Noah's family members. His dad. His sister Honora . . .

And he had a horrible feeling that he was about to be the next Gold to die.

Chapter 9

Claire's heart pounded fast and hard as she watched River try key after key from that big ring, but none of them turned the knob. She pounded on the metal wall next to the door frame. "Hello? Is anyone in there?"

"If they are, they probably can't hear you over the engines," River said.

Claire could barely hear the other woman's soft voice over the rumble of the motors that emanated from the building, along with the fumes. Since they were this bad on the outside of the building, she could imagine how bad it must be inside. She pounded harder on the metal. But if someone was inside, they were probably unconscious now or . . . dead.

Then finally a key fit and the knob turned. Claire pushed on the steel door before River could, swinging it inside the building, into a cloud of exhaust fumes.

"Noah!" she yelled.

"Noah!" River echoed, then coughed.

Claire's lungs burned, too, but she had to get to Noah. She

had to find him because she was certain now that he was in here. If he'd been outside, he would have heard her pounding on the door the first time or would have seen her running across the cemetery to the house. Or when she and River had driven back here on the service road between the buildings that River had pointed out, he would have seen her car.

She blinked, trying to clear her vision, as her eyes burned and watered from the fumes. "Noah!" She walked farther into the building with River close behind her.

The door slammed shut behind them, expunging the little light they'd had, plunging them nearly into darkness except for the glow of the truck headlights shining through the exhaust smoke. River ran back to the door and fumbled with the knob. "It's stuck!"

"We need to open the overhead doors," Claire shouted back at her. Already it was getting hard for her to breathe. Her lungs burned, and her head felt fuzzy, unfocused.

Where would the controls be for the overhead doors? There had to be remotes inside the vehicles. She tried to open the door of one of the trucks, but it was locked with the keys inside, the engine rumbling along. She went around it to head to the other truck, but she tripped and landed across a body. A long, broad body: Noah.

But he didn't move. He didn't react.

Was he already dead?

She reached out to find a pulse on his neck, but her fingers found something wet instead. He was bleeding.

"I found him!" she shouted at River.

But there was no reply. Had River already succumbed to the fumes? Or had whoever slammed the door behind them grabbed the other woman?

What the hell is going on now at Gold Memorial Gardens? That call from Claire made no sense to Luke. Why would engines be running in the maintenance building with all the doors shut? Maybe someone had left them running and then gone out for lunch or something. But clearly Claire didn't think that was the case, and neither did Luke.

Not when it involved the Golds.

Nothing ended well with them. It always ended with death.

Maybe he was crazy for getting involved with River. He'd already felt disloyal to his younger brother who'd loved her so much. And he'd worried it would be awkward for his niece Sarah and even for Jackson. He'd moved Jackson to Gold Creek with him so that the kid could have a fresh start and a hopeful future.

But the kid who died had been Jackson's age. And every time Luke had tried to sleep last night, he'd kept seeing Jackson lying in that grave partially covered by dirt. He'd promised his best friend, Jack, that he would step up if he had to, that he would take care of his godson if, God forbid, something happened to both him and Adele. As Jack and Adele had pointed out to him, *godfather* wasn't just an honorary title; it was a responsibility. Luke already felt like he'd failed Jack. That he should have been the one who hadn't survived that last deployment instead of the man who'd had a wife and a son. He couldn't let his best friend down again. He had to keep Jackson safe.

Luke had once thought Gold Creek was so safe, but after all that had happened, he should have known better. He should have known that no place was safe. Claire Underwood knew that, which was probably why she'd sounded so urgent on the phone. And she'd been running, too, because she'd been breathing heavily. And then the phone had disconnected.

He could have tried calling her back, but instead he'd rushed out of his office to the sheriff department SUV and headed, with lights flashing and siren blaring, over to Gold Memorial Gardens. Once he pulled through the gates, he didn't stop at the house. Instead, he took the service road that led back to the maintenance building.

And he wished like hell now that he hadn't cleared it as a crime scene. But the techs hadn't found anything in the building but Tyler's duffel bag and signs that he'd been sleeping on the couch. No sign of a crime.

Until now.

Because he trusted Claire's judgment that something was wrong. That those vehicles shouldn't have been running with all the doors shut. When he pulled up to the building, all the overhead doors were open. But smoke, or exhaust, hung thickly in the air like a dense fog. When he shoved open his door, he coughed against the burn of it, and his eyes stung and began to water. "What the hell . . ."

He coughed again and called out, "Claire? Noah?"

"In here," River yelled back from inside the building.

Even with the doors all open, the smoke was so thick he could barely see them. River and Claire. "Get out of there!" he said.

But they weren't paying attention to him; they were leaning over a body lying on the ground. No. Claire was leaning while River was doing chest compressions.

"Oh, my God!"

It was Noah lying on the ground; Noah, who apparently wasn't breathing on his own. Then Luke heard the squawk of his radio and the sirens. They'd called an ambulance.

But would it get here in time?

The grave digger was coming. Noah could see him moving across the cemetery, the light wavering in and out as he passed in front of the lantern he carried in one hand. And then the shovel clacked against a tombstone as the old man, the ghost, passed it.

And another clack.

And another . . .

The sharp noise reverberated inside Noah's skull, making him groan with pain. He reached up to touch his head. Was it smashed like Tyler's?

Was he dead, too?

And would he spend the rest of eternity walking the memorial gardens like Lyle McGinty did?

Was that his hell or his heaven?

Noah wasn't ready yet to go to either place. He wasn't ready to die because until now he hadn't realized how little living he'd really done. While he'd dated over the years, he'd never had a big romance, nobody he would have brought home to his family.

Maybe that was because he'd been worried his father would steal her away like Gregory Gold I had stolen Noah's nephew Garrett's girlfriend. They were both dead now.

Noah didn't want to be dead, too. He had to fight. He forced his eyes open; they were burning yet like they'd burned earlier when he'd awakened for a few minutes in the maintenance building.

All the machinery and trucks had been running. Who'd started them? Who'd hit him over the head?

He reached up again and touched a bandage that covered a big lump. He'd definitely gotten hit over the head. With what?

And who had done it?

The same person who'd killed Tyler? The poor kid had definitely been murdered.

Noah blinked and tried to clear his vision of the water running from his eyes. He had no idea where he was. While he could smell some of the fumes yet, they weren't as intense as they'd been earlier. Maybe it was just what was left in his hair or his nose.

But there was a tube in his nose, pumping in oxygen. And an IV ran from a pole to a needle in the crook of his elbow. And something wound tightly around his bicep and beeped as numbers appeared on a monitor next to the IV.

He was in a hospital, lying on a bed.

How the hell had he gotten from the floor of the exhaust-filled maintenance building to here?

He peered around; the chair next to his bed was empty. Nobody sat at his side. But then a shadow fell across him, and he turned to the other side to see someone tall standing over him. That someone held a pillow.

Noah jumped and struggled to sit up in bed. Was this person going to finish what they'd started in the maintenance building?

"Who . . ." he began, his voice just a weak rasp. "Who are you?"

"You don't recognize me, Uncle Noah?" a deep voice asked.

Even the nephew and niece who weren't that much younger than him called him Uncle; his mother had insisted on them showing him respect.

He blinked fast enough to clear the moisture from his eyes. "Wynn?" The person who'd brought Claire to the cemetery and then to the building where he'd shown her some bizarre, grotesque collection of dead animals. "You . . ."

Son of a bitch. He wanted to say that, but his voice gave out.

"Dr. Gold, actually," Wynn said. "I'm going to be working here at Gold Memorial Hospital. Sounds kind of like the family business, doesn't it? I'm pretty sure that Grandfather probably built it, like he built everything else in this town. Like he owned everything else."

And that was probably why Wynn had been hired. Because he was a Gold. But was he a good doctor? Or a killer?

"I didn't expect you to be one of the first patients coming

into the ER after my hire," Wynn said. "What happened, Uncle Noah? Do you remember?"

Wynn wasn't wearing a white coat or even scrubs. In his khakis and button-down flannel shirt, he didn't look like he was working at a hospital. He looked like he'd been out for a hike. Or maybe for a walk in the memorial gardens.

Noah shook his head and flinched at the pain that shot through it with the movement. "No . . ."

"I didn't realize you were so distraught," Wynn said, and clicked his tongue against his too-white teeth. "I guess the still waters running deep thing is really true with you."

"What . . . ?" he managed to rasp. He needed water. His throat was so damn dry.

"First your father dies, then your sister . . ." He made the clucking sound with his tongue again. "It makes sense that you would be upset. Depressed. That you would lock yourself in the building where you spent so much time and try to kill yourself."

Despite the dryness of his throat, Noah managed a short chuckle. And he shook his head again though his stomach flipped from the pain. "I didn't . . ."

"No, you weren't successful in pulling it off," Wynn said, and he sounded disappointed.

At least to Noah.

Noah, who was seeing his nephew so much more clearly now and not just because his eyes had stopped watering. He'd always thought Wynn and his sister, Taylor, were different from the rest of the family because they hadn't wanted anything to do with the family business. They'd gone their own ways. Wynn into medicine and Taylor into . . .

He had no idea.

But he could see now that Wynn was more like the Golds

maybe even than his father Lawrence was. He was manipulative and dark.

Noah managed to work up enough saliva to speak. "Is that why you have the pillow? Gonna finish me off?"

Wynn looked down at the pillow and his dark eyes widened as if he hadn't realized he'd been holding it. "Oh, no, I just thought you might need another one."

And Noah remembered that probate over his father's estate wasn't settled yet. Gregory Gold I had set up his will to pit his survivors against each other just like he'd done when they were alive. An heir had to survive the probate period in order to inherit. If they died before, their share went back into the estate and the percentage everyone else inherited got bigger.

Had Wynn wanted a bigger share? Was that why he'd tried to kill him?

"And I just want to help you," Wynn said in such a smarmy voice that Noah felt sick again. "We're working on getting a psychiatric placement for you, so that you can get the help you need. So that you don't try anything like this again."

"Fuck you," Noah said, his voice gruff but stronger.

Wynn chuckled. "You always were the oddest one of our family, Uncle Noah. Someone should have realized before now that you were struggling."

Noah snorted now. "You're a sick bastard, Wynn."

His nephew gasped as if he was offended. "What are you talking about? I'm just trying to help you. Something I should have done sooner, but I've been so busy with school and residency. That's why I took this job here at the hospital. I should have moved back to Gold Creek years ago. Then maybe all these horrible things wouldn't have happened and wouldn't keep happening."

"Not going to keep happening," Noah said, shaking his head

again. He wasn't going to die or let anyone else close to him die. Was that what had happened to Tyler?

Had the poor kid just been in the wrong place at the wrong time? Maybe he'd seen or heard something he shouldn't have.

"No, it's not," Wynn said as if agreeing with him. "We'll get you help."

"Fuck you," he said again stronger. "And get away from me."

"What's wrong? Why are you getting so upset? Is it because your plan got thwarted? Because you're alive?"

And if he said yes, Wynn would probably help finish him off.

"I didn't try to kill myself." And he reached up to the back of his head. "Somebody tried to kill me."

Wynn widened his dark eyes again even as a slight smirk crossed his mouth. He looked like he thought this was all so damn funny.

"Was it you?" Noah asked.

Wynn laughed now. "You must have some brain damage from the lack of oxygen." He shook his head pityingly. "That's too bad."

"I know what you did," Noah said.

And the slight smirk slipped off Wynn's face as he narrowed his eyes. "What are you talking about?"

"Years ago . . . Claire Underwood . . ."

"Claire Underwood. There's a name I've not heard in years. Well, except for a short while ago when she was brought into the hospital with you."

Noah reached out for the railing on the side of the bed and levered himself up. "Claire's hurt, too?" He flinched, trying to rack his brain. He'd been alone when he'd walked into the maintenance building. He'd left her back at her mother's grave.

Which had been too close to where Tyler died. Had the killer returned to the scene of his crime and attacked her?

"Is she all right?"

Wynn shrugged as if he wasn't concerned. "I don't know. I'm not technically seeing patients yet. Just accepted the offer."

So he had no reason to be at the hospital or in this room with Noah.

"I need to see Claire," Noah said. And he needed to get the hell away from his creepy nephew until he was stronger, until he could deal with him. Because Wynn was big like Noah and could easily overpower him right now.

Wynn clutched that pillow yet, his fingers clenched into it so that his hands looked like fists.

And Noah drew in a deep breath.

"How do you even know Claire?" Wynn asked.

"CPS," Noah said. "She works for CPS."

Wynn shrugged. "What does that have to do with you? You have no children. Hell, I don't know if you ever even dated anyone. What's your preference, Uncle? Women? Men? Blond? Brunette? I realize now that I've never taken the time to get to know you. And here you could have died today, probably would have died if not for Claire Underwood." He made that tsking sound again. Was he disappointed that Claire had saved him?

"Claire saved me?" Noah asked.

Wynn nodded. "Yes. As long as you have no adverse effects from all that carbon monoxide you inhaled. Same for her and River. They're both here, being treated. Being smaller than you and female, they might have even more adverse effects than you're having."

The only adverse effect Noah had was waking up to his nephew looming over him with a pillow.

Where the hell was a call button? Should he have one so he could summon a nurse if he needed her?

Where the hell was everyone?

Because Noah didn't trust his nephew. And he certainly didn't want to be alone with him.

"I . . . I need to check on them," Noah said. "Can you get a nurse?"

Wynn shook his head.

"You won't get a nurse?"

"I mean that it's pointless to ask," Wynn said. "With all the rules around privacy right now, there is no way anyone will tell you how they're doing. After all, Claire Underwood is nothing to you. And River . . . well, she would have had to put you down as a person with whom medical staff could discuss her condition."

Condition. Medical staff. How badly had Claire and River been hurt trying to save him?

"Claire . . ." he began again, and cleared his throat. "She told me what you showed her all those years ago. That collection." He shuddered at the thought, and he'd never even seen it himself.

"Your collection," Wynn said. "I guess that should have been a tip-off for how much you've always struggled with your mental health."

"Fuck you," Noah said again.

Instead of being offended, his nephew laughed.

"That was yours," Noah insisted. "All those helpless animals. And you showed it to a teenage girl who'd already been through hell. You're the psychopath."

Wynn sighed. "You're obviously suffering some kind of break from reality right now. I really should see about getting that psychiatric hold in place. They can keep you for up to seventy-two hours."

Noah shook his head. "You're the one who needs the help, Wynn."

"I told you, that collection wasn't mine. I didn't even know it was there. Claire and I stumbled across it when I was looking for someplace where we could fool around. She was such a beautiful girl. Still is, even though she looked so very weak and helpless when they brought her in here, like you are so very weak and helpless." He tightened his hold on that pillow again.

And Noah had a horrible feeling that his nephew was going to go after Claire next, after Wynn used that pillow to finish the job he'd probably started in the maintenance building.

Wynn was going to kill him.

Chapter 10

Claire had used her CPS credentials to get administration to give her Noah's room number. She hadn't been lying since he actually was involved in one of her cases. He was the last person Tyler had texted. Was he the last person that Tyler had seen?

Had he killed the teenager and then tried to kill himself when she'd confronted him with her suspicions and accusations?

But why had there been blood on the back of his head? Had he passed out from the fumes and fallen? Or had someone knocked him out and then turned on all the machinery?

She stopped in the hall outside his room, surprised that the door was shut. Shouldn't the nursing staff be monitoring him more closely? He hadn't been breathing when she'd found him in the building. Once River had opened all the doors, they'd given him CPR until the paramedics arrived. Fortunately, they hadn't taken long because she and River had been fighting to breathe themselves because of the overpowering fumes.

Because their levels had dropped so much, the paramedics had insisted on giving them both oxygen as well. But she had no idea how long Noah hadn't been breathing. How long his brain had been deprived of oxygen.

Was he conscious yet?

She drew in a deep breath now and then turned the knob and stepped inside the room. After the brightness of the hall, the room seemed dark. The blinds were drawn across the window and the curtain pulled, so that the only light came from the machines monitoring Noah's vitals. And one of those machines beeped fast and loud, like his pulse was racing.

Once her eyes adjusted to the dim light, she saw the man standing over his bed, a pillow clasped in his hands. "Get away from him!" she shouted. "Security!" The door had shut behind her, so nobody could probably hear her. She turned to run for help, but a hand shot out and grasped her arm.

"Wait. You two are both overreacting," the man said. "I'm just checking on my uncle, seeing if he needs an extra pillow."

"Uncle?" She looked up at the dark-haired man who clasped her arm too tightly. He was definitely a Gold; he looked so much like Noah but with finer features and a thinner build.

"I'm Wynn," he said. "Well, Dr. Gold now, and you're Claire Underwood, right?"

She ignored his question and said, "You can't have a family member as one of your patients." She knew that because of a doctor who'd tried to explain away his children's injuries as their physician. It was that case that had caused her relocation because she hadn't cared who he was; unfortunately, the judge had and had discounted the kids' injuries and their explanations of what had happened. Just as a judge had once done with her.

So she might have gone to a reporter she knew and got some media attention on that doctor and his golfing buddy the judge.

And that might have gotten the judge removed and another, less partial one, assigned to the case.

"Uncle Noah is not my patient," Wynn said. "I'm not even on staff yet. I've just accepted the offer. I was here when you were all brought into the ER, and I wanted to make sure that my uncle is all right."

"Is he all right?" she asked. That was why she was here; to make sure that he had regained consciousness. She peered around Wynn to the bed he'd been standing over with that pillow. But he hadn't used it on his uncle. Noah was awake, his eyes open, and the machines hooked to him showed that his heart was beating. Fast. He was breathing now on his own, too.

"Physically, yes," the doctor replied. "But the psychiatric evaluation will really tell us what's going on."

"There will be no psychiatric evaluation or hold or whatever you're threatening," Noah said, his voice gruff. "I am fine mentally, better than I am physically."

"We have to make sure that you won't try to harm yourself again," Wynn said in a patronizing tone.

"I haven't *ever* tried to harm myself," Noah said. "Someone hit me over the head."

Wynn gave him a pitying look that made Noah's heart rate increase on the monitor.

She could understand why he was upset. She would be, too, if she hadn't harmed herself and someone thought she had.

"Uncle Noah, you were found alone in that maintenance building," Wynn said. "Nobody else was in there with you."

"How do you know that?" Noah asked, and his dark eyes narrowed with obvious suspicion of his nephew.

"Wasn't he alone, Claire?" Wynn persisted.

She nodded.

"Then I must have heard that when you all were brought

into the ER," Wynn said. "The doctor who treated you put in orders for a psychiatric evaluation."

"That I don't need," Noah said. "I might have been alone in that building when I was found, but I wasn't alone when I went in there after seeing Claire in the cemetery. Someone else was inside the building." He cocked his head to peer around his nephew and focus on Claire. "Did you see anyone else around?"

She shook her head. "No. I heard the engines going and went up to the house. River found keys to it and helped me get inside the building."

"How did you know I was in there?" Noah asked, and now he looked at her with suspicion.

"You were heading there when you walked away from me in the cemetery," Claire said. "I had a few more questions for you." She'd actually wanted to check on him then after their conversation. She'd felt badly for basically calling him a psychopath. And if he was one, he wouldn't have tried to harm himself.

"Questions or accusations?" Noah asked. "Tell her, Wynn, that that sick collection you showed her all those years ago was yours."

Wynn shook his head, and that pitying look crossed his face again. "It wasn't mine. I really believed it was yours. And I had no intention of showing it to her. I was totally surprised to find it there."

"That's not how I remember it," Claire said. He'd been amused and patronizing, just like he seemed now, with that slight smirk on his face. "You thought it was funny and wanted to scare me."

"Isn't that why you came out to the cemetery?" Wynn asked. "Why any of the teenagers ever came out there? To see the grave digger's ghost and scare themselves silly?"

"So you knew the collection was there," Noah said. "Why would you think something so cruel and disturbing was funny?"

Wynn shook his head and sighed. "I didn't think it was funny, and I didn't know it was there. But yes, it didn't really affect me to see it or surprise me. I grew up in a funeral home. So did you, Noah. And even though you didn't grow up in a funeral home, Claire, you saw worse things than some dead animals even back then. So what was the big deal?"

Goose bumps rose on her skin at his callous disregard for the lives of those animals. If anyone was the psychopath in the Gold family, it was probably Wynn. But he was a doctor. He was supposed to be helping people. And yet she'd found him holding that pillow like he'd been about to press it down over his uncle's face.

"I'm not really concerned about the past right now," Claire said. "I'm concerned that a kid died in the cemetery last night, and that Noah could have died in that building today." And they needed to find out who'd killed Tyler and who might have tried to kill Noah if he hadn't tried to kill himself. He was so offended that they thought he might have harmed himself that Claire was beginning to believe him. Was the person who'd killed Tyler the same one who'd gone after Noah?

"You were the one who brought up the past to my uncle," Wynn said to her. "You told him about that collection and that I thought it was his. Why did you bring that up?"

She felt as cornered as she'd been that day in the room off the maintenance building where the fuel was stored. But she'd gotten away from Wynn that day, and she intended to get away from him now. "I don't think any of that is relevant right—"

"You thought it was relevant because whoever would have some sick collection like that is a psychopath," Noah said, and he stared at his nephew's face, as if watching him for a reaction.

Claire considered it smarter to drop the discussion and not

make Wynn so aware of her suspicions. After she'd been so blunt and open with Noah, he'd nearly died. She didn't want anyone else getting hurt, especially not herself, and if Wynn had been holding that pillow with the intention of using it on his uncle, he would have no qualms about killing her. Or Tyler.

Was he the one who'd killed the teenager? But why?

Wynn's brow furrowed, and he looked offended now. That macabre collection had to have been his. "Well, it's not like who-ever collected those skeletons actually killed the animals—"

"Really?" Claire said, unable to contain her skepticism. "Some-body just found that many dead carcasses and decided to keep them? That makes no sense."

Wynn shrugged. "People collect all sorts of things. I had a mentor in med school who collected appendixes. He kept the ones he removed in glass jars of formaldehyde."

"So doctors and serial killers have a lot in common appar-ently," Noah remarked. And he glanced at the pillow his nephew held yet.

Wynn tossed it onto the foot of his uncle's bed. "I just came by to check on you. I'll let you get some rest now." He focused on Claire. "You should leave, too, let him get some sleep."

Claire didn't know what else to say to Noah or to ask him. And despite or maybe because of his irritation with his nephew, he looked exhausted. His skin was pale except for the dark cir-cles beneath his eyes. "I agree. Let's let him rest." She walked back to the door to the hall and waited for Wynn. She was not about to leave him alone with Noah.

Even though *she* wasn't going to keep Noah awake with any more conversation, she was going to find the sheriff and have Luke talk to his friend. Maybe he could get the truth out of him about everything that had happened while also protecting him from his creepy nephew.

That nephew stepped out into the hall and waited for her to

join him. Then he pulled the door shut. "He really does need a psyche eval," Wynn told her.

She nodded. "I'm sure the doctor who is able to treat him will make sure that he has one."

Wynn's mouth curved into that smirk again. Then he leaned close to her and said, "Now that we're both living in Gold Creek, we can get close again, Claire."

"We were never close," Claire told him. She'd only met him at the cemetery all those years ago because she'd wanted to ask him what had happened to Peyton. She'd been pretty sure that her friend had considered one of the Golds a friend or maybe even more than a friend. What had happened to *her friend*?

Had he died like Tyler and been buried in someone else's grave? She needed to find out the truth about Peyton's disappearance as much as she needed to find out who was responsible for killing Tyler Hicks and maybe for almost killing Noah Gold as well.

Even as exhausted as he was and with all the machines hooked up to him, Noah had been tempted to jump out of bed and stop Claire from leaving with his nephew. But they'd disappeared before he'd been able to unhook his IVs, and then the door had opened again to a nurse who'd finally noticed the change to his vitals. Right behind her had been the psychiatrist who'd been asked to evaluate his mental state.

The shrink wasn't sure who had requested the evaluation: the doctor who was really treating him or Wynn. But Noah had no fears about passing it. He knew what to say and what to keep to himself.

He told the truth about not wanting to hurt himself and that he wasn't depressed. But he didn't share how upset he'd been that Claire had called him a psychopath or that he sometimes saw and heard a ghost, like he had while he'd been locked in that building. He was pretty sure that Lyle had been trying to wake him up.

Or maybe that had just been Claire pounding on the locked door, trying to get inside to him. She'd saved his life.

He realized that now that his head had cleared more. He could have died; he would have died if not for her and River. He owed her for saving him. If only she didn't have so many suspicions about him . . .

The psychiatrist asked quite a few questions, so clearly, he had suspicions, too. But Noah must have eased them because the doctor suggested no seventy-two-hour hold like Wynn had threatened. Noah was free to go home once he was medically cleared to leave the hospital.

When the door opened a short while after the psychiatrist left, Noah hoped that it was the doctor who could release him to go home. But Luke stepped inside the room, and from the expression on his face, the sheriff apparently had as many suspicions about him as everyone else seemed to have.

Noah groaned.

"Are you all right?" Luke asked with concern. "Do you need the doctor? The nurse?"

"The doctor, so I can get out of here," Noah said. He did not want to be in this hospital room with a door he couldn't lock and his weird-ass nephew hanging out at his bedside with a pillow he didn't need. At least at the house he could lock and barricade his door to make damn sure nobody got inside his room.

"I don't think you're going to be able to leave tonight," Luke said. "You were unconscious for quite a while. You weren't even breathing when River and Claire rescued you. They were doing CPR when I arrived at the scene and continued doing it until the paramedics arrived."

He let out a breath now in a ragged sigh of shock. He'd already realized that Claire had saved his life, but he hadn't known exactly how close he'd come to dying. Then he shuddered. "Damn."

"They were exhausted, and because they weren't able to move you out of the building, they inhaled too much of the noxious fumes themselves. Even though River opened every door, there was too much carbon monoxide lingering yet," Luke said. "Despite how big the building is, it looked like it was full of fog. If the space wasn't so big, with such high ceilings, you definitely wouldn't be here right now. You would have died before Claire got River and the keys to unlock the door."

Noah remembered briefly opening his eyes to that fog. But he hadn't been able to remain conscious for long. The situation had been toxic for him and for his rescuers.

Claire had looked tired when she'd walked into his hospital room a short time ago, but she'd looked tired that morning when he'd seen her at her mother's grave. He'd figured then that she hadn't slept any better than he had after she'd found Tyler. And now she'd risked her life for his.

And his sister had as well.

"How is River?" he asked.

Luke released a shaky sigh now. "She's okay. Thank God. Sarah already came too close too many times to losing her mother since they arrived in Gold Creek."

"What about you?" Noah asked.

"I'm fine," Luke said. "The paramedics got there shortly after I did. I wasn't in the building for very long."

"What about you and River?" he asked, and he was surprised that he was so curious about their relationship. He'd made it a point to never get involved in his family's love lives; he'd learned from the way his dad had gone through marriages and women that relationships were complicated. Or more likely his dad had made the relationships complicated.

Noah hadn't wanted to be like Gregory Gold I in any way, so he'd become a loner. When he'd lain on the concrete floor, helpless to save himself, his life might had flashed before his eyes. But he couldn't be sure because there hadn't been much to see. He hadn't lived or loved much. His longest lasting and most meaningful relationship was with a ghost.

Maybe he needed to call that psychiatrist back and tell him a few more things. But he didn't want to be held for seventy-two hours because of the grave digger. He had to get back to the cemetery, not just to maintain it but also to make sure that nobody else died in it.

"What do you mean?" Luke asked.

"How do you feel about nearly losing River as many times as *you* have?" he asked.

Luke bit his lip and shook his head, as if he was too emotional to put his feelings into words. But they were clear in the tears that glistened in his eyes. He loved River. He cleared his throat and said, "She's really not mine to lose. We've only gone out a few times. We've both been so busy and . . ."

"And what?" Noah prodded.

"I wonder if she'll always be Michael's girl."

Noah shrugged. "A part of her will be, but she left that girl in her past, Luke. She's an adult now with a child of her own that she's done a damn good job raising. Sarah's a neat kid. Funny. Smart. Strong."

"Thank God for that," Luke said. "She's been through a lot since they came here. She's seen things and been put into situations that no teenager should have been."

"She's resilient," Noah said, and a sense of pride in his niece surged through him.

"What about you?" Luke asked. "I thought you were resilient, too."

"I am," Noah said. Then he groaned and continued. "Don't tell me you think I locked myself inside that building. You should damn well know me better than that."

Luke arched a dark eyebrow. "Should I?" he asked.

"Yeah, we've known each other for years. We've gone fishing together," Noah reminded him. "You know I wouldn't try to kill myself."

"You don't talk much," Luke said. "You don't let anyone in."

"Neither do you. That's why we get along," Noah said. "Because we're so much alike."

Luke chuckled. "Okay, you might have me there."

"Let River in," Noah urged him. "Don't get hung up on the past. Enjoy the present and look toward the future."

Luke chuckled again. "You must have taken a real hard blow to the head. You're actually chatty right now."

Noah laughed, too, then flinched. Whatever pain meds that nurse had given him to bring his vitals back down were wearing off now. But the machines were beeping steadily along like they had while he'd talked to the psychiatrist. The only person who'd upset him had been Wynn.

"While I feel like talking, let me fill you in on a few things," he said. And he told Luke about his conversation with Claire, the collection of dead animals, and his nephew's strange behavior in the hospital.

Luke nodded. "Claire already told me some of this. She came to find me right after she left your room."

He grimaced, not with pain, but with regret that she'd left before he'd had the chance to thank her for saving him. "She was alone? Wynn wasn't with her?"

Luke shook his head. "No. But she was definitely unsettled about finding him in your room holding a pillow."

"She wasn't the only one. My father's will isn't settled yet,"

Noah reminded him. "Only the heirs who survive the probate period will inherit, and that percentage gets bigger with every heir that dies."

"Fuck your old man," Luke muttered. "Did he want you all to kill each other?"

"Lord of the flies . . ." Noah muttered. Maybe that collection Wynn had shown Claire had belonged to his father; he'd certainly been a sadistic son of a bitch in some ways.

"But Tyler Hicks wasn't an heir," Luke said. "Where does he figure into this?"

"Was he murdered?" Noah asked even though he was pretty certain he had been, especially since Claire had found him nearly concealed in that open grave.

Luke sighed. "I don't know. I have to check in with the coroner, but I've been a little busy. Do you have any idea what happened?"

"To Tyler?"

"To you."

"I went back to the maintenance building after talking to Claire and found a note on the door to my office. It was sending all my staff home, saying that the cemetery was closed on police orders."

"There was no note found on the door," Luke said. And maybe he doubted him again, because his eyes narrowed.

Frustration elicited another groan from Noah. "It was there. And while I was reading it, someone hit me over the head. Then I heard the engines starting, but I passed out before I could shut them off."

"The doctor said you took quite a blow to the back of the head, but she couldn't say for sure if you were hit with something, or if you hit your head when you fell."

"I was hit with something," Noah said. "I remember that. I was standing up when I got hit and then my legs just gave out."

As the pain had radiated throughout his skull. "And I was sure that there was someone else in the building. I could hear them." He could feel them, too, but he didn't want to sound like a kook.

"But you didn't see anything," Luke said.

He shook his head and flinched as that pain radiated throughout his skull again. The pain meds had definitely worn off. "No."

"Who would want to kill you, Noah?"

"I just told you," he said, his voice rising a bit with irritation. "Because of that will, any member of my family might want me dead."

"Not River," Luke said defensively. "She was really worried about you and put herself in danger to save you."

Noah felt two twinges—one of guilt that she'd been hurt and one of appreciation that someone in his family actually cared about him. His father had never paid him any attention, and his mother and sister Honora had paid all their attention to his father and had had none left for him.

"River is all right?" he asked, needing assurance.

"Yes."

"Please, keep her safe," Noah implored him. "And Sarah."

"What about you?" Luke asked.

He sucked in a breath. "I'm going to be a lot more careful now. I won't turn my back when I hear there's someone around, someone who won't identify themselves." Because there was only one reason why that person had hid themselves in the building, because they hadn't wanted him to see who they were just in case he'd survived. Like he had, but that was thanks to River and to Claire Underwood.

Noah had to make damn sure that he didn't give the killer another chance to take him out. But the only way to keep himself and everyone else safe was to figure out who had tried to kill him and who had killed Tyler Hicks.

*   *   *

The killer watched while Claire Underwood walked out of the hospital to an Uber that was waiting for her. She was going to be a problem. If she hadn't shown up when she had, Noah would already be dead. She couldn't get in the way next time. And there would be a next time. Noah had to die, and like today, it had to look as if he'd hurt himself.

As if he was responsible for Tyler Hicks's murder—because the person who was really responsible could not be held accountable for it. There was too much work to do.

Too many lives yet to take . . .

Chapter 11

Despite the doctor giving her a clean bill of health, River's hands shook. She was upset over what had happened to Noah, over how close her brother had come to dying. But she was also upset over how that door had slammed behind her and Claire. She'd left the key in the lock on the outside, and the door had locked, shutting her and Claire inside with Noah and all those toxic fumes.

If she hadn't found the controls for the overhead doors and been able to open them, she didn't think any of them would have survived. Was that what the person had intended?

Before the door slammed shut, she'd noticed a shadow cast across the concrete floor. A long, tall shadow that had blocked out the light coming through the open door. And she'd thought of the grave digger. Legend had it that he was tall and skeletal thin with that unsettling glass eye. Legend and her memory. She'd seen him once on that night she was supposed to meet Michael in the cemetery. She was sure she'd seen the grave digger, and seeing him had made her even more determined to follow through with the plan and run away that night. But she'd had to run away alone.

Until her brain had cleared, she'd been thinking that it could have been the ghost who'd slammed the door shut and locked it. So she hadn't mentioned it to Luke. But now that her mind had cleared, she suspected that someone other than a ghost had been hovering around that building. And knowing that Luke needed all the facts, she waited for him outside Noah's room. When he stepped out, she clasped his arms.

"You're shaking," he said, and he closed his arms around her. "Are you all right?"

She nodded. "I just . . . I just had to process what happened. And there was something I didn't tell you . . ."

He tensed and stepped back. "What? What did you remember?"

She hadn't forgotten, but she didn't correct his misassumption. She just told him about the shadow and the slamming door.

"Damn it. That means that someone else was really involved in this," he muttered.

"You thought he locked himself in there?" she asked because the thought had flitted through her mind, too. She'd been gone a long time; she didn't really know her half brother all that well.

He shrugged. "I didn't know what to think. He insists that he didn't do it. He actually thinks that someone could have tried to kill him because of your father's will."

Father. She'd never really believed that Gregory Gold I was her father, probably because nobody else had believed it. She didn't look like the Golds. She looked like her mother. But her daughter looked like a Gold, nearly identical to her cousin except for the dimple in her chin. That and her deep-set eyes were all her father. She also looked like her uncle Luke.

But Sarah was definitely a Gold and so was River. Could someone really try to kill them because of that will in order to inherit a bigger share of the estate?

"We need to get back to the house," she said. "Sarah will be home from school soon." And she wanted to make sure that nobody tried to hurt her daughter.

Luke nodded. "I'll drive you."

"Me, too," a gruff voice said as Noah stepped through the door behind Luke. Actually, he staggered as if his legs were weak. He was wearing jeans and a flannel shirt that was misbuttoned. He must have dressed in a hurry. And he looked pale except for the dark circles beneath his eyes.

"Noah!" she exclaimed. "You need to get back in bed."

He grimaced as if the thought brought him pain. "Not here. I want to go home. I'll feel safer at home."

River snorted. "Really? You're safer here."

He shook his head. "At home I can lock my bedroom door."

"But the doctor won't let you go home yet," she said. "You were out for so long." She shuddered as she remembered doing CPR with Claire Underwood. Thank God the CPS investigator had known what she was doing because River would have had no idea. She'd just done what Claire had told her to do. She stepped around Luke to hug her brother. "I'm so glad you're all right."

"Thanks to you," he said.

"Thanks to Claire Underwood," she said.

"I want to thank her," he said, and he gazed in first one direction down the corridor and then the other. "Where is she?"

"She called an Uber to take her back to her vehicle," Luke said. "She left it at the maintenance building."

"We need to get back there," Noah said, his voice sharp with urgency. "Now."

Was he worried about Claire's safety like River was worried

about her daughter? But Claire wasn't a Gold; she wasn't in the danger that Sarah could be in, that River and Noah could be in.

But then Tyler Hicks wasn't a Gold, and he was dead. So maybe nobody was safe at Gold Memorial Gardens and Funeral Services.

As Toby drove the van through the gates, Sarah could see through the windshield, over the console from the back seat, that once again there were sheriff and state police vehicles in the parking lot.

"Shit," Toby said as he gripped the steering wheel.

"Why are they back?" Gigi, who sat in the passenger seat, asked. And she turned toward Sarah, as if she figured she would know.

Probably because her uncle was the sheriff. But she hadn't really talked that much to her uncle Luke yet. It was still awkward between them. She knew that he'd urged her dad to convince her mom to give Sarah up for adoption because he'd thought they were too young to be parents. Maybe her dad had been too young and that was why he'd bailed. But her mom had always been mature for her age, more mature than Grandma Fiona and even Great-Grandma Mabel, who was ancient. Mom was the best mom Sarah could have had, and she loved Sarah so much that she'd agreed to stay here in the place she'd hated so much she hadn't been able to wait to leave. She'd run away from it, but for Sarah she'd agreed to stay instead of going back to Santa Monica.

Gigi leaned farther over and looked past Sarah, who wasn't alone in the back seat. Jackson was with her. He'd gotten permission from Mrs. Sebastian to spend some time with her. Studying. That was what he'd claimed they were going to do, but they didn't even have any classes together. She was ahead because of being homeschooled, and he was a bit behind because of the tragedies in his life. So maybe she should help him study, get him caught up. But they weren't going to get any studying done tonight.

"I haven't talked to Luke," Jackson replied.

"No, because he wouldn't have let you come here if you did," Sarah said. "Not after Tyler died here last night."

"Miss Mary knows about that, too," Jackson said, "but she let me come here."

"She's getting old," Gigi said. "Maybe she forgot what happened."

Jackson sighed and shrugged. "I don't know how old she or Pastor Sebastian are. People in my life don't get old."

Sarah felt a twinge in her heart. And not just for Jackson who'd lost too many people he loved. "Tyler won't be able to get old now," she said.

"That sucks," her cousin Toby said. "But how'd *you* even know Hicks? He was a dealer."

Sarah shrugged. "I had him in a couple classes. He seemed really nice and smart. I didn't think he'd used drugs, let alone dealt them."

"You liked him?" Jackson asked, and his voice was a little gruff.

She shrugged again. "I didn't really know him. I just talked to him a couple of times. But he seemed nice. And even if he wasn't, he still didn't deserve to die like he did."

"Do you think someone else died?" Gigi asked, her eyes wide. "Is that why they're here again?"

Sarah stared beyond her, through the windshield, to all the state and sheriff vehicles parked in the lot. "I don't see a coroner's van," she said. She didn't even know where all the techs were because it wasn't like they were going in and out of the house. Nobody was even standing under the portico leading to the lobby doors. So where were they?

Then a vehicle came down the service road from the maintenance building. A woman was behind the wheel. She wore glasses, and most of her curly hair was pulled back. But she wasn't driving a coroner's van or one of the sheriff or state police vehicles. It was just an old hybrid with a few dents in it. She didn't stop at the gates but drove fast through them, as if she couldn't wait to get away from this place.

That was how Sarah's mom had felt all her life until she finally ran away when she was pregnant with Sarah. But she'd come back for her dad's funeral, and she'd agreed to stay for Sarah and maybe for Luke Sebastian, too.

The sheriff's SUV pulled into the lot behind the van they were all sitting in yet.

Jackson groaned when he noticed it. "He's probably going to be pissed that I'm here."

"Well, bad shit keeps happening around here," Gigi said. "Can you blame him?"

"Bad stuff happens everywhere," Jackson said.

Sarah reached out and clasped his hand, squeezing it. He'd been through too damn much in his sixteen years. Instead of whining about never knowing her dad, she should have been grateful that she'd always had her mom and still had her.

But then her mom climbed out of the passenger side of the sheriff's SUV, and she stumbled a bit and fell back against the door as she pushed it closed, like she was so weak.

Sarah shoved open the sliding door on the van and jumped out. "Mom! What's wrong? Are you all right?" Were all these crime scene techs here because of her?

Her mom turned and rushed toward Sarah, throwing her arms around her. She was shaking. And now so was Sarah.

"Mom, what happened?" she asked. "Why are the police here again?"

Luke moved around the SUV from the driver side, but he

wasn't alone. He had his hand on Uncle Noah's elbow, either helping him or not wanting him to get away.

"What happened?" she asked again, but she asked the sheriff now.

"Did you arrest Uncle Noah?" Toby asked. He and the others had followed her out of the van and stood around her and her mom. "Did he kill Tyler?"

"No!" Sarah said at the same time her uncle Noah did. She liked him; he was quiet, but when he talked, he was really snarky funny. And he was the only one in her family besides her mom who didn't care about being in charge, who wasn't all caught up in the money and the power of the family business.

"I did not kill anyone," Noah said.

"*He* was nearly killed earlier today," River said. "Someone hit him over the head and locked him in the maintenance building with all of the equipment running." She coughed as if getting choked up just thinking about it.

"I would have died if not for your mom, Sarah," Noah said.

"If not for Claire Underwood," her mother said, correcting him. "She came up to the house for the keys because she heard all those engines running and suspected you might be inside."

Claire Underwood?

"You and this woman rescued him?" Sarah asked, and she grasped her mom's thin arms. She'd obviously put herself in danger.

"Yes, they did," Noah replied. "They even did CPR to get me breathing again."

"Wow, that was close, Uncle Noah," Sarah said. She wasn't a hugger, but for her mom and Jackson, but she stepped forward to hug him. He didn't close his arms around her, just patted her shoulder, but she was fine with him not being a hugger, either. And she stepped back and said, "I'm really glad you're all right."

"Me, too," Toby said.

"Yeah," Jackson said. "That sounds like a close call."

"And like a crazy is on the loose again," Toby said.

Gigi let out a shaky little sigh. "That's why all the state police vehicles are here again."

"And while the crime scene techs are finishing up here, you should all go over to our house, Jackson," Luke said. "I'm sure Miss Mary would be happy to have a house full of kids again."

"But she said I could come here," Jackson said.

"Because she can't say no to you," Luke said with a smile. "She won't be able to say no to you all hanging out there for a while."

The sheriff was trying a little too hard to get rid of them, which concerned Sarah. But she was most concerned about her mom. She hugged her again. "You both got checked out at the hospital, right? You were okay to leave?"

"Yes, we were checked out at the hospital," Mom assured her. "And we're fine. Or at least *I'm* fine. Noah should have stayed but insisted on coming home so he could recover in his own room."

"I'm fine, too," Noah said with a slight smile. "I'm already recovered." But he still looked pale and shaky, and his eyes were bloodshot, too.

Mom glanced at him and grimaced, then she focused on Sarah again. "The sheriff is right. You would be safer—I mean, it would be better for you to go to his house for a while. He'll tell you when it's sa—when it's clear to come back."

Her mom hadn't misspoken. She was worried about Sarah's safety. Maybe it was just because a kid died here last night. Or maybe it was because of what happened today with her and Noah. There was another killer on the loose.

"Mom, will *you* be safe?" Sarah asked.

River smiled but it didn't reach her eyes, and she didn't meet

Sarah's gaze, either. "Of course." Then she smiled at Gigi and Toby. "I'll tell your parents that you'll be home a little later."

Toby snorted. "Like they would even notice."

"They would be worried," River insisted, but she couldn't know that. She didn't really know any of her family very well since she'd been gone so long.

Even Grandma Fiona was weird. Sarah remembered what she'd said the night before, how it would be bad for business if nobody else died. But was that just because they had to have funerals to make money or because if more Golds died, the shares of the inheritance to the survivors got bigger?

Sarah hugged her mom again. "Please, be careful," she whispered to her.

Her mom met her gaze now and held it, and the intensity in her green eyes scared Sarah. "You too," she said.

Were they all in danger?

Was that what her mom was worried about, that someone had tried to kill Noah and maybe her and that Sarah could be next?

Luke watched as the Gold Memorial Gardens and Funeral Services van pulled through the open wrought iron gates and drove off with the kids inside it. Once it disappeared from sight, some of the pressure on his chest eased, and he breathed a little deeper.

"Are you sure it's safe for them to be at your parents' house?" River asked, her voice shaky with fear.

"Safer than they'll be here," Noah answered before Luke could.

River gestured at the police vehicles parked in the lot. "But here we have protection."

"They'll be wrapping up soon," Luke said. At least that was the update he'd received via text message.

Noah started walking off toward the service road, and Luke reached out to grasp his arm. "You can't go in the maintenance building yet. It's still an active crime scene." It had nearly been the scene of his murder.

"And why would you want to?" River asked, and she shuddered.

"I don't want to go in the building," Noah said. "But I should, to find that note."

"If it was there, the techs would have found it," Luke said.

Noah turned around and glared at Luke. "It was there."

"What note?" River asked. "Noah, did you leave a note?"

"I didn't leave it," he said. "It was on my door telling my crew to go home, that the police had closed down the cemetery. I was reading it when someone hit me on the head. That's why I was alone in the building and why no one would have found me . . ."

"If not for Claire Underwood looking for you," River finished for him. "She really did save your life."

"And I would like to thank her," Noah said. "Didn't one of you say she had to come back here for her car?"

"It's gone," Luke said. "We actually passed her on our way here."

"Where was she headed?" Noah asked.

Luke shrugged. "I don't know."

"I want to talk to her," Noah said, and he started to pull away from Luke. "My truck is parked on the other side of the home." But when he started walking away from Luke, he staggered again.

Luke grabbed his arm, steadying him before he fell. "Careful."

"You need to go lie down," River said. "You shouldn't have even left the hospital."

The doctor had said that, too, but had reluctantly signed Noah's release papers. Luke understood why his friend wanted to be home even though he probably should have stayed in the hospital. Noah wanted to be somewhere familiar, somewhere he could lock his door. But the maintenance building was familiar to him, and he'd wound up locked inside with toxic fumes. He could have died.

"Maybe the two of you should go to the Sebastians with the kids," he suggested.

River smiled. "I'm not sure your parents would appreciate having a bunch of houseguests."

"They loved having the house full of kids when they were younger," Luke said.

"Well, they're older now, and we're not kids," Noah said.

"You're not kids," Luke agreed. "But I'd like to see you both get older. And I'm not sure that can happen here, in this house. You're not safe, not with the crazy way your dad wrote up his will."

River shivered, and he reached out to slide his arm around her shoulders. She wasn't just cold; she was shaking. He was shaking a little, too.

"Tyler didn't die because of that will," Noah said. "And whoever tried to kill me might not have gone after me because of that will."

River and Luke both tensed.

"Why else would they go after you?" Luke asked. Despite knowing Noah since they were kids, he really didn't know him well. Luke had been gone a long time, and Noah had always been a quiet guy who kept to himself and to the cemetery.

"Tyler," he said. "He texted me. He wanted to talk to me. Maybe someone thinks that he did."

Luke shook his head, disgusted with himself for not considering that. While he'd been an MP in the Marines, he didn't have much experience with investigations like this. With murder investigations.

The crime scene techs weren't the only ones who'd sent him a text. The coroner had, too. **Not an accidental death.**

He knew the doctor was talking about Tyler Hicks. The kid hadn't died because the high winds had knocked a tree limb down on his head. Someone had purposely smashed in his skull.

Why?

Because they hadn't wanted him to talk to Noah or to CPS?

"Do you have any idea what he wanted to talk to you about?" Luke asked.

Noah shrugged. "I figured he was going to tell me why he was crashing in my office in the maintenance building. And maybe about the money that I found in that bag."

Luke had that bag with money in the evidence room right now. "How do you think he got that money?"

Noah sighed. "Dealing drugs. That was why I fired him, because I caught him dealing out by the grave digger's grave."

"But why would anyone go after *you* over that?" River asked.

"Maybe they thought he was going to tell me who he was dealing for," Noah said.

Luke groaned and pressed his hand to his forehead. "Drugs. Murder. Why the hell did I think it would be safer for Jackson in Gold Creek than anywhere else?"

"Because you forgot what this place is really like," Noah said. "When you were gone, you idealized it."

River expelled a shaky breath. "*I* did not do that."

"No, *you* did just the opposite. You demonized it," Noah said. "I used to think it was somewhere in the middle of those two things, but now I think you were right, River."

"Then I shouldn't have come back here," she said. "And I damn sure shouldn't have brought Sarah with me."

Luke felt a pang of loss over the thought that he might never have seen River again or have ever seen his niece if she hadn't returned for her father's funeral. He had to make Gold Creek safe for them and for Jackson, too, and for everyone who had voted for him.

Some of the people in this house had voted for him, might have even coerced other people to vote for him. Had they done that because they'd thought he wasn't up to the job and that they could get away with murder?

Chapter 12

Once Claire picked up her vehicle from the crime scene at Gold Memorial Gardens, she'd intended to head back to her place. Or maybe to the CPS office; it wasn't as if Mallory would fire her for returning to work, especially when she had other open cases besides Tyler Hicks's.

But instead she found herself pulling up to a farmhouse with a wooden plaque, engraved with the surname *Sebastian*, dangling from chains off the mailbox. She'd been back in Gold Creek for a few weeks; she probably should have stopped by to visit before today. She'd used the excuse that she hadn't had time because she'd been too busy with work. But after going into the carbon monoxide–filled building to rescue Noah, she'd almost really had no time for anything anymore.

She could have died. The ER doctor had told her that and so did her pounding head and her heart that continued to beat a little too fast. She wasn't sure why she was so affected; she'd been in dangerous situations before. She'd been attacked. Choked. Nearly run down by a vehicle.

So maybe she wasn't upset that she could have died but that

Noah Gold could have, which was even more upsetting to her, that Noah Gold's well-being had affected her so much.

Coming back to Gold Creek had been a mistake; it was bringing back all kinds of emotions and memories that Claire had locked away since she'd left. So coming here, to the Sebastians, was a mistake, too. But she opened the driver's door and stepped out onto the gravel drive. She walked across it toward the little walkway lined with purple and white hyacinths and hydrangeas. On the edge of the lawn was a row of lilac bushes bearing both purple and white flowers. Had Mrs. or Pastor Sebastian left those flowers on her mother's grave? They'd both known her mother as everyone seemed to know everyone else in Gold Creek, but they'd not been close. If they had left them, they'd probably done it for her, because she had been Claire's mother.

Her heart beat a little harder yet as she climbed the porch steps, and it wasn't because of physical exertion. She was remembering that night a CPS investigator brought her here. She'd been shaken and devastated then but also somewhat relieved as well, which had made her feel like a terrible person. Her hand trembled a bit, but she fisted it and knocked on the storm door. The interior door was open, so she could see inside, see the glow of light from the kitchen, and she could smell the scent of cinnamon and apples and some kind of chicken dish as well.

Her stomach growled, reminding her that she hadn't eaten all day. After last night, after finding Tyler Hicks in the open grave, she'd had no appetite then or this morning. And then she'd made the mistake of going back to Gold Memorial Gardens.

What was it about this place that had her making mistake after mistake?

A woman with bright white hair stepped out of the kitchen, her gaze focused on the door. When she saw Claire, her eyes widened, and she gestured at her to come in. "Claire!" she exclaimed, and she rushed forward to close her arms around her, just like she had that night so long ago.

That night Claire had stood stiffly within the older woman's embrace, not certain that she deserved or even needed comfort or compassion. But then she found herself closing her arms around Mary Sebastian's petite body. The woman seemed even smaller than Claire remembered, but her grasp on Claire was tight and comforting as well.

Claire released a shaky sigh. "I'm surprised you remember me with all the kids who've come through your home."

Mary pulled back and reached up to cup Claire's cheek in her palm. "I would never forget you, sweet girl."

Had she been sweet? She didn't remember that; she honestly didn't remember much of her time in this house. She hadn't been here that long before CPS had found her maternal grandmother who'd agreed to have Claire come live with her. On a trial basis, as long as Claire was not as much trouble as her mother had been.

Claire hadn't wanted to be anything like her mother then or now. Her mom had been desperate for a man, so desperate that she would keep one no matter how horrible he was or what he did. But they were gone now. And for years Claire had been gone, too. From here . . .

From the memories of this place.

The only thing Claire had probably been, during her time with the Sebastians, had been quiet, due either to shock or that somewhat disturbing sense of relief she'd felt.

"You were so kind to me," Claire said. That she remembered very well. Both Mary and Pastor Sebastian had been incredibly kind to her. She'd actually felt safe here. Maybe that was why she'd come here today, for that feeling of security. "I hope you know how much I appreciated you and Pastor Sebastian."

"You were very sweet," Mary said again, "and you made that very clear to us."

"Speak for yourself, Mary," a man's voice said.

Claire tensed for a moment until she saw the big grin on Pastor Sebastian's gently lined face. He and Mary had both aged, of course, in the years since she'd seen them. Mary had seemed to shrink, though, getting shorter and slighter while Pastor was tall yet and looked even taller for being a bit thinner than she remembered. He reached out and closed his arms around her. "Claire, I'm so happy you're home."

Even though she'd felt safe here, this had never been home, and not just because she hadn't lived here long. The other place she'd lived in Gold Creek with her mom and stepdad in that trailer in the woods certainly hadn't been home, either. Even after she'd left to live with her grandmother, that house had never felt like home, either, because that trial basis had hung over her head, making her nervous that she might do something that would have her grandmother sending her away.

She hugged him back and then stepped out of his embrace. "I'm not sure I'm going to be staying," she said.

"But we heard that you're working here now," Mary said. "That you're with Child Protective Services."

She nodded. "Yes."

"That is definitely God's work you're doing, Claire," Pastor Sebastian praised her with a wide smile.

She shrugged. "I don't know about that," she said. "Maybe if it was possible to do more, to make more of a difference, but parents and even judges don't always comply with our recommendations."

"Sadly, I remember that all too well," the pastor said, and he hugged her again. "God knows, though, that you're doing *your* best. And that's what counts with Him and with us."

Tears rushed to her eyes, and when she shut them to hold

back the tears, she saw Tyler Hicks staring up at her with that blank expression, with that crushed skull. And Noah . . .

Lying on the ground, blood matting his dark hair to his head.

She drew in a shaky breath and murmured, "Sometimes my best isn't good enough." If only she could have gotten to Tyler sooner . . .

"Oh, Claire," Mary said. "You were always much too hard on yourself."

"Much too hard," Pastor Sebastian agreed. "You're one of the good ones, Claire. You're living your life in service, helping make this world a better place. A safer place."

Tears stung her eyes, but she shook her head, unwilling to accept his praise. She hadn't made anything safer for Tyler Hicks.

"Come into the kitchen," Mary said. "Dinner is almost ready, and I made an apple crumble, too."

Claire's stomach rumbled, and she smiled. "Your cooking was one of my favorite things about staying here."

"Not my sermons?" Pastor Sebastian asked.

Her smile widened. "I don't remember any of those."

"Saying you slept through them?" he asked.

"Saying that you weren't very preachy for being a pastor," she said.

He shrugged. "I only preach to those who need it and who actually want to hear it."

She wasn't sure if he hadn't preached to her because she hadn't needed it or because she had but wouldn't have been willing to listen. "Luke said you've retired," she remembered. "So nobody's willing to listen anymore?"

Because she knew they still needed preaching, particularly whoever had killed Tyler Hicks and tried to kill Noah Gold. Yet that person was the least likely to seek out help or guidance. They were more likely to go after another victim.

Or back for the one who'd survived.

Noah had to be in the hospital yet. But was he safe there, especially with his creepy nephew on staff? Remembering how she'd found Wynn in Noah's room, that pillow clutched in his hands, had a shudder passing through her.

"You're cold. Come into the kitchen." Mary said again, "It's warm, and the apple crumble is fresh from the oven. You can have dessert first. With the job you have, you've definitely earned it."

She'd lost Tyler, so she hadn't earned anything. But she followed Mary into the warmth of the kitchen. Pastor Sebastian walked in behind her. "What about me?" he asked. "May I have dessert before dinner?"

"With your cholesterol and blood pressure, you probably shouldn't have any dessert," Mary said.

Claire doubted that Mrs. Sebastian would deny her husband anything. They had had a sweet and loving relationship; it was the only one she'd ever witnessed growing up. Her mother and stepfather's relationship had been toxic, and her grandmother had been alone and bitter.

"How do you think my cholesterol got high?" the pastor asked, and he gestured at the big pan with steam rising from the surface of the crumbled oats and brown sugar and pecans. It sat on the counter next to a big clear canister of home-baked cookies.

That had been one of the biggest surprises for Claire when she'd stayed at the Sebastians. That there was so much homemade food and that it was so good; her mother hadn't ever cooked. The other big surprise was that she hadn't had to lock her door.

That hadn't been the case in her own home, and she knew that there weren't many foster homes around even now where that was the case. The Sebastians were exceptional people. While the Golds were the richest in the town, the Sebastians were the most respected, and rightfully so for as much as they served the community and all the children they'd made feel safe again.

"So you shouldn't have any crumble then, Peter," Mary said, but she was smiling.

"Ah, Mary, I'd rather have your crumble and die a happy man than deprive myself."

Mary laughed.

And then the storm door squeaked.

Mary looked through the doorway and smiled. "Jackson. You're just in time for dinner and dessert."

Claire turned to see four teenagers standing just inside the storm door. She knew about Jackson; Luke had told her that the kid was his godson. But were the others just friends of his or what she'd been all those years ago? "I thought you didn't foster anymore," she said to Pastor Sebastian.

"These aren't fosters," the pastor said. "This is Luke's godson, Jackson." The boy was tall and good-looking with black skin and short cropped hair. "And these are his friends: Sarah, Toby, and Gigi Gold."

The two girls, who could have been twins, certainly looked like Golds with their black hair and dark eyes. The girl with the shorter hair had a dimple in her chin, though, while the one with the longer hair did not. The boy was tall and too thin for his big bones, but he would be as good-looking as the other Golds when he got older, like Noah with his thick dark hair and soulful eyes. Hopefully, he wouldn't have Wynn's soulless eyes.

Golds.

She couldn't escape them since she'd come back to Gold Creek. But she shouldn't have expected that she would. This was, after all, *Gold* Creek in *Gold* County, and the town and the county hadn't been named that because of any mineral found around here. Nothing was taken from the ground in Gold Creek, but for many years the Golds had been putting everyone in the ground.

"This is Claire Underwood." Mary introduced her to the kids. "She once stayed with us a long time ago."

The kids exchanged glances with each other. While they might not know the specifics, they knew there was a reason she'd stayed here, that she'd once been a foster kid.

"And now she works for Child Protective Services," Pastor Sebastian said, pride in his voice.

Her heart warmed with pleasure. Her grandmother had died before she'd finished college, so there was no one in Claire's life to be proud of her, to praise her. She hadn't realized how much it would mean to have someone do that, to have someone care.

"You're not here about Jackson, are you?" the girl with the chin dimple asked. "He's never been in any danger since he's come to live here with the sheriff and the Sebastians. The killer—*killers* around the Gold Memorial Gardens and funeral home never had any interest in him."

But clearly this girl did.

"There is no case for Jackson . . ." She had no idea what his last name was. He was Luke's godson, not his son. But everybody in the office would have been talking if someone had called in a report about the kid living with the sheriff and the Sebastians.

"I saw you just a little while ago," the girl named Sarah said. "You were driving out of the cemetery. You were the CPS investigator for Tyler Hicks."

She nodded. "What do any of you know about Tyler?"

Jackson shrugged. "Nothing really. I haven't lived here very long."

She focused on the Golds. "What about you? He died in the cemetery last night. Was he meeting one of you there? Were one of you bringing him food when he was staying in the maintenance building?"

Gigi shuddered. "God, no." Then she flushed and looked at Pastor Sebastian. "Sorry, Father."

He smiled. "I'm not a priest, Gigi. And I'm not even a pastor anymore."

"You still do funerals," the girl said.

"And you give sermons on Sunday a lot," Jackson added.

"Ah, so you are still preaching," Claire said with a glance at the pastor.

He chuckled. "Only when I am coerced into it."

"Or someone asks," Mary said. "Or you feel compelled to step in when someone needs some guidance."

Claire wasn't distracted. "What about either of you?" she asked Sarah and Toby.

Sarah glanced at Jackson. "I'm new here, too. Tyler was in a class of mine, but we just talked a little bit about the work, teacher, that kind of thing. He was pretty quiet and seemed nice."

Toby snorted. "He was trouble. He sold drugs out in the cemetery by the grave digger's grave."

Pastor Sebastian made a noise. "Drugs are an abomination. They take so many lives and souls."

Toby glanced at Pastor Sebastian, and his face flushed. "I only know that because of what other kids told me. I never go out there. I know better. He should have, too. Uncle Noah fired him because of the drugs."

Claire's shoulders sagged with disappointment. She wasn't getting any new information about Tyler. Had he had any friends? Or just customers? And why had a quiet kid who'd seemed to enjoy school been selling drugs? She still had more questions than answers.

And Sarah stared at her like she had a question of her own. "What?"

"You're the one who helped my mom save my uncle Noah," she said. "Thank you for doing that."

Claire shrugged. "I wasn't even thinking. I just reacted."

"Most people would have done nothing," Jackson said.

"Yeah, that was cool that you saved him," Toby said.

Heat flushed Claire's face, and it wasn't from the heat of the warm kitchen. She just nodded.

"See, you do deserve dessert first, Claire," Mary said. "But eat dinner with us, too." She turned toward the kids again. "All of you need to sit down and grab a plate. I made plenty."

Pastor leaned close to Claire and murmured, "She loves having all the kids around again."

Claire saw the grin on his face and the warmth in his hazel eyes as he stared at the kids. "She's not the only one," she said.

"It's good to have them around, even better to have Luke and now you back in Gold Creek."

Despite this visit with this very sweet couple, she couldn't say that it was good to be back. Because of all the memories and Tyler's death, it wasn't good. It was hell. And while she'd lived through it once, she wasn't sure she would survive a second time. No. Coming back here had definitely been a mistake.

Noah had insisted that River and Luke didn't need to help him inside the house. But it took him a ridiculously long time to walk the length of the portico to the lobby doors. He had to draw in a deep breath and gather his strength before he could push open those doors. When he stepped inside, he found his half brother, Lawrence, and his stepmother, Fiona, waiting for him.

"This isn't good for business," Lawrence said, and he made the same tsking sound with his tongue that his son had in the hospital.

"What isn't good?" Noah asked.

Fiona gestured toward the doors. "All the police vehicles parked in the lot and the techs and sheriff and deputies going over the cemetery and over your maintenance building."

"You do know that I could have died?" he asked. He probably would have died had it not been for Claire Underwood. He owed her a thank-you, but that didn't seem like enough for his life. But what had he actually done with his life besides spending entirely too much of it here?

"Of course," Fiona said. "But you're home, so you're fine. And if you actually hurt yourself, you need to admit that and if you actually hurt that boy, so that we can get back to bus—"

"What the hell are you talking about?" Noah asked. "I haven't hurt anyone. And I can't believe you think that I would have." But *he* was hurt right now and not just physically anymore. "I was one of the few who was actually defending you from all the people, including my own mother, who thought you killed my father, Fiona." Disgust churned in his stomach. Then he pointed at Lawrence. "And did you send your strange son to the hospital to finish me off? Was that why he was standing next to my bed with a pillow?"

Lawrence gasped, and his dark eyes widened with shock. "Of course not. That didn't happen. You're delusional, Noah. Maybe it's the aftereffects from inhaling all those fumes."

Noah shook his head, then grimaced when pain shot through his skull. "I'm not delusional. Someone else caught him in my room and probably saved me from him trying to smother me." So Claire had saved him twice, and he hadn't even thanked her. "You're the delusional ones to think that I could have hurt a kid or myself."

Why the hell had he come back home to this? To the suspicion and the accusations.

He'd thought he could lock himself in his room and keep them all out. But first he had to get to his room. He regretted now that he hadn't had River and Luke walk him into the building. Hell, he regretted coming back at all.

And where was everyone else?

His mother?

Maybe she hadn't even heard about what had happened today. She rarely left her room now. Despite not being married to his father anymore, she'd struggled with his death. Then her daughter died, and her grandson was arrested for waving a gun around and threatening other family members.

Fiona sighed and rushed forward, touching his arms. "Of course we know better. We do," she assured Noah. "It was just that everyone was so convinced that you'd locked yourself in that building, that you were trying to end it all. And after everything that has happened, we've learned that we can never assume what someone else is capable of doing."

Murder. A lot of his family had been capable of murder. And there might still be a killer among them. Wynn?

Lawrence?

Fiona?

He couldn't trust any of them except River. He knew she had a good heart, but he didn't want her in danger. And as for Claire Underwood . . .

He could definitely trust the woman who'd already saved his life. But he suspected that if she kept pushing to find out what happened to Tyler Hicks, that she would be in danger, too, if she wasn't already. He hated that she'd driven off on her own.

After losing her mom and stepdad so long ago, maybe she was as alone in the world as he felt. Or maybe, unlike him, she lived a full life and had someone significant in it. While he only had these people . . . his family . . . with one or more of them probably capable of killing him just to inherit more of his father's estate.

River should have gone inside with Noah despite his assurance that he was fine. He wasn't fine. He could have died. And a boy not much older than Sarah was had died.

She wrapped her arms around herself and waited while Luke talked to the techs who'd come up to report to him about their findings. Cynically she didn't think they'd found much because Luke wasn't rushing off with lights flashing to make an arrest. He didn't know who was responsible for Tyler's death or the attempt on Noah's life.

"River, you're cold," Luke remarked. "You shouldn't have waited outside for me." He touched her arms, running his hands up and down over the sleeves of the sweater she wore. "But I am actually relieved that you did stay out here, so I can make sure you stay safe."

"And Sarah?" she asked. "Was it a good idea sending the kids off to your parents?"

He nodded. "I feel like they're safer there than anywhere else."

"But they have to get there," she said. "And they're driving one of the company vans." Not that many weeks ago she had driven one that had been rigged so that she'd lost control of it and crashed.

He flinched as if he'd been injured in that crash, too. Or maybe he was regretting sending the kids off like he had. "Text Sarah. Make sure they're fine. And I'll personally drive her and Gigi and Toby back here unless you want them to stay there. And maybe you'd consider staying there, too?"

Yearning filled her. When she'd been dating Michael, the Sebastians had always been so warm and kind and uncomplicated, unlike her family. She was tempted to go there and stay. She'd always hated the house by the cemetery. But it was her and Sarah's home now. "I don't think it's a good idea for Sarah and Jackson to spend too much time together," she admitted. She liked their friendship, but she didn't want her daughter to be like her and her mother and her grandmother: a mom too soon.

Luke nodded. "I agree."

"Of course you do." He hadn't approved of her brother and her becoming parents in their teens.

"River." He glanced around, maybe to make sure all the techs were gone. And they were.

"What?"

"I can't keep apologizing for how I handled things in the past," he said.

"I'm not asking you to," she said. "As a mother myself now, I understand what you were thinking at the time. And I'm not upset or angry about it anymore."

"I just wish we knew what happened to Michael," he said. "Did you check the funerals with burials around the time he went missing?"

She shook her head. "I was trying to figure out the password to sign onto Lawrence's computer when Claire came running into the lobby, worried about Noah."

"She was right to be worried."

River nodded. "Yes, she was. And I'm worried, too, now."

"I'll check on the kids," he said.

"Good. But I'm not worried just about Sarah."

"No, you need to worry about yourself, too," he said.

"And my mother . . ."

He grimaced a bit. "I know she's your mom, so of course you're going to worry about her, too."

"She was why I came back, why I stayed." She hadn't come back because the man she hadn't really believed was her dad died. She'd returned because she'd been worried about what would happen to her mother after Gregory Gold I died, and then once she'd arrived, she'd stayed because it had been clear that her mother was Luke's number one suspect.

"I'm not sure what exactly I worry about with my mother," she admitted. "I think she can take care of herself much better than I realized she could." And she was worried that her mother might have taken care of something else, like maybe Michael Sebastian.

Had she done something to him so that River wouldn't run away with him? She felt guilty for even thinking that about her mother, though, and was not about to bring up that suspicion to the sheriff.

"What about Tyler Hicks?" she asked instead. "Why would someone hurt that poor kid?"

Luke shrugged. "I don't know. I have no idea what if anything is related to anything else that's happened. Did the same person who killed Tyler go after Noah? Or are there two separate killers? And Michael . . ."

"Is he alive and living somewhere else or is he buried somewhere like Tyler would have been buried had Claire Underwood not found his body?" River finished the question for him, the one that was plaguing her. "I'll try to get those records about the funerals."

He nodded. "Be careful."

"You too," she said.

Because if the same person who'd killed Tyler Hicks had killed Michael, then that person had been killing for a long time. And they were probably very good at hiding their tracks. They were also someone who spent a lot of time around the cemetery, around the grave digger's grave.

Was the grave digger's ghost capable of murder? She already knew that members of her family were, but she'd thought they were all dead now. Maybe their ghosts were haunting the grounds, too.

But she didn't really believe that a ghost could kill. So she was pretty sure that the killer was alive and well and uncomfortably, dangerously, close to home.

Chapter 13

Claire found herself actually smiling as she pulled into the driveway of the little bungalow she'd rented on the outskirts of the village of Gold Creek. She'd enjoyed herself at the Sebastians. The food had been amazing, just as she'd remembered, and the company had been even better.

Once she'd stopped interrogating the kids about Tyler, they'd relaxed around her. They'd talked about what teachers they had and had been so stunned that some of the ones who'd taught her were still teaching. She'd pretended to be offended that they thought she was so old, but she really hadn't been. Sometimes she felt so old. And it had been funny to watch them scrambling around for compliments to make up for the offense.

She stepped out of her vehicle with a smile on her face. Then she thought of all the things she had yet to do. Like make sure that Tyler's siblings were safe. She would need a lot of evidence to prove that they weren't, or a judge wouldn't remove them from the home. With the mother and stepfather vouching for each other's whereabouts the night Tyler died, she wouldn't be able to use his death as a reason unless Luke found evidence to prove they were lying and that one of them had killed him.

But if that was the case, why would that person go after Noah, too? Unless they thought Tyler had told him something or he'd seen them.

Remembering that night in the cemetery, the howling wind, the tendrils of moss slapping her, the falling limbs, she shuddered. Then she blew out a shaky breath and headed toward the door of the bungalow. In front of the house, a white picket fence partitioned off a little courtyard with an arbor over it. She pushed open the gate and stepped onto the brick patio. The setting sun streaked through the cedar boards of the arbor except in one place . . . where the shadow of a man blocked the light and blocked her access to the front door. She turned to run back to her car.

To get away.

This had happened before: parents tracking her down where she lived, threatening her, trying to hurt her.

Even that doctor who'd sworn he was such an upstanding citizen that he wouldn't have hurt his kids had tried to hurt her. That was another reason she'd moved.

She'd realized she wasn't safe anywhere so she might as well come back to the place where she'd felt the least safe.

And she'd definitely been right. She was the least safe than she had ever been here in Gold Creek, and that was confirmed when a big hand closed around her arm and stopped her from escaping.

Sarah liked being at the Sebastians. They were probably close to her great-grandmother's age, but they were a lot more normal than GG Mabel had ever been. They sat down and had family meals together. They joked and laughed and asked questions. They cared.

Not that GG Mabel didn't care, and Sarah's mom certainly did, but Sarah had never had that two-parent, male/female unit that so many other kids had. Toby and Gigi had two parents that were still married, but they were odd. Uncle Gregory III was a little too slick and secretive and their mom, Karen, was really *a Karen*. Just super-bitchy and condescending and really obviously jealous of Sarah's mom. River was gorgeous, though, and nice, and that made some people hate her because they knew they would never be her.

During dinner Claire Underwood had said nice things about her without seeming at all jealous. She'd given Mom a lot of the credit for saving Uncle Noah.

"That CPS investigator was pretty cool," Sarah said to Jackson as they finished drying the dishes that Gigi and Toby were washing. They'd been appalled that the Sebastians had no dishwasher, but they'd stepped up to help. She'd thought they were spoiled rich kids when she first met them, and they were. But they were trying to be more real now.

Jackson let out a shaky sigh and nodded. "Yeah, really cool when you know what happened to her."

"You mean today?" Sarah asked. "Being in that building with Mom and Uncle Noah?"

He shook his head. "No. Luke told me that she stayed here with the Sebastians because her parents died in a murder-suicide thing. Super sad."

Jackson knew sad. He'd lost his parents tragically, too, but neither of them had been responsible for the other one dying. That was extra tragic and made Sarah rethink her whole yearning for that two-parent thing.

"Stepdad," Pastor Sebastian said as he walked into the kitchen. He had on his coat like he was heading somewhere. "It was Claire's stepdad who killed her mother and then himself. I think he knew eventually he would have charges pressed against him."

"For what?" Toby asked.

"He was not a good man. Let's just say that," Pastor Sebastian replied. "And his death spared Claire from having to deal with any more trauma than she already had."

Sarah's morbid mind could fill in the gory details about their deaths and the motive for them. And she cringed a bit. "Poor Claire. I'm surprised she wanted to come back here."

"I'm surprised anyone wants to be in Gold Creek," Gigi said. "It's not safe. So many people have died."

"I thought it was over after Grandma Caroline died," Toby said. "That there wouldn't be any more people dying since she was behind everything. But now that drug dealer and almost Uncle Noah."

"My mom and Claire could have died, too," Sarah said. "It sounds like the building was really toxic when they went in to rescue him."

"You don't think he hurt himself?" Pastor Sebastian asked. "And that maybe he had something to do with that kid's death?"

"No," Sarah said. "Absolutely not."

Toby shrugged. "I didn't think all the other people in our family who killed and did crazy stuff could have done it, either . . ."

"But they did," Gigi finished for him. "That's probably why the sheriff wanted us to come here."

"Because we're not safe at home," Toby said.

"You can stay here," Jackson said, then glanced at Pastor Sebastian. "I mean . . . if it's cool with you and Miss Mary."

"You know we would love that, and that you would all be safe here. But I do have to leave now to meet with some grieving parents," Pastor Sebastian said.

So he must have been asked to officiate the funeral for Tyler Hicks. He still did a lot of them.

He smiled at them all and said, "But none of you should be

worried about your safety. Luke will make sure nothing happens to any of you."

Jackson clenched his jaw and closed his eyes, and Sarah could almost imagine what he was thinking, what he was remembering. But he waited until Pastor Sebastian left the room before he said, "Luke tries his best. But he couldn't protect and save my dad when they were deployed together. And I don't think he can protect and save any of us from a killer, either. We have to look out for ourselves."

"That's true," a deep voice said.

But it wasn't the pastor who'd walked back into the kitchen. Uncle Luke stood there; he'd heard what Jackson had said.

Jackson grimaced. "Shit, Luke. I wasn't bashing you. I was just being real."

"I know," Luke said. "I agree with you. I didn't protect or save your dad. I'm not even sure what happened to my younger brother, Sarah's dad, so you're right. You all have to be careful. Look out for yourselves. Don't do anything stupid like going off somewhere alone."

Toby snorted. "Like every bad actor in every horror movie ever made."

Luke smiled. "Yeah, like that."

"And like Uncle Noah and Tyler," Sarah said. "They were alone when they were attacked."

"You don't know yet that the boy was murdered, do you?" Pastor Sebastian asked. He must have met Luke at the door and come back into the kitchen, but he was hidden behind Luke's taller and broader body.

"I'm meeting with the coroner after I make sure the Gold kids get safely back home," he said. "So I'll know more then."

Sarah was sure he had a pretty good idea now, or he wouldn't have been so concerned about their safety, which made her more concerned. "Why are you so worried, Uncle Luke? Do you think someone is purposely killing kids in the cemetery?"

"Sarah, we don't know for sure what happened to Tyler Hicks," Luke said, but he didn't quite meet her gaze. "And he is the only *kid* who has died in the cemetery."

The body she and Jackson had found weeks ago had belonged to a creepy private investigator. He'd definitely not been a kid. But still . . .

"You kids shouldn't be worried about all of this," Pastor Sebastian added as if he was trying to make them feel better.

"If Tyler wasn't murdered, why don't you want us going out in the cemetery alone?" she asked her uncle.

"Until we know what happened, it's just not smart to take unnecessary risks," Luke replied.

"Like the kids in those crappy horror movies," Toby said, and chuckled.

But Sarah didn't laugh. She wasn't finding any of this funny right now because something else was going on. She stepped closer to her uncle and asked, "How do you know that no other kids have died in the cemetery? What if my dad died there that night he was supposed to run away with Mom? What if he's buried in someone else's grave like Tyler nearly was?"

Uncle Luke's throat moved like he was trying hard to swallow, and his eyes glistened a bit. He blinked and said, "I don't know, Sarah. But your mom and I are going to find out what happened to him. Just like I will find out what happened to Tyler and who's responsible."

Who's responsible . . .

Because he said that Sarah was sure he knew Tyler had been killed and obviously he didn't want her or Jackson or Toby or Gigi to be next.

With his hand on her arm, he could feel her shaking. He'd scared her again. "Claire, don't be alarmed. It's just me," Noah said. "And I'm really sorry for just showing up like this."

"How did you find me?" she asked, her voice a raspy whisper.

Was that from the fumes she'd inhaled earlier that day? His throat felt raw, too, and his head was pounding and felt a little light. He released her arm and stumbled back to drop down onto the bench under the arbor. As he did, he knocked over one of the potted mums he'd brought with him.

She didn't even notice it as she crouched down in front of the bench, in front of him, and peered into his face. "Are you okay?" she asked now with concern. "Why aren't you in the hospital?"

He released a shaky sigh. "Give me a minute. I'll answer one question at a time."

"I should take you back to the hospital," she said. "Or call an ambulance—"

He touched her shoulder now, stopping her from jumping up. "I'm fine . . . because of you, because you saved me earlier today. I came here to thank you for that." He moved his hand from her shoulder to lean down and right the potted mum. It was purple, like the one she'd had at the cemetery, while the other one was pink. "I realize now that these are kind of a lame thank-you gift." He owed her so much more than flowers. "But this one looks like the one you brought to your mother's grave."

She touched the purple blooms. "I was going to bring it back here, but I must have left it at that building."

"When you rescued me," he said.

She ignored his remark and asked again, with that raspiness back in her voice, "How did you find me?" She straightened up and stepped back, as if fearful of him. "Luke and the Sebastians don't even know where I live."

"I didn't ask them," he said, which was apparently a good thing since he would have been wasting his time. "My family owns a lot of houses and buildings in Gold Creek. I checked with the property manager to see if you might be renting one of them."

"You went to a lot of trouble," she said. "Why?"

"To thank you," he said. "You saved my life, Claire. Maybe more than once today."

She shivered. "More than once?"

"I don't know what Wynn really intended to do with that damn pillow," he said. "That's why I didn't want to stay in the hospital. I insisted that they release me to come home."

"Where Wynn is probably staying, right?" she asked. "Is that safe? To be in the same house with him?"

He shrugged. "I don't know. But I feel like he has more access to me in the hospital than in the house where I can lock and barricade my bedroom door."

Claire released a shaky breath and nodded. "I always have to have a lock on my bedroom door."

Noah felt a twinge of sympathy for her, for all she'd endured when she was young, if the rumors were true about her stepdad. But he didn't ask her; she'd already been through so much. And he didn't want to bring up a past that probably already haunted her. But he was so damn impressed with how strong she was to overcome that and to go into the career that she had.

"But why would your nephew want to hurt you anyways?" she asked.

He sighed. "My dad liked pitting my family members against each other."

"But he's dead now," she said, her voice gentle as if she'd assumed he'd forgotten and needed to be reminded. Or that he would be upset that the old man was gone.

Noah wasn't upset. "Yes, but his will stipulates that only his heirs who survive the probate period will inherit. For every one of us who dies, like my sister and my half . . . or step . . . brother . . ." He wasn't sure what Gregory Gold II had been to him since he hadn't really been his father's biological son. "And my stepbrother's mother, they were heirs who've died, leaving a bigger share of the estate for the others."

"So Wynn might want to kill you so that he inherits more?" she asked. "Your family business isn't just in Gold Creek. I've seen Gold funeral homes all over the state."

"And the country," he said.

"So the estate has to be huge, and Wynn is a doctor. I can't imagine he wants that much to do with the family business that he would kill for it."

He shrugged. "I don't know. Maybe he was just messing with me with that pillow. He has a sick sense of humor."

She shuddered. "I know."

"So why did you ever date him?" he asked, and he flinched at the faint note of jealousy in his voice. He'd never been the jealous type. He hadn't cared who was more important to his dad or more favored. He hadn't wanted more power or money. The only control he'd wanted was over the cemetery, to take care of it in a way that honored the history of it, the grave digger and the dead within.

"I didn't *ever* date him," she said.

"But you were with him at the cemetery the night he showed you that sick collection of his." It had to have been Wynn's. It certainly hadn't been Noah's.

"I told you earlier today why I was there with your nephew and some others that night," she reminded him. "I was looking for a friend who went missing after going there."

Noah nodded, then flinched at the pounding in his head. "Yes, you said that. He went missing like Michael Sebastian. I don't remember any report about a missing kid back then though. But I guess there wasn't one about Michael going missing, either. Everybody just thought he'd run away."

"They thought the same thing about Peyton," she said. "He was staying with the Sebastians, too, when I was because his stepfather kept beating him up. Do you remember Peyton Shusta? He wore a lot of black eyeliner and bleached out his long hair so that it was so blond it was nearly white?"

That face popped into Noah's mind as an old memory. Maybe he'd passed him on that double staircase before, long ago. He nodded. "I seem to remember him hanging around the house."

"The house?"

He nodded. "He must have been friends with Wynn or Wynn's sister, Taylor. I don't remember him around River. I don't think she ever hung out with anyone but Luke's brother, Michael."

"I didn't think to ask River about Peyton," she said.

"You two were a little busy saving me," he said. "And I really appreciate it."

"I wish I could have saved Tyler, too," she said. "His death makes me wonder even more about what really happened to Peyton. If I hadn't found Tyler, we would all think he'd just gone missing, too. Maybe even that he ran away."

He remembered those long moments walking around the cemetery in the windstorm, trying to find Tyler. What if they never had? What if they'd never learned what had really happened to him? He would always wonder, just as Claire had wondered about her friend and now River and Luke were wondering what had really happened to Michael. "You don't think Tyler just fell in that grave?"

"No, and you don't think so, either," she replied with such certainty in her voice. "Not with the injury he had to his skull. He couldn't have walked anywhere."

Noah touched his head and flinched. "I hope he didn't feel any pain."

"You are," she said. "You should be resting, not here."

"I wanted to thank you," he said. "And I wanted to make sure you were okay."

She shrugged. "I'm fine."

"You lost a kid on one of your cases," he said.

And she was the one who flinched now. "I don't know why

this is bothering me so much," she said. "I've lost other kids. And I never even met Tyler. I never got the chance." She stepped closer and then settled onto the bench next to him. "What was Tyler like?"

"He really was a nice kid. A hard worker. I liked him. A lot. He reminded me a little of myself and of Lyle McGinty. Tyler had been happy in the cemetery."

She shuddered. "Happy in the cemetery?"

He grinned. "Yeah. I am. Tyler was. And Lyle . . ."

"The grave digger," she said. "You think that's why people claim to see his ghost? That he isn't really digging their graves, that he's just taking care of the place? Like you?"

He sighed. "We do have to dig graves, but only after the people have died. And if Lyle is haunting the place . . ." He wasn't about to admit to seeing him himself. "Then I'm sure it's just because he's taking care of the cemetery and doesn't want to leave it."

"Like you?"

He shrugged. "I'm happy there. So was Tyler."

"Maybe he felt safe there," she said.

"But he wasn't," Noah said. Someone had hurt him.

"If you liked Tyler so much, why did you fire him?"

"I couldn't have him dealing drugs on the property, on the grave digger's grave. Especially not there."

"Why especially not there?" she asked. "I saw how you looked at it earlier and hear how you talk about him . . ."

"He saved my life once," Noah admitted. "When I was little, I once got out of the house before everyone else was awake, and I probably would have gotten lost in the swamp or drowned in the ponds if he hadn't found me." Noah touched one of the mums he'd brought her. "Guess I should bring him some flowers, too."

"So he wasn't the monster the legend claims he is?" she asked.

He shook his head. "Not to me."

"So who is the monster? Who do you think Tyler was dealing for?" she asked.

"His parents."

She tensed. "What?"

Noah sighed. "I don't have any proof. Just gossip. But I know that his parents deal drugs. His stepdad is a piece of work."

"Damn it. I need to get the other kids out of that house," she said.

He nodded. "Yeah, you should."

"I didn't find any criminal records for either parent," she said. "How could they have gotten away with dealing drugs all these years?"

"Luke just became sheriff a few months ago," Noah said. "And Buzz had other people doing the actual street dealing. He's a middleman, or so the gossip goes."

She stared at him for a moment, but his face was probably in shadow while the fading sunlight illuminated hers. She was really beautiful. "How do you know all these things?" she asked. "I thought you kept to yourself."

"I live in a house full of people," he reminded her. "And a lot of them like to gossip, even my sister."

"River?" Claire asked. "She doesn't seem like the type."

"Not River. Honora. My sister who recently died. Her son, Garrett, has issues with drugs."

"Do you think he would talk to me?" she asked. "Or to the sheriff? That he would testify that Tyler's parents are dealers or middlemen or whatever they are?"

"He's in rehab right now," Noah said. "And he won't talk to Luke without a lawyer. He's up on charges for assault with a deadly weapon or something like that."

"Then maybe he will talk to Luke and strike a deal or something," she said.

Noah tilted his head to study her face; the excitement in her voice flushed it, making her even prettier. "I wouldn't count on Luke being willing to reduce the charges. Sarah and River are the people Garrett assaulted or tried to. He almost shot them."

"Wow, your family is fucked up," she said.

Noah laughed, then flinched as the sound reverberated in his aching skull.

"And you shouldn't be anywhere around them," she said.

"Will you let me stay here?" he asked, shocking himself with his audacity.

Her eyes widened behind the lenses of her black glasses. "Wow, you must have gotten hit really hard on the head."

He chuckled again, then groaned. "Really, the only reason I came here was because I wanted to thank you. You risked your life to save mine. I owe you more than flowers for that."

"Well, since you know my landlord, maybe you can get me a break on my rent," she said. Then she laughed. "Just kidding."

"Seriously, doing what you do for kids, you deserve a break," he said. "Were you working this late?"

Her smile slipped away. "No. I should have been. But I was actually with the Sebastians and with Jackson and Sarah, Toby and Gigi."

"That's right," he said. "Luke sent them over to his folks to keep them safe."

"It does feel safe there," she mused almost wistfully. "It was the first place I felt safe after . . ."

The horrific murder-suicide involving her parents; people had talked about it for years even after she left town.

"I'm sorry," he said. "It must be rough being back here with the memories and all."

She shrugged. "Memories go with you wherever you are. But when I'm not here, it's easier to pretend that they're not real. But now . . . it's too real."

"I'm sorry," he said again. But he found himself asking, "Why did you come back?"

"I was being harassed over a case," she said. "Guy following me, threatening me."

Noah sucked in a breath. "Damn. I'm sorry. When you saw me standing here, you must have thought he found you again."

She nodded. "He's not the only one who's harassed me." She sighed. "I should be used to it by now."

"Why don't you quit? Why do you keep doing it?" he wondered aloud.

She smiled, but even as it turned up her mouth, her lips pulled down again at the corners. "I think you know."

"To help kids like you once were," he said.

She nodded. "And the Tylers."

He felt like she'd punched him. "I wish I'd helped him. He wouldn't talk to me about his family though, just his little siblings. He loved them."

"They loved him, too," she said. "They were there last night. I talked to them. They insist nobody's hurting them."

"But you shouldn't trust the parents," he said.

"I shouldn't trust anyone," she said.

"Not even me?"

"Especially not you, Noah Gold."

"Why?" he asked. "Because you still think I'm a psychopath who collected dead animals and killed Tyler?"

She shook her head. "No, because I *don't* think that anymore. I don't think that at all."

"Then why not trust me?" he asked, and he leaned closer to her, staring at her mouth. He wanted to kiss her. Badly. Maybe he had taken a harder blow to the head than he'd realized because how could he be thinking about kissing anyone right now let alone the woman who'd accused him of being a monster? But that woman had also saved his life.

"I've been wrong before," she said. "I could be wrong about you."

He shook his head. "No. You're not."

"Then if I'm right, you're in a lot of danger, Noah. Somebody tried very hard to kill you and they almost succeeded. Do you think they're going to stop trying now? I think that they might keep trying until they succeed."

A sudden chill rushed over him as he realized how right she was. He was in danger. And in coming here, he might have led that danger right to her. He'd had the feeling that night in the cemetery that someone else had been out there, watching them.

And he had that feeling now, too.

"I'm sorry," he said. "I shouldn't have come here." And hopefully he hadn't put her in danger by doing so. But if he stayed, that someone might try again to kill him and get her instead or just kill them both.

Chapter 14

Claire stood in the courtyard watching as Noah drove off in a truck with *Gold Memorial Gardens* scrolled on the door. The truck had been parked across the street, so she hadn't noticed it when she'd driven up. He'd gone from staring at her mouth to running off practically within seconds. That was her fault, though; she must have scared him with her observation that he was still in danger. And because he was, she shouldn't have let him leave.

But yet she couldn't imagine him, or anyone else, staying with her. She hated sharing her space with anyone. She'd barely slept in college until her roommate had started spending more time at the frat houses instead of their dorm. And she'd gotten an off-campus apartment on her own as soon as she'd been able to. Thanks to being her grandmother's only heir, she'd had enough money for college. She could have even bought a house of her own instead of renting, but she liked moving around from county to county within the state. It was safer than staying in any place too long.

Even though she'd only been back in Gold Creek a few weeks, she already felt she'd stayed here too long. She was feeling again. Too much. Regret, grief, and guilt over a kid she'd never met and over another that she'd lost long ago. But she could handle the regret, grief, and guilt much easier than she could what she'd felt for Noah when she'd sat on the bench with him. Just as Lyle McGinty hadn't been the monster legend claimed he was, Noah wasn't either, or so Claire thought. Even though they'd shared a couple of laughs, it hadn't been as uncomplicated as her dinner at the Sebastians. He'd kept looking at her mouth, and she'd wondered what it would have felt like to kiss him.

Maybe she was the one who'd been hit on the head. Or the fumes had affected her. It was good that he left. Even if she could bring herself to trust him, she didn't have the time or interest in a personal relationship. The few times she'd tried to get involved with someone had ended with somebody getting hurt. Not her. She really didn't have the capacity to get attached to anyone, to let herself trust or even care enough to let them get close to her.

But she didn't want to hurt anyone else. And Noah had already been hurt. And just like she'd shared with him, she was afraid that he was going to get hurt again. That whoever had tried to kill him would try again.

And again . . . until they succeeded.

Noah's only reason for visiting Claire had been to thank her for saving his life. And now his visit might have put her life in danger. Even if he hadn't been followed to her house, he'd been able to find her, so other people would be able to as well.

He'd been filled with gratitude earlier for her saving his life. Now he was filled with guilt. The last thing he wanted to do was put her or anyone else in danger. So it was good that she'd immediately shut down his idiotic request to stay with her.

Even as a joke, it had been stupid and totally out of character for him to make.

Maybe he was more messed up from the attempt on his life than he'd realized. Not only had he been physically hurt but he was also struggling with the realization that he hadn't lived as much as he wished he had. He was thirty-eight years old and hadn't had a serious relationship. And the one relationship that meant the most to him was with the ghost of the man who'd cared as much about the memorial gardens as he did.

Tyler had cared, too.

But Tyler was gone, just like Lyle McGinty. Would he see Tyler now when he went back to the cemetery?

Of course that was where he was heading now. It didn't take long to get there since Claire's little bungalow wasn't far from Gold Memorial Gardens. He drove through the open wrought iron gates and through the brightly illuminated parking lot. But he didn't stop there, by the house. He continued driving down the service road to the maintenance building.

He knew it was a crime scene and he probably wouldn't be able to get access to it. But he didn't entirely trust that Luke's techs had searched it that thoroughly. He had to find that note he'd found taped near the computer.

Maybe someone would be able to analyze and match that handwriting to that of whomever had tried to kill him. Was it the same person who'd killed poor Tyler? Or was it someone else?

A member of his family who'd seen an opportunity to take him out. Lawrence and he kept clashing over how to manage the gardens. The easiest way for Lawrence to win that argument was to get rid of him. Permanently.

Father had always left the gardens and the cemetery to Noah. He'd trusted him to take good care of them. He had even once remarked that Noah was more like the grave digger's kid than his. However, Gregory Gold I's will had required them all to take DNA tests, and Noah was biologically a Gold. But that was the only way he was like them.

He would never kill anyone to ensure his place in the family, to get a bigger percentage of the money and the power. But he couldn't say the same about the rest of them, except for River. Despite or maybe because of all the years she'd been gone from Gold Creek, she was the only one he really trusted. And the kids.

Sarah, Toby, Gigi.

He didn't want something happening to them like what had happened to Tyler or even what had happened to Garrett. Was someone targeting teenagers in the cemetery?

Was that what had happened to Sarah's father? And Tyler? And to Claire's friend?

As much as possible he'd stayed out of the investigation into his father's death and into the other deaths that had followed. But he couldn't stay on the sidelines this time and not just because someone had tried to kill him although that did piss him off. It had also made it pitifully obvious that he'd spent too much of life on the sidelines.

Until he'd nearly died, he hadn't realized how little of his life he'd spent actually living. So he had to find out who had tried to kill him and who had killed Tyler.

And he also wanted to help his sister and Sarah get answers about Michael Sebastian. And he didn't want Claire to wonder about her old friend anymore, either.

The lights of the pickup truck glanced off the dark metal of the building. The yellow tape, wrapped around the building, sharply contrasted with the charcoal paint. He wasn't supposed to break that tape and go inside, but with as long as Luke's techs had been there, they had to be done processing it now. They probably also hadn't missed anything, and he was wasting his time going through it again.

Or maybe he was just stalling. He wasn't eager to go back inside the house with probably more than half of his family thinking he killed the kid and then had tried to kill himself. Even River had seemed to have some doubts. But one person might not: the person who tried to kill him. If it was a family member.

He really hoped it wasn't. He really hoped that the old man wasn't still manipulating them all from beyond the grave. Gregory Gold I would love that too much, that even after he was dead, he was still around, influencing them, making them do what he wanted them to do.

But did he really want them to destroy each other?

He'd been the one who insisted that they all live together. Even his ex-wives had remained in the house with their kids and grandkids. He'd never been willing to let anyone go even when he'd gotten tired of them, or they'd gotten too old.

Unlike his father, Noah wanted to get old. He wanted to live a long life like Lyle McGinty, just one that was a little bit fuller than his currently was. So before getting out of the truck, he grabbed the crowbar he'd stashed under the seat earlier. He wasn't going to be the one getting hit if someone snuck up on him again.

But because he was gripping the crowbar, he couldn't juggle his phone or a flashlight, too, as he pushed open the driver's door. So he left the truck running with his headlights illuminating the dark building, reflecting off the yellow tape and lighting up some of the woods behind the building. Before he closed the door, he reached for the visor inside the pickup and pushed the button for the overhead garage door opener.

It chugged and grinded as it rose, the faint light from it and the headlights glancing off the equipment inside the building, casting shadows across the concrete floor. A sudden chill rushed over him, and it wasn't just because the temperature had dropped with the sun.

It was windy again, the branches and leaves rustling. And it was damp, with mist rising from the grass and moving through the trees and across the cemetery. And within that mist, he thought he saw a light flicker. But when he looked again, it was gone.

Lyle?

Or someone else?

Someone human?

"Hello?" he called out.

But nobody answered him back. Not even an owl or one of the coyotes he sometimes heard in the woods made a sound. Just that wind.

As it increased in velocity, it began to howl again like it had the night Tyler died. Just last night.

It felt so much longer ago.

Luke still didn't have any answers about how the kid had died. Maybe the autopsy hadn't even been done yet.

Hopefully what had happened to Noah hadn't slowed down the investigation into Tyler's death. The kid deserved justice. And his siblings deserved to be safe. Maybe he would reach out to his nephew once the rehab allowed visitors. Maybe he would try to get Garrett to tell Luke about the Buczynskis, if his nephew actually knew anything about them. There were, undoubtedly, more drug dealers than them in Gold Creek.

And maybe there was more than one killer, too.

He grasped that crowbar a little more tightly as he headed into the building. Was this crazy, going back to the scene of the crime? Despite what too many thought, he hadn't committed the crime; it had been against him. And he had to figure out who was responsible.

Was it even safe for him to go back inside his house? Sure, he could lock his bedroom door. But eventually, even though he had an ensuite bathroom, he was going to have to come out. He was going to have to come back here because he still had work to do. And given the velocity of the wind, he was going to have even more cleaning up to do.

Using the light from his pickup, he found the switches on the wall that turned on the overhead lights. He blinked and squinted against the harsh glare of the fluorescent bulbs. With the lights above and the ones on the truck in his face, he was nearly blinded.

But he could hear. Either the building or the trees made strange creaking noises. The wind kept howling, the force of it making leaves and twigs ping against the metal roof and walls of the building. Leaves tumbled across the concrete floor and over a dark brownish red patch, which must have been where the blood from his head wound had soaked into the cement. His head pounded now as he stared down at it.

What had hit him?

He hadn't seen it. He hadn't seen anything but that shadow out of the corner of his eye. Then he'd read the note taped to his office door. The tape or the note might have fingerprints on it. He walked over to the door, and he could tell that it had been dusted for prints.

The techs had gone over everything well. He doubted he would find that note anywhere. But he looked through the trash that had been spilled across the floor. The techs had looked through that, too. He checked in toolboxes and cases. And each time he needed to use both hands and put down the crowbar, he looked behind him before he did. But this time he was alone in the maintenance building.

But out there . . .

With the truck lights shining so brightly into the building, he couldn't see anything beyond those high beams. Maybe he should have shut off the engine. But there was something comforting in the sound of it running, reminding him that he could escape from here quickly. He didn't have to walk back to the house, which was something he usually enjoyed doing, walking through the cemetery at night.

Hell, maybe some of the kids who swore they'd seen the ghost of the grave digger over the years had actually seen him instead. He actually hoped that they'd seen the ghost, though, because then he wasn't alone in the sightings. And maybe he wasn't crazy.

While he'd answered that psychiatrist's questions honestly today, maybe he should have volunteered some information, too. But he'd been too worried he would wind up in a strait-jacket for that seventy-two-hour hold Wynn had threatened.

He groaned at the thought of his nephew, of having to see him and the rest of his family again. But he'd stalled out here as long as he was able, and that was probably really all he'd been doing: stalling the inevitable. The techs had gone over the crime scene more thoroughly than he ever would have been able, and if they hadn't found the note, then the person who'd written it must have taken it after they struck him over the head. So there probably had been fingerprints or DNA on it, something that would have identified who they were.

But the why mattered as much to Noah as the who. Why try to kill him?

Was the motive over the estate or over Tyler? What had the kid wanted to tell him that night?

He wasn't going to find any of those answers out there, so he shut off the lights with one hand. Then he hit the control that was next to the door, so the door started descending. He ducked beneath it and stepped out of the building. The wind whipped around him, plastering his clothes to him, stinging his skin. He needed to get some rest because he was going to have to get up early and clean up the gardens.

As the door descended behind him, he started toward the bright lights of the truck. But before he could go around it, the engine revved, and the truck surged toward him. Between the door closing behind him and the truck hurtling toward him, Noah was trapped.

Luke wasn't sure what was worse—the morgue or the embalming room at the funeral home. Or the cremation ovens.

Hell, the morgue was better than most of the places in that house by the cemetery. But still he held his breath, trying not to breathe in the smells of chemicals and blood.

"You said it was definitely murder?" he asked the medical examiner.

Without looking up from his computer in a corner of the morgue, the white-haired doctor said, "What I texted you was that it wasn't natural causes." He tapped the keyboard. "I just emailed you the report. You should have it in your inbox soon."

"Can you give me the highlights?"

The doctor sighed. "It's been a long day, Sheriff, and it's already dark outside."

"He's just a kid, and there are other kids in the parents' household. I and the CPS investigator need to know if they're in danger."

The doctor slid off the high stool and turned toward the sheriff then, giving him his full attention, and said, "I'm sorry. I should have considered that."

"So you think Tyler's siblings could be in danger?"

He shrugged. "I haven't examined them, but I did find a lot of old bruises and healed fractures on Tyler. I can't say for certain, but I definitely suspect someone had been abusing him for a while."

Claire wasn't going to be happy about that; Luke certainly wasn't. "Okay. And his death? What is the *unnatural* cause?"

"A blow to his head crushed his skull. It would have killed him instantly."

So he hadn't walked or even dragged himself over to that

open grave. Someone had tossed him into it just like Claire believed. Hell, maybe his old foster sister should be the sheriff. She probably had more experience with investigations like this than he did.

"What was it? A tree limb?" Several of them had fallen in the cemetery. Maybe the crime had been one of opportunity; someone had struck him with a fallen branch.

The coroner shook his head. "No bark or anything in the wound. And it's slightly concave. The object was wide but had a curve to it."

"Like a rock?"

The man shook his head again. "No. More like a . . ."

"A what?" Luke prodded when the medical examiner trailed off as if almost reluctant to speculate on the weapon. Or afraid to?

The doctor sighed. "The blade of a shovel."

Luke tensed as suspicion and dread flitted through his body. There had been a recently dug grave, so it would make sense for there to be a shovel lying around it. Tyler hadn't died far from it.

But graves weren't dug like they'd been years ago. They had that small backhoe now that Noah, more times than not probably, carefully used so that it wouldn't ruin the grass or any of the flowers. Noah used the backhoe. But maybe sometimes he had to use a shovel, too. Had he used one on Tyler? Or had someone else used it?

Someone who was rumored to still carry that shovel through the cemetery at night. The shovel in one hand, the lantern in the other, the grave digger walked around looking for his next grave to dig, his next victim to bury.

That was the legend the teenagers told, but this was the first time Luke had seriously wondered if it was true. If the grave digger was real.

Chapter 15

Maybe Claire should have let Noah stay with her. While she'd never had anyone else in the house with her, not even to visit, it felt empty to her in a way that it hadn't before. It was eerily quiet, and the lights didn't seem quite bright enough to dispel all the shadows.

Maybe she just needed to replace the bulbs with ones that had higher wattages and cast a bright white glow rather than the yellowish one that barely illuminated the space. Or maybe she was just uneasy after the past couple of days.

Tyler Hicks had died. And Noah nearly had as well. He wasn't safe at Gold Memorial Gardens or in that house next to it. But he was probably right that he wasn't safe at the hospital, either, not with his weird nephew now on staff there.

But if Claire had let him stay here, she would have been the one who wasn't safe. Even though she found herself believing that he hadn't hurt himself or Tyler Hicks, she couldn't be sure that she was right to trust his word. She couldn't be sure about anything. So it was better not to trust him or even her own instincts. She needed facts. Proof. Evidence.

She needed Luke to share what he'd found out. Her cell rang just as she reached for it. "Claire Underwood," she answered.

"Luke here, Claire," the sheriff said. "I'm just leaving the coroner's office."

She didn't even have to ask; he filled her in on the autopsy results. But she felt no satisfaction in being right. Instead of waiting to conclude the interviews with the younger kids' teachers and doctor, she should just remove them from the house if she could get her supervisor to sign off on a removal. She had a feeling that Mallory might not have the guts to follow through without those interviews and some other compelling evidence that the younger kids were being mistreated like their older brother had apparently been.

Was that why Tyler had died? His parents had been afraid he would talk to CPS this time?

"But what about Noah?"

"What about Noah?" Luke asked.

She hadn't realized she'd spoken aloud. "If Tyler's stepdad or mom killed him, why would they go after Noah?"

"They could think that Tyler talked to him."

"He suggested that," she admitted. "But his father's will put a target on his back, too."

"On all of theirs," Luke said. "I worry about River and Sarah, too."

"Toby and Gigi are nice kids, too," she said. Spoiled maybe but good.

"They are, but Sarah is my niece," Luke said.

"Michael's daughter," she said. "Do you think there could be a serial killer responsible for his disappearance and my friend Peyton's and Tyler's deaths?"

"A serial killer?"

She thought of that macabre collection Wynn had shown her all those years ago. "Yes."

"We don't know that Michael and your friend are dead," he said. "We need to focus on Tyler Hicks right now."

"And Noah," she said, her stomach suddenly flipping with nerves. "You should check on him."

"He should be locked up in his bedroom right now sleeping," Luke said.

"No. He was here just a short while ago."

"Damn," Luke said. "He wasn't really supposed to leave the hospital, and he definitely shouldn't be driving."

"I should have let him . . ."

"Let him what?"

She should have let him stay. "Make sure he got home."

"I'll do that," Luke said.

"Let me know when you know if he's okay," she said. She didn't wait for his reply, just disconnected the call. She didn't want to waste any of his time. For some reason she had a feeling that he needed to find Noah.

As soon as possible . . .

She just hoped Luke wasn't too late. She walked over to her front door and peered through the glass out into the courtyard where the mums he'd brought her sat in the glow of the porch light. The blooms were such brilliant colors; the purple and the pink flowers were visible even in that dim light. He'd given them to her as a thank-you for saving his life, and then she'd let him drive off with what was probably a major concussion and dangerously low oxygen levels. She shouldn't have let him leave. Or she should have at least driven him back to his house to make sure he got safely home.

But she had a feeling that even if he'd made it home, he wasn't safe. Not in that house, not with those people: his family.

Noah's shoulder burned from scraping across the concrete as he'd squeezed beneath the overhead door just before it com-

pletely closed. If he hadn't, he would have been crushed between the door and the truck that had rammed into the door
just as he'd escaped into the building.

Ignoring the pain in his shoulder and his head, Noah scrambled to his feet. The person who'd hopped inside his running
truck could open that overhead door again; the opener was on
the visor. The faint light from the opener was already beginning
to fade. He used what was left of it to find the crowbar he'd
dropped. He picked it up and gripped it in both hands.

And he waited.

But the door didn't open again. Maybe it couldn't. It seemed
slightly crumpled from the truck hitting it. And the truck must
have still been there; he could hear the motor running and the
horn blaring. The airbag had probably gone off.

Was the driver injured?

He hoped like hell that they were. But he wasn't about to go
outside and check. Unfortunately, he'd left his cell phone in the
cupholder in the truck, or he would have called 9-1-1. There
was a landline in his office. Just as the light began to fade from
the opener, he reached that door. Then he was plunged into
darkness. He took one hand off the crowbar and fumbled
around for the doorknob. But as he started to open it, another
door creaked open. And he was no longer alone.

Hell, he was never alone around here. There was either someone trying to kill him or the ghost of the grave digger. And
sometimes Claire.

God, he wished she'd let him stay with her. He might have
actually been safe there. Or he would have made her unsafe.
He'd felt then like he felt now, like someone else was out there.

A bright light flashed on and then bounced around the
garage. Noah pushed open the door to his office and slammed
it shut behind himself. There wasn't a lock on it. So he would
have to slide something in front of it, something to barricade

himself inside and away from whoever the hell was trying to kill him.

"Noah?"

The voice was familiar. But that wasn't necessarily a good thing. That didn't mean he was safe, just that whoever was trying to kill him was someone he knew. But he'd already figured that had to be the case.

"Noah? Are you in here?"

"Luke?" Luke was the sheriff as well as a friend. And he wasn't a Gold, so he couldn't be the one trying to kill Noah. But he was involved with River and was Sarah's uncle, so Noah still hesitated for a moment. Maybe Claire Underwood's world-weary cynicism was contagious, or maybe nearly getting killed was rightfully making him suspicious of everyone.

"Noah? I need to know if you're in here, if you're hurt," Luke said, his voice gruff with what sounded like genuine concern.

He also sounded close, so he was probably about to open the door anyway since Noah hadn't had time to barricade it. So Noah opened it. That bright light shone in his face, blinding him. He held up his hand to block it.

And he heard a gun cock. "Put down the crowbar!"

"What?" Noah hadn't even realized he was holding the crowbar in that hand. But he hesitated to drop it. "What are you doing here, Luke?"

"Checking on you," he said. "Now put down the crowbar."

Noah's fingers were numb from grasping it as tightly as he had, so he had to ease them slowly apart to drop it onto the concrete. It fell with a clang and kicked back against his leg. He flinched. Of course the weapon he'd chosen to defend himself would wind up hurting him. "Really? You're just out *here* checking on me?"

"Yeah, I stopped at the house first, but River checked your

room, and you weren't in it," Luke said. "So I figured you might be out here even though I told you to stay the hell away from it."

"Your techs aren't done with it?" Noah asked.

"For now maybe," Luke said. "But you still shouldn't have come out here. Hell, they shouldn't have released you from the hospital. You have a concussion, and you could have died from carbon monoxide poisoning. Did you black out? Is that how you drove your truck into the building?"

"I didn't do that," Noah said. "I left it running to come in here and look for that note I saw, the one I was reading when I got hit over the head. And when I started back out, the truck engine revved and it shot right toward me. I got back under the door just in time." And it hadn't stopped like it was supposed to when something was under it. Maybe he'd been under the sensor though that would have stopped it since he'd just barely gotten beneath the door before it met the concrete. He was probably lucky that the damn door hadn't crushed him.

"You're saying someone drove the truck at you?" Luke asked. "Who was it? Did you see them?"

"The headlights were on high beam, like your damn flashlight. I couldn't see inside the truck. Hell, I was pretty much blinded."

Luke lowered his flashlight a bit more, then moved it over the wall until he found the switches. He must have already holstered his gun once Noah dropped the crowbar. Luke used the sleeve of his shirt to touch the switches and turn on the overhead lights. "I should get the techs back out here and have them process the truck for fingerprints."

"I left my cell in it, or I would have called you right away. I was heading for my phone when you came in," he said. "You scared the hell out of me."

"Good," Luke said. "I can't believe you don't realize how much danger you're in."

"I nearly died. Of course I realize it," he said.

"Then why are you going off on your own?" Luke asked. "I warned the kids not to do that earlier today, and they all agreed that would be idiotic, like the thing the bad actors in the horror movies do before they get brutally murdered."

Noah chuckled. "Sarah?"

"Toby is actually the one who said it," Luke said. "But you're missing my point. You shouldn't have gone off anywhere alone."

"I'm always alone," Noah said. Realizing he probably sounded pathetic, he added, "I like it that way." Even though he had a crew that maintained the grounds with him, he gave them their assignments in the morning and spent the rest of his days working alone.

"If you like it that way, why did you go see Claire?" Luke asked.

"She told you?" Noah asked. Had she complained to the sheriff that Noah had sought her out and showed up on her doorstep like some stalker? Like one of the parents on her cases who'd harassed her?

"I called her about Tyler's autopsy results, and she asked me to check on you, to make sure you got home safely. She was worried."

Maybe he should have felt guilty that he'd worried her when she clearly had a stressful job and life already, but he felt a flash of warmth instead that she actually cared. She was a caring person, though, or she wouldn't have chosen the job that she had.

"I went to see Claire to thank her for saving my life," he said.

"And ironically you put it in danger again instead," Luke said.

A jab of guilt struck him now. "She's all right, though? She's safe? Nobody followed me there?"

Luke sucked in a breath. "I hadn't thought about that. Did

you see anyone on the road behind you? Anyone who might have been following you?"

Noah shrugged. "No steady lights. But I didn't see anyone out there, either." He gestured toward the slightly crumpled overhead door. But he had seen something in the darkness, that wavering light and a slight mist.

"What?" Luke prodded. "You saw something."

Noah shrugged again. "I don't know. I've just had this feeling like someone is watching me." And he didn't think it was the grave digger this time.

"Of course someone is watching you," Luke said. "That's how you got hit over the head and nearly killed in this building. And how someone got into your truck and nearly ran you down with it. You're in danger."

"Why?" Noah asked. "What did Tyler's autopsy tell you? Was he murdered?"

Luke sighed and gave a slight nod. "I shouldn't tell you all this."

"You told Claire."

"Claire is working on Tyler's case. And there are other kids in that household."

"So Tyler was being abused?"

Luke clenched his jaw and nodded.

"Fucking Buzz," Noah said. "I remember him being a bully in school. Of course he would have bullied his stepson. I shouldn't have fired Tyler. I should have tried to do more for him." But he'd liked his solitary life, liked not getting involved, not participating in all the drama that his family thrived on.

"You know how you can do more for him?" Luke asked.

Noah had an idea. But he asked, "How?"

"By staying alive," Luke said. "The kid reached out to you with that text. He liked you. He came here when he was on the run. He wouldn't want you getting killed, too. So stop putting yourself in danger."

"If being alone puts me in danger, I would have been in danger all the time," Noah said. "This isn't about me. Hell, whoever's going after me might not even have anything to do with Tyler." It could be a member of his family. Hell, whoever killed Tyler might be a member of his family. Buzz was a bully, but he wasn't necessarily a killer.

"Just do me a favor then," Luke said. "And don't take any more unnecessary risks. And stick close to River and Sarah. You can all keep each other safe."

River was another teenager that Noah hadn't helped when he'd been able. He was five or six years older than his younger half sister, so he hadn't been able to protect her from the school bullies. But he should have protected her at home from the bullies in their family, from his sister Honora, who'd been so jealous that she was no longer Daddy's only girl. He'd been at college when River had run away, but he wished he'd been there for her then.

So he could do his best to protect her and Sarah now and the other teenagers, Toby and Gigi. But that didn't help him feel any better about Tyler. There had to be something he could do for him.

"Will you be careful?" Luke asked him.

Noah sighed and nodded. "Yeah, of course. That's why I had the crowbar."

"It wouldn't have done much good against that truck," Luke said. "You got lucky that you didn't get run down. And you got lucky earlier today when Claire and River rescued you from this building. But eventually, Noah, your luck might run out."

Noah had never considered himself a particularly lucky person to begin with, but maybe he had been. Maybe it had been luck that day that Lyle McGinty had saved him from wandering into the marsh. So if his luck went back that far, it might be close to running out now.

*   *   *

Noah Gold wasn't easy to kill. Maybe it was because he didn't really deserve to die. He hadn't been like the others. And if he had seen something when Tyler Hicks died, surely he would have told Luke or someone about it already.

But for some reason, killing Noah Gold had become a challenge now, one that the "grave digger" couldn't walk away from until the challenge was won, until Noah was dead.

Chapter 16

Feeling a twinge of guilt, River slipped out of the showing room where the service was being held for Susan Hughes. She hoped she wouldn't be missed, but there hadn't been many mourners so her presence would probably go unnoticed. Susan's great-niece had shown up, and Estelle McGinty was here, too, with her couple of blue-haired cronies. Instead of being annoyed, River smiled. Of course they had complimented her on how nice a job she'd done on Susan.

Her mother had smiled with pride, too, as if she'd done the work herself. She had taught River how to do it, though. Fiona was in there with Lawrence, representing the Gold family and trying to undo the damage they were worried Tyler Hicks's murder might have caused. Instead of burying Susan in a "used" grave, they were going to cremate her after Pastor Sebastian concluded the service, and they would inter her ashes in one of the mausoleums.

Since Fiona and Lawrence were busy with the funeral, River had a chance to try to log on to their computers again. So she softly closed the showing room doors behind herself and turned toward the hall.

"Where are you going?" a deep voice asked.

She nearly jumped at the sound of her brother's voice. "Noah?" She turned to find him sitting in one of the chairs spread about the lobby area. He had dark circles beneath his eyes, and the bandage on his head had a dark stain from where blood had seeped into it. "Are you all right?"

He nodded.

"You should be sleeping in," she said.

"I did."

She smiled. "Not long enough."

"I had to make sure my crew was cleaning up the cemetery," he said with a glance toward the French doors. "It was another windy night last night."

"A dangerous one, too," she said. Luke and Noah had both filled her in on his other near miss at the maintenance building. "I hope you met them here."

He nodded. "I did. On the patio here. Luke wants me sticking close to you."

She must have flinched slightly.

"What?" He stood up and walked toward her. His dark eyes narrowed, and he asked, "Where are you going?"

She could trust Noah. She lowered her voice and whispered, "Lawrence's office. I need to check some records."

"Well, let's go," he said with a smile. Then he gestured for her to lead the way down the hall.

She glanced back at the showing room doors to make sure nobody had overheard them. Then she rushed off down the hall to Lawrence's office. When she reached for the knob, though, she found it locked. "Damn. Do you think he knew I was in here yesterday trying to log in to his computer?"

Noah sighed. "Knowing Lawrence, he was probably standing right behind you, and you didn't even notice him."

She chuckled. "I kept checking to make sure he didn't sneak up on me."

"Yeah, but he's really good at it." His forehead furrowed a bit. "Kind of reminds me of whoever has been trying to kill me."

"He's our brother. You think he would do that?"

"Don't you?" Noah asked. "I have a feeling he really likes being in power and will do anything to maintain it. Isn't that why you were trying to get into his computer?"

She shook his head. "I was trying to get into the burial records. I wanted to find out who was buried around the time Michael disappeared."

He released a shaky breath. "Oh."

"Tyler being put in that grave made me wonder if that was what happened to Michael."

He nodded. "I get it. It makes sense. But you don't need Lawrence's computer to dig up the burial records." He gestured for her to follow him now as he slipped back down the hallway and climbed the stairs to the second story.

"Where are we going?" she asked.

"My laptop's in my room," he said as he pulled a keychain from his pocket and unlocked the door at the end of the hall, on the other side of the family dining room.

He was her brother, and they'd grown up together. But she didn't think she'd ever been in his room before. He'd always been older and such a loner that she hadn't ever considered reaching out to him. Any time that she'd started to try, his sister—their sister, Honora—had reacted like River was competing for his attention like she'd always thought River was competing for their father's attention. And she'd made some cutting remark that he didn't want their father's white trash stepdaughter pestering him.

Step. She'd always been *step* to them, not even the *half* that she genetically was.

"It's okay," Noah said. "I can bring the laptop into the dining room if you're uncomfortable coming in here."

She hadn't realized he was holding the door for her. She shook her head, trying to shake off the memories. "I'm sorry. I was just thinking about the past," she admitted. "About Honora, and how I wasn't ever welcome in some places."

He blew out a breath. "I was worried that you were scared to come in here," he said. "That you thought I would hurt you."

"No, that's not the case at all," she assured him. And she stepped into the room and closed the door behind herself.

"But I did hurt you," he said, "when I didn't stick up for you all those years ago. I'm sorry I didn't."

She smiled. "You were never mean to me," she said. "You were just sometimes in your own little world." She looked around at that world now. He had so many botanical pictures on the dark paneled walls, or maybe they weren't pictures at all but different plants pressed between glass. "These are beautiful," she said. Even the tendrils of moss that he'd collected, that she'd always thought so creepy hanging from the trees, looked beautiful as he'd displayed them.

"Yes," he agreed. "This is actually *my* collection."

"Of course," she said. "I can't imagine anyone else in our family being interested in the beauty in nature the way you are."

"Lyle was."

"Lyle?"

"Lyle McGinty, the grave digger," he said. "But he wasn't actually family." He picked up a framed photograph from the desk in the corner of the big bedroom suite and handed it to her. "That was him."

The color picture was so old that it had faded to nearly black and white. But even faded, the blooms of the flowers were still bright in the backdrop of the cemetery. But the man and the toddler he held were centered in the picture. The man was tall and slim. He wore jeans, and a long-sleeved shirt with suspenders. His hands were big and gnarled looking, and his face was gaunt, with one eye gleaming oddly, reflecting back the flash of the camera.

River shuddered as she stared at him. He must have been alive because he was holding the child, but he looked like a skeleton, like a specter. The ghost she tried to forget she'd ever seen.

"He saved my life that day," Noah said. "I'd slipped outside before anyone woke up and just got into the marsh when he caught me and stopped me. If I'd gone any deeper, I might have gotten lost or wound up in one of the ponds on the other side of it." He shuddered now.

She focused on the little boy the man held. His bare arms and legs were chubby and, even in the faded picture, the scratches on them were visible. But he wasn't crying. His big dark eyes were round with fascination as he stared up at the very old man holding him. One of the toddler's chubby hands was wrapped around one of the man's suspenders. The little boy's mouth was curved into a smile. There was a faint smile on the old man's face, too.

"He wasn't the monster people make him out to be," Noah said, his voice deep with respect and almost reverence. But then he owed the man his life.

She smiled and nodded. "No. His legend took on a life of its own."

"A nightmare," Noah said. "But that wasn't how I ever saw him."

"Did you ever . . ." She couldn't bring herself to ask him; he would probably think she was as flighty as her grandmother and her mother. Well, at least her grandmother. Fiona had revealed herself to be much more cunning than anyone had realized.

"What?" he asked. "Did I ever see his ghost?"

"Yes."

He shrugged. "Maybe I just want to see him, to think he's still taking care of the place with me."

So he had.

So maybe she wasn't crazy. Or maybe Noah was.

She really had no clue anymore about anyone.

He opened his laptop. "What burials did you want me to look up?" he asked.

"The ones that happened around the time Michael disappeared."

His fingers hovered over the keyboard.

And she gave him the date. The exact date.

"You're thinking he's buried out there somewhere?" he asked.

"Like Tyler nearly was, yes," she said.

He didn't argue with her that Michael could be alive and out there somewhere living his best life. Or maybe just living.

He tapped in the dates. Then his forehead scrunched up. She looked over his shoulder to read the screen. "I see a couple burials before that date," he said, pointing toward a spreadsheet of plot numbers, dates, and names. "But those graves would have been covered shortly after the service. And there was nothing until nearly a week after the day he disappeared."

"So you don't think he's buried in someone else's grave?"

He shrugged. "I don't know what to think."

"I don't want to think about it," she said, her heart aching as she considered what might have happened to the boy she'd once loved. "If Michael was killed, like Tyler, maybe that person hid his body until there was a burial."

"That's possible, but we can't just dig up graves to find out unless we have a court order." He tapped on the keyboard, scrolling back a few years earlier.

"What are you looking for?" she asked.

"Claire mentioned a friend who went missing after coming out to the grave digger's grave one night," Noah said. "He was staying at the Sebastians with her. When he didn't come back, everyone assumed he ran away."

"Like Michael."

He nodded. "I'm not sure what night he went missing. I do know that Claire stayed with the Sebastians after her mother died, so I would think he disappeared around that same time frame. There were a lot of funerals then." He sighed. "Do you remember a kid named Peyton? He wore eyeliner and had bleached hair."

She nodded. "Yes. He was Wynn or Taylor's friend, I think." And because he was a friend of theirs, she hadn't talked to him. Her niece and nephew hadn't wanted anything to do with her, so their friends hadn't, either.

"Did Michael know Wynn and Taylor, too?"

She nodded again. "Yes, Michael is—was a year and a half older than me, so he was in Wynn's grade. Taylor was a year behind me." She didn't like to think about high school, how much she'd been teased and bullied over being one of the ghoul family. But kids would always find reasons to bully other kids, like Sarah had been bullied in Santa Monica, which was why she'd chosen to homeschool there instead of attending in-person classes. But Sarah loved going to school here with Toby and Gigi and Jackson. She had family and friends in Gold Creek. But there was also danger here, in this city and maybe even in this house. While Noah seemed to be suspicious of their niece and nephew, River still had suspicions about her mother. But maybe she would rather think Fiona was involved because she knew her mother wouldn't hurt her or her daughter.

But River didn't trust the rest of her family to not harm Sarah or herself, especially with a bigger share of her father's inheritance at stake. "Did Luke tell you to stick close to me?" she asked.

Noah grinned. "Maybe. Did he tell you to stick close to me?" he asked.

She grinned. "Maybe." But her grin slipped away as she remembered that she should get back down to the service. "I need to go back to Susan Hughes's funeral."

"Go," he said. "I think you'll be safe there with the other people around."

"Come with me," she said.

He shook his head. "No. I have something I need to do."

"Remember that Luke doesn't want you going off alone."

"I know," he said.

She stepped out of his room and closed the door. And it was only when she was walking down the stairs that she realized he had just acknowledged what Luke wanted but hadn't agreed to it. But after yesterday Noah had to know how much danger he was in and wouldn't take any more unnecessary risks.

Claire knocked on the open door of her supervisor's office. Mallory looked up from her desk. "I'm heading out to meet the sheriff at Tyler Hicks's house. Are you going to tag along to that, too?"

"Excuse me?" Mallory asked, her voice sharp.

"You went with me to all my interviews this morning like I was a trainee," Claire said. "Why?"

Mallory's face flushed, her cheeks turning pink. "I was advised to keep an eye on you."

"Who advised you to do that?" she asked. She didn't think the sheriff was worried about her safety, at least not for the interviews with the Buczynski children's teachers and pediatrician.

"Someone who was concerned that you might not be impartial during those interviews."

"Impartial? I ask the same questions we ask every time we interview teachers and pediatricians."

"I know, Claire. And the teachers and the pediatrician didn't believe there was any abuse happening with the younger kids."

"But their older brother is dead, and if one of the parents is responsible, then they should be removed from the household."

"A court referee or a judge will make that decision, not you, Claire. And based on the interviews today, they are not going to issue a removal order."

Mallory was right. But Claire still didn't believe the kids were safe in that household. "We'll see how the interview with the sheriff and the parents goes," she said. "I'm leaving for it now. Are you coming along?"

Mallory sighed. "No. What else were you doing earlier?"

"What do you mean?" Claire asked. "You were with me earlier."

"Since we got back to the office, I saw that you were pulling up some old records."

"So you actually know what I was doing," Claire said with a smile. "You really are watching me closely."

"Why were you pulling up those records? Who are Peyton Shusta and Michael Sebastian? And what about the search you did for kids who went missing or ran away? What are you looking for?"

The truth. Claire shrugged. "I was curious how many there have been."

"You know a lot of kids run away," Mallory said. "Sometimes they do that to avoid us, like Tyler Hicks probably did, and that was why he was in the cemetery. And sometimes they do it to avoid the abuse they probably are getting at home, and they don't trust us to handle that for them."

Claire understood that. It was hard for abused kids to trust any adults, especially when the ones who were supposed to love and protect them were the ones hurting them.

"We didn't help Tyler Hicks," Claire said. "He slipped through the cracks."

"And what was your search about? Trying to find out if other kids have? But why go back so far?"

Claire shrugged. "Just being thorough. You've never looked up old case files?"

"No," Mallory said. "There are more than enough current cases to keep me busy. You can close the door on your way out, Claire."

Claire needed to be on her way. Luke had agreed to let her sit in on his interview with Tyler's mom and stepdad, but she was worried that he might change his mind if she was late. Despite the interviews she'd conducted with her supervisor, she still wasn't sure that Tyler's siblings were really safe. Making sure that they were was her top priority, but she also wanted justice for Tyler.

And for whoever else might have died like he had.

A twinge of guilt struck Noah that he'd ignored Luke's advice to not take any unnecessary risks. But to him, this was a necessary risk. He'd failed Tyler when he was alive, so he was even more determined to do something for him in death.

He peered through the windshield of the van he drove, looking for the address he'd taken off Tyler's employment records. He slowed down to read the numbers on the battered mailboxes. He found it and turned into the gravel driveway leading back to a ranch house with moss-stained siding and roof. Two vehicles were parked near the porch.

He braked, shifted into park, and shut off the ignition. Then he drew in a deep breath and pushed open the driver side door. When he slammed it shut again, a dog started barking. It could have been in the Buczynskis' house or in the neighbor's house. Or maybe it just set off a chain reaction because he could hear dogs barking in the distance, too. While their house was set a bit farther off the road, so were the other ones near it. A few had campers near the houses with electrical cords running to outside breakers.

Sometimes he forgot how rich and privileged he'd grown up. Unfortunately, most of his family, with the exception of River, were all too well aware and tended to lord their wealth over less fortunate people. Was that what the Buczynskis would think he was doing?

He hoped not, but after seeing where Tyler grew up, Noah understood him even more. This was probably why he'd had to work at such a young age and probably why he'd sold drugs in the cemetery, too, to help support his family.

Guilt gripped Noah again and compelled him to climb the nearly rotted steps of the front porch. While the siding was stained and the wood rotting, the doorbell was bright and shiny. One of those video ones probably. So he didn't even have to push it before the door swung open.

"What the hell are *you* doing here?" a woman asked, her eyes red and swollen. "You have some fucking nerve, you freak!"

"Mommy?" a child called out fearfully from behind her. Apparently, Claire hadn't been able to remove Tyler's siblings from the house yet.

"Buzz!"

"Mrs. Buczynski," Noah began. "I'm here to offer my condolences and something else—"

A man shoved the woman aside and reached for Noah, slamming his hands against Noah's chest, pushing him back. Then he fisted his hand and swung it.

Noah ducked. "I want to offer—"

"You killed him!" the woman shrieked. "You killed my son!"

"No—"

The man reached out again, but instead of shoving Noah, he grabbed his shirt and jerked him forward. Noah lost his footing and fell into the house. He rolled onto his side to catch his breath from the fall.

"Buzz!" the woman yelled.

And for a moment Noah thought she was going to get her husband to stop, but then he looked up, into the barrel of a gun that the woman held, directed right at him.

Luke was going to be pissed that Noah hadn't taken his advice.

Chapter 17

Claire had worried that she would be late getting to the Buczynskis but when she stepped outside the DHS building where CPS was located, she found Luke waiting in the parking lot for her.

"I thought it would be smarter to ride together," he said through the open window on the driver side of the sheriff department SUV.

"Really?" she asked with skepticism as she hopped into the passenger seat.

He nodded. "Yeah, what's up?"

"You tell me," she said. "Are you the one who made my supervisor go on all my interviews today with me?"

He shook his head and shifted the SUV into drive. "I wasn't concerned about you talking to teachers and doctors. I just don't want you talking to the Buczynskis without me."

While she struggled to trust anyone, she couldn't think of a reason that Luke would lie to her. "Mallory, my supervisor, said someone advised her to keep an eye on me because they didn't think I could be impartial on Tyler's case."

"Could it have been the Buczynskis?" he asked, as he headed in the direction of their house. She shrugged. "Maybe, but then that doesn't make her very impartial, does it?"

He sighed. "No, it doesn't. Did you find any reason to remove the younger kids?"

"No. So maybe they're safe." But she needed to investigate thoroughly to make certain that they were.

"The coroner said that Tyler had a lot of healed fractures and old bruises."

"We have to be able to prove somehow that someone in that house is the one who hurt Tyler," she reminded him. "We have to make sure we get the truth out of the Buczynskis."

Luke snorted. "I haven't been sheriff long, but I do know that getting the truth out of anyone isn't that easy."

She chuckled. "Now that is the truth."

He chuckled, too.

"I looked up Michael today," she said.

And his slight grin slipped away. "You did?"

"And my friend Peyton Shusta, too," she said. "Have you looked them up?"

"I believed Michael ran away with River all those years ago," he said. "And her mother let me believe that. I still tried to find him, but I figured he was using a different name. When he was on the run from CPS with my mother, they used a lot of different names."

"Was there ever a police investigation?" she asked. "For him or for Peyton?"

Luke shook his head. "Not for Michael. Like I said, everyone believed he ran away. And he was eighteen then, so I think the sheriff at that time figured an investigation would be a waste of time. I don't know about Peyton, but I can look him up, too."

"I would appreciate that," she said. "He was staying with the

Sebastians then, too. His stepdad treated him like a punching bag because he was different."

"Like we think Tyler's stepdad treated him," Luke said. "But it wasn't because he was different, just because he wasn't his child?"

"Or it had to do with the drugs that Noah caught Tyler selling in the cemetery," she said. If the Buczynskis were involved in drugs, that would get the kids removed from their custody, too. "We need to find out what went on in that household with the drugs and if Buzz was beating on Tyler if we're going to be able to get Tyler's siblings out of the house."

"I want to know if he killed him," Luke said.

"Of course Tyler deserves justice, too." But she wasn't as sure that the stepdad committed murder. Could there be another killer out there? One who'd been killing for a while maybe?

"And Noah does, too," Luke said. "Somebody nearly killed him."

"Why?" Claire wondered aloud. "It doesn't make any sense. He swears he didn't see anything the night Tyler died and that he didn't get the chance to talk to him. Unless it isn't about Tyler at all."

"That damn will of Gregory Gold's." Luke slowed the SUV and turned into the Buczynskis' driveway. Then he cursed again when he saw the van already parked there, the van with *Gold Memorial Gardens and Funeral Services* written on the side of it. "It has to be Noah."

"Why would he come here?" she asked. "You heard the way they talked about him. They blame him for Tyler's death." Which gave them a motive to try to kill him. "Oh, my God. They could be the ones." She opened the passenger side door to jump out.

And just as she opened it, a gunshot rang out.

"Stay here!" Luke yelled at her, and as if he didn't trust her to listen, he reached over the console and pulled her back onto the passenger seat. He was also talking into the radio on his lapel as he pulled on his bulletproof vest. "Shots fired—"

"Look, Luke!" Claire said, and she pointed toward the house and the front door that was opening.

"Get down!" he shouted at her, shoving her below the dash just before he jumped out of the SUV.

She wanted to tell him to wait for backup, wanted him to stay back and stay safe with her. But she was more concerned about Noah and those little kids right now. Hopefully, the kids were at school yet. They'd been there earlier when Claire had talked to their teachers.

But Noah . . .

He had to be in that house where those shots had been fired. Had they already killed him?

The dog barked. The kids cried, and that gunshot echoed inside Noah's skull. Just the sound of it, not the bullet.

Fortunately.

Mrs. Buczynski hadn't fired the gun into him, but she'd come damn close to blowing off his head. There was a hole in the matted carpet near it. Noah looked from that hole to the kids who were sitting on the couch, holding each other as they cried in fear. They had to be scared because he was pretty damn scared himself.

"Tammy, what the hell did you do?" Buzz yelled at her from where he stood near the front door he'd opened. "The fucking sheriff is here now. And I think that CPS lady is with him."

Oh, God, Claire was with Luke.

They had to stay back, or Tyler's mother would probably shoot them. Noah had thought she was just grieving earlier, but now he could see the wildness in her eyes, how dilated her pupils were. She was on something.

"That bitch isn't taking the kids I have left," Tammy yelled. And she started toward the door that Buzz had opened moments ago.

Worried that Tammy would start firing at Claire, Noah jumped up from the floor then and grabbed her. He wrapped his arms around her thin body and closed his hands over her wrists, trying to wrest the gun from her grasp.

"Get off her!" Buzz yelled. And he launched himself at Noah, knocking him to the floor again.

Noah brought Tammy down with him, and as she fell another shot rang out. Then a burning pain exploded in his side.

And somebody was screaming.

He didn't know if it was Tammy, Claire, Buzz, or those poor kids.

And then consciousness slipped away from him.

Luke watched as the ambulance took off, lights flashing, sirens wailing, with Noah in the back. He wished he could go with him. Or that Claire could have gone with him.

But they, along with some other officers who'd showed up, were talking to the Buczynskis. Well, Claire was talking to the kids, in their bedroom where she'd taken them so that they didn't have to see the blood on the floor, and until moments ago, the man who'd been lying in that blood.

"This isn't my fault," Mrs. Buczynski said, her eyes were wild, her face flushed. And she was shaking. "He forced his way into our house. He was beating up my husband. I want to press charges."

"You shot him," Luke said.

"I have the right to defend my home, and I didn't shoot him. I shot in the air to get him to leave."

Luke gestured toward the hole in the floor that the techs were processing. "That isn't the air."

"I don't know, it all happened so fast." She was sitting on the couch with her arms behind her, but she kept leaning forward like she was going to fall off or fall asleep.

Luke had cuffed her and her husband, who was sitting in the back of a patrol car with a deputy who was taking his statement. They needed to be interviewed separately.

"We heard a shot when we drove up and then your front door opened," Luke said.

"Yeah, yeah," she said. "When you showed up, he tried to get the gun away from me."

Noah had probably been trying to protect Luke, and he might have also known that Claire was with him, too. Luke wasn't sure how serious his friend's wound was. A shot in the stomach could be really bad; Luke knew that from his deployments. And there had been a lot of blood.

"That was when . . . that was when it went off . . ." Her eyes weren't just dilated now, they were starting to roll back into her head.

"Mrs. Buczynski, what did you take?" he asked.

She shook her head and nearly toppled over on the couch. "Noth . . . nothing . . ."

He glanced at one of the techs. "We're going to need paramedics again." In the chaos after the second shot, he'd rushed into the house to secure the scene. He'd taken the gun and then handcuffed the Buczynskis. And sometime during that chaos, Claire had rushed in.

She'd ushered the kids out of the room and had come back with towels that they'd pressed against Noah's wound. The paramedics must have taken them with him. They probably should have taken Mrs. Buczynski, too, but he hadn't realized then that she might need medical attention.

"Don't let that bitch take my kids," she murmured. "Don't let her take them a . . ."

"Ms. Underwood will make sure that they're safe," he said. "They're not safe here. You could have shot them instead of Noah. You could have killed your own kids, Mrs. Buczynski. Is that what happened with Tyler? Are you responsible for his death?"

She started crying then, hysterical sobs. He didn't know if it was grief or an admission of guilt.

Chapter 18

His blood was on her hands. Literally. Claire's skin was stained with blood from his wound. She'd pressed those towels against it, and then, when the paramedics arrived and pushed her aside, she'd thought she'd wiped it off. But the kids kept staring at her hands and then she noticed it, too.

"He'll be okay," she said. She didn't know if they cared, but she did. She might care a little too much about Noah Gold because it didn't seem like he cared that much about himself since he'd come here. He hadn't had a reason. She did; she needed to make sure these kids were safe.

"Where's Tyler?" the little girl asked.

"Tyler's gone, honey," Claire said. "He's not coming home."

"He's dead, stupid!" the boy said through his tears. "Somebody killed him."

"Do you know who?" Claire asked.

"Mama thinks it was that guy she shot," he replied. "That was what she said."

But he didn't sound like he believed it.

She could have asked the little boy more about his brother's murder, but he hadn't been there that night. So whatever he knew would have been hearsay.

"Do you have a grandma or a grandpa? An aunt or uncle? Somebody I can call for you?" she asked. She had a few names of their family members on both sides, but she wanted to see which one they would prefer. "That will let you stay with them?"

"Is Mommy going to jail?" the little girl asked.

Claire hoped so, but she just shrugged. "I don't know. But I want to get you two out of this house for a while." Maybe forever.

"Nana Blue," the little girl said. "She and Mommy fight a lot, but she loves us."

The little boy nodded. "Yeah, call Nana Blue."

"I will," she said. Blue was Tammy Buczynski's maiden name. Claire had already reached out, leaving a message for the woman to call her back about Tyler. Hopefully, she would pick up or respond this time.

Claire needed to find a safe place for these kids, and then she had to get to the hospital. She had to find out if Noah was going to make it. He'd been breathing when she and Luke got to him; she hadn't had to do CPR on him this time.

But the blood . . .

She stared down at her stained hands. She didn't want that to be the last she saw of Noah.

It was lucky he didn't get through the swamp to those ponds. One of them is deep. Some say it's just about bottomless.

Lyle was holding him up, close to his chest, where his old heart pounded fast and hard. "He's fast. You're going to need to keep a good eye on him, Mrs. Gold."

The old man started to hand Noah off to his mother, but Noah clung yet to Lyle, clutching one of the worn suspenders in his chubby hand. He didn't want to let go.

He didn't want to let him go.

But he slipped away . . . into the mist and the fog . . . just a flickering light and that occasional scrape of a shovel.

"Lyle . . ."

"Lyle!"

"Noah!"

He jerked his eyes open and stared up at the man leaning over his bed. There was no glass eye gleaming in the light, no skeletal thin face. But there was amusement in the dark eyes that stared down at him. "Lyle? Were you calling out to the grave digger?"

Noah blinked and stared around him.

"Yeah, you're back in the hospital," Wynn said. "I don't know if you're lucky or unlucky."

"I'm alive?" He remembered the searing pain in his side and reached for it. There was a bandage on it, but it wasn't even that big a one. He didn't even have an IV or a machine hooked to him this time. Or maybe Wynn had disconnected them. He stared at his nephew. "What are you doing here? Did you bring me a pillow again?"

Wynn chuckled. "No. You've not had any trouble sleeping. In fact you've been in and out of it since the shooting."

The shooting. Everything came back to him, and he sat up. "The gun went off. Was anyone else hit?"

"Just you," Wynn said. "Which does make you unlucky. But it's really just a flesh wound. Went straight through your side without hitting anything vital." He made that annoying clicking sound with his tongue.

"Disappointed?" Noah asked him.

Wynn chuckled. "I'm a doctor, Uncle. I don't need any more

money than I make myself, so I don't have to get rid of you to get a bigger cut of the estate, if that's what you're thinking."

"I'm thinking about those animals you showed Claire." And that his nephew was a sociopath.

Wynn sighed. "That was a long time ago. You and she need to get over the past. For that matter, so does River."

"Are you talking about Michael?" Had Lawrence figured out that Noah had searched those old burial records for her?

Wynn nodded. "Yeah, why does she care about some druggie like him? He let her raise her kid alone. Why does she give a damn what happened to him?"

"Druggie?" a deep voice asked.

Wynn jumped and stepped back from the bed, whirling toward the door that the sheriff had opened. "I'm sorry, Sheriff, but Michael wasn't squeaky clean like you and the Sebastians. Everybody knew that, even River."

Noah hadn't known it, but then he hadn't paid that much attention to his siblings' friends. "What about Peyton Shusta?" he asked.

Wynn tensed. "What about Peyton Shusta? He was a freak."

"He was your friend, wasn't he?" Noah asked. "I remember him being in the house before."

"My friend?" Wynn shook his head.

But Noah had definitely seen the kid that Claire had described to him. "But you called him a freak. You knew him."

Wynn shrugged. "That was a long time ago. I don't really remember. Like I just said, you and River need to stop living in the past. And Claire Underwood, too."

"You know he was Claire's friend."

"I know Claire mentioned him, and that's how you know about him," Wynn conceded. "But that's all I know about him. And now I better get to my patients. I just stopped in here to see how you were."

"How is he?" Luke asked.

"He's not my patient," Wynn said.

"But you must know," Luke persisted.

And Noah wondered why the sheriff was so interested in his release. What had the Buczynskis claimed happened at their house?

"It was seriously just a flesh wound," Wynn said. "No organs were affected. The bullet passed through."

"He lost so much blood."

"Flesh wounds will do that," Wynn said with a careless shrug.

And it was clear to Noah that his nephew didn't really care about him or probably about anything else. Why had he chosen to become a doctor? Just for the money and prestige?

"He'll be released soon," Wynn said, then brushed past the sheriff on his way out of the room.

Noah waited until the door closed behind his nephew before focusing on the man he thought was his friend. "What's the deal? Do you intend to arrest me? Is that why you're so concerned about when I'm getting out of here?"

"I would be arresting you right now—"

"For what?" Noah sat up more in his bed, grimacing when the bandage pulled at his skin and probably the stitches over his gunshot wound. "Why would you arrest me?"

"For the story that Mrs. Buczynski and her husband told me, how you forced your way into their house, and you were trying to kill Buzz. So Tammy, terrified for her husband and her kids, found the gun someone must have left at their house and fired a shot into the air."

"That's all bullshit," Noah said.

"I know," Luke said.

"How do you know?" Noah had a feeling that it wasn't because Luke trusted him any more than Claire did.

"For one, they have a doorbell camera and I was able to get a judge to have them turn the footage over to me," Luke said, "and for another, Claire got the truth out of Tyler's younger half-siblings when she and her supervisor drove them to their maternal grandmother's house."

The image of those poor kids crying in fear popped into his head, and he closed his eyes. But then he saw their older brother lying in that grave with his head nearly crushed. "Did their dad kill Tyler?"

"They don't know that, but they do know that their dad was hurting Tyler," Luke said, "and they said that Buzz pulled you into the house, which is what the doorbell footage showed, too. But even before he did that, their mom grabbed her gun, the one they're never supposed to touch. They saw everything."

Noah sighed. "I didn't know they would be home—"

"Why the hell did you go there? Were you trying to get killed?"

Noah shook his head. "I wanted to offer them a free funeral for Tyler, and one of the better burial plots. He loved the cemetery." He could hear how lame and weird that sounded. But to him, having a nice plot, near the fountains and flower gardens, with the lushest grass, meant a lot. And it would have to Tyler, too.

"Obviously, neither his mom nor stepdad cared about Tyler," Luke said. "Or the mom would have used that gun to stop her husband from beating on her son."

"You said that the kids know that Buzz was abusing Tyler."

Luke nodded. "They weren't getting hurt like Tyler was, mostly because he was taking the blows for them, but Claire was able to place them with their grandmother now and will go for a permanent removal. And I'm pressing charges against both parents and getting court-ordered drug tests, too. A search of the house revealed a lot of drugs, more than for personal use."

"So they are dealers?"

Luke nodded again.

"And they were the ones who were probably forcing Tyler to deal in the cemetery," Noah said. "I wish he would have told me."

"He was probably scared to blow up his whole family," Luke said. "And they knew that was what would have happened."

"So that's why they killed him," Noah said. "You do think it was one of them, right? And that they must have thought he told me what was going on and that's why they were trying to kill me?"

"I have techs going back over the doorbell footage," Luke said, "trying to determine if they were home or gone when Tyler was killed and when you were attacked."

"You don't sound convinced that they are responsible," Noah said, and that chilled him. He had so hoped that this was over.

"Buzz and Tammy could have killed you," Luke said.

Noah groaned. "I know."

"But they didn't," Luke said. "They had time. She could have shot you when you were on the porch and dragged your body inside. She could have shot you in the head instead of shooting near your head. She and Buzz are horrible people, but I'm not sure they're killers."

Neither was Noah, or he wouldn't have shown up at their house. He'd thought he could get through to them, that they would do what was best for Tyler. "Then who and why?" he asked.

Luke sighed and shook his head. "River said you pulled up burial records for around the time that Michael disappeared and around the time that kid Peyton Shusta disappeared."

"Yeah. But what will you be able to do with that information? Can you get a court order to dig up other people's graves on a suspicion that those kids might have been murdered instead of running away?"

"No. Claire found a few more kids that had gone missing over the years, too," Luke said.

"So you think there's a serial killer in Gold Creek?"

"Or it's the grave digger's ghost like the legend has claimed all these years," Luke said with a little chuckle.

But Noah wasn't amused. He shook his head. "The grave digger wasn't a killer." Lyle McGinty had saved his life, and that memory played through his head again. "The grave digger wasn't a killer," he repeated. "This isn't the grave digger."

If there was a serial killer on the loose in Gold Creek, it was someone else.

Someone alive.

Rumors were swirling around Gold Creek. Everyone had seen the police and the ambulance at the Buczynskis' house. Everyone knew they'd been arrested and that the children had been removed from the home. Now they knew about the drugs, too.

Or maybe a lot of people had already known about those. They'd certainly known that Tyler was dealing them, but if they'd known for whom, nobody had admitted it.

Not even Tyler.

It was too late for Tyler. He was dead. And he would have been buried had Noah not interrupted. But maybe Noah wouldn't have to die. The Buczynskis had tried to kill him.

Had shot him.

So surely they would be blamed for the attempts on his life and for taking Tyler's life. And all of this would be over now.

The "grave digger" wouldn't have to do any more damage control. And the rest of the dead would stay where they were, undisturbed ... and undiscovered. And it would never be proven that they were dead instead of just *gone*. Runaways ...

That was what everyone thought they were. But they hadn't run fast enough or far enough to escape the "grave digger."

Chapter 19

A few days had passed since the shooting at the Buczynskis, and Claire was sitting in her cubicle at the CPS office, typing up her reports. The kids were safe with their grandmother, who was deeply regretful that she hadn't done more to protect Tyler from his mom and stepdad, so she was determined to keep the younger ones safe. Their safety was Claire's main concern, so she was relieved that they weren't in any danger now. She'd also heard from Luke that Noah would be okay, too. It was just a flesh wound, but she hadn't gone to see him.

She wanted to close this case and put it and all the feelings it had brought up behind her. But Luke had to finish his investigation into Tyler's death. If the parents were involved, they wouldn't ever be getting their children back. As it was, the drugs found in their house would keep them in prison for a while along with the assault charges for trying to beat up and shoot Noah. Had they tried to kill him, too?

Or had that been a member of his own family?

Even though he hadn't been hurt too badly, she couldn't

stop thinking about him, worrying about him. And she hated that she couldn't get him off her mind.

"Claire, can you come in here?" Mallory asked.

Claire swallowed a groan and stood up. As she passed the other cubicles, some of the CPS coworkers avoided her gaze and a couple gave her commiserating glances. She just shrugged. It wasn't as if she could be in trouble; she hadn't done anything wrong.

She stepped into her supervisor's office, and Mallory gestured at her to close the door. She complied and waited.

Mallory's face flushed as Claire stared at her. Then she said, "If you were sent here to replace me, I'm not going to fight it. You are better at this job than I've ever been."

Claire laughed. "I don't want your job." In other counties, she'd been offered the supervisor role before and had turned the position down. She didn't want the paperwork or the responsibility that came with it. She just wanted to investigate the cases.

"Why not?"

Claire sighed. "I was not sent here to replace you. I was sent here because I'm too good at my job, and that means that I piss off too many people."

Mallory nodded. "I know that. I've heard that, but now, after working with you, I realize that some people deserve to be pissed off."

Claire felt a little flicker of hope that maybe coming back here hadn't been the mistake she'd started to think it was. Maybe she would be able to work with Mallory after all. "Who told you to shadow me?" she asked. "Who warned you about me?"

"Besides your prior supervisor?" Mallory shrugged. "Just a friend who had offered some advice."

"Not one of the Buczynskis?"

"Of course not," Mallory said. "But I should have listened to you about them. And Tyler's case should have been a priority one. That's why I'm wondering if I'm right for this job."

"We can only work with the facts that we have," Claire said. "You can't beat yourself up for what you weren't told, for what you didn't know."

"Your instincts are just better than mine, though," Mallory said.

Claire sighed. "I've just been doing this longer. That's all." And sometimes she thought it was too long. But while she hadn't saved Tyler, she had gotten his siblings out of that home.

"I will trust you from now on," Mallory said. "I'll trust your instincts."

Claire's instincts were telling her that there was more going on in Gold Creek than the Buczynskis dealing drugs. She wasn't as sure as everyone else seemed that they were responsible for Tyler's death and those attempts on Noah's life, and if they weren't, that meant there was another killer out there.

She needed to trust her own instincts on that because she had a feeling that Noah wasn't out of danger yet. And because she was so concerned about him and his safety, she wasn't out of danger, either.

She was in danger of getting more personally invested than she'd ever been. Not in a case or a child but in a man. That was why she'd stayed away from him these past few days. She didn't like how much she was feeling. She didn't like feeling at all. It was better to be dead inside.

Noah kept having that same dream over and over again about Lyle. Even after his release from the hospital, he continued to have it. He'd even awakened a few times and peered out his window to the cemetery and he'd seen Lyle. That wavering light, the glass eye glinting in the mist as the ghost moved over the grass, heading toward the marsh.

Toward the ponds.

And so, once the sun began to rise, he called the sheriff. "You up for some fishing this morning?"

"It's not morning yet," Luke said.

Noah chuckled. "Look out your window. It's morning. And I really think we should go fishing."

Luke groaned. "You just got out of the hospital."

"A few days ago."

"You're still healing."

"I'm better," he said. He'd been directing his crews but taking it easy himself. But he wasn't getting any sleep, and he wouldn't until he did what he felt the grave digger was urging him to do. But he didn't want to build up Luke's hopes because he wasn't sure.

"You sound tired," Luke said, and his own yawn rattled the phone.

He was tired. Ever since he'd left the hospital and stopped taking his pain pills, he hadn't been able to rest. He just kept thinking, mostly about Claire Underwood.

He hadn't seen her since the shooting. He hadn't really even seen her that day. He'd just known that she was there because of what Tammy Buczynski had said about that bitch coming for her kids.

And Tammy had been right. Claire had taken them away. They were safe now. If only she'd gotten to Tyler in time . . .

If only Noah had . . .

But his interest in Claire wasn't just because of Tyler. It was because she was beautiful and strong. And she used her strength to protect others and to fight for the truth.

And it was past time Noah found out what the truth was. Maybe that was why he kept seeing the grave digger when he was asleep, and even when he was awake, because Lyle McGinty was trying to lead him to the truth. Whether that was out there or maybe locked up in Noah's mind.

"I'm going out fishing," Noah said. "To the ponds beyond the marsh. You can join me or not, but I need to know."

"What?" Luke asked, and he sounded wide-awake now. "What's going on?"

Noah saw the grave digger again, but this time just in the picture frame on his desk. The old photo was fading, but it was still possible to tell that the bottoms of the old man's jeans legs were wet. From the marsh.

Noah had come close to disappearing forever that day like Michael had and Peyton and maybe Tyler would have had Noah and Claire not been out in the cemetery looking for him when he died.

"I just think it's time we went fishing," Noah said.

"You're really determined to do this," Luke said. "With or without me?"

"Yes."

"Wait for me," Luke said.

"You still don't want me going off alone, not even after the Buczynskis have been arrested?" Noah wasn't sure that they weren't responsible for anything that had happened to him except for that gunshot wound.

"We'll talk about that when I see you," Luke said.

But he didn't have to; Noah had a feeling he knew what Luke had to share, that the Buczynskis hadn't tried to kill him and probably hadn't killed Tyler, either.

Someone else had. Someone who had probably killed before and might kill again if they weren't finally stopped.

Sarah didn't mind waking up early on Saturdays anymore. She liked going into the dining room with all of her family gathered around that long, formal table. She felt like it was a board meeting sometimes because they talked about the family business, but she liked the business no matter how morbid it was. Or maybe she liked it because it was so morbid. She could even imagine this scene as a graphic novel with everybody saying one thing and thought bubbles showing that they were thinking something else entirely.

She smiled at the thought, and Gigi, sitting on one side of her, giggled. She probably knew what Sarah was thinking, like she could see her thought bubble, because she'd told her about this image in her head before. Gigi wasn't just a cousin to her; she was a friend and maybe even closer than that, like a sister. Not her mom's sister who might have meant to kill Sarah, but a real sister.

"I can't believe Noah was going to offer someone a free funeral and a prime burial plot without discussing it with me," Uncle Lawrence said to Grandma Fiona. He was supposed to be in charge now, but it was clear that Grandma Fiona was really the boss.

"Was that why he went to Taylor's house—when he got shot?" Sarah asked her mom, who sat next to her.

Her mom's face was pale, as if she felt sick remembering that her half brother could have died yet again. She nodded. "Yes."

Sarah glanced around the table and to the open doorway, but there was no sign of Uncle Noah. He'd been getting around the house and had gone to the cemetery a few times over the past couple of days, so she'd thought he was getting better even though he had dark circles around his eyes.

"He offers them a free funeral and plot and they shoot him?" Fiona asked, an eyebrow raised in a perfect arch over one of her eyes. It was like she practiced or something.

"It wasn't like that," River said.

"It makes him look even guiltier," Lawrence said.

"I thought the boy's parents killed him," Fiona said. "So surely, nobody is accepting this offer Noah made."

River cleared her throat. She did not enjoy these family

breakfast meetings as much as Sarah did. "The grandmother found out that was his reason for being there, and she is considering it," she said.

"How do you know?" Lawrence asked.

"Claire Underwood, the CPS investigator, gave her my phone number, and she reached out a couple of days ago."

"This is something that I should be deciding," Lawrence said. "Not Noah." He glanced around then. "Where is he?"

"Fishing," River said.

Fiona snorted. "Fishing? Isn't that what you were doing when you were checking the burial records with him a few days ago?"

River's face wasn't pale anymore; it flushed pink. "How do you know we checked those?"

"After the subterfuge that's happened in this family, Colson Howard suggested we have monitoring software on all the business records so we can tell who's accessing what, you know like how someone accessed that van you were driving and you nearly died," Fiona said to River, but she didn't sound like she was all that concerned.

She sounded almost like she was warning or threatening her own daughter.

Sarah bristled. "You better not be saying my mom is in danger again."

"The only danger your mom is in is blowing her chance with the sheriff because she won't stop obsessing over the drugged-out kid who let her down all those years ago," Fiona said, her voice harsh. "If Michael had loved either of you, he would have stepped up to take care of you. He wouldn't have left you and then run off on his own."

"Luke and I both want to find out what happened to Michael," River said. "Nobody's seen him since that night."

"So you think what? That he was buried in someone else's

grave? And what about his car? Where did that go?" Fiona asked. "You know he just took off, but you don't want to admit it."

"Claire had a friend who went missing from here, too," River said. "Peyton Shusta."

Taylor gasped. Taylor was about Sarah's mom's age. With long black hair and sharp features, she looked like Honora, which freaked Sarah out sometimes because just seeing Taylor reminded her of how she'd found her aunt Honora with her head broken open on the stairs that led to the basement preparation rooms and cold storage. She'd sent Sarah a text, acting like she was Gigi and trying to trick her into meeting her. Had she intended to kill her?

This family was definitely messed up. But it was still her family. And after all the years that it had just been Sarah, Mom, and GG Mabel, Sarah liked having the rest of them around.

But Taylor and her brother, Wynn, were a lot like their dad, Lawrence, and just that weird that you couldn't quite figure out why they were weird. Wynn wasn't at breakfast; he was probably at the hospital where he was working now. Sarah had no idea what Taylor did; half the time she forgot she was even here.

"You knew Peyton?" River asked her.

Taylor tensed and shrugged. "I don't know."

"He would have been about your age or Wynn's," River said. "Which one of you was friends with him?"

"Wynn and I had different friends," Taylor said. "I don't know who his were and he doesn't know mine." She jumped up from the table then and rushed out of the room.

"Yeah, that doesn't seem suspicious at all," Sarah muttered sarcastically, and her mom glanced at her, but it wasn't to tell her to be nicer. She nodded in agreement instead.

"There is nothing suspicious at all," Fiona said, and her usually soft voice sounded sharp like the wind when it whipped through the cemetery breaking branches and sending a cyclone of leaves across the grass. "There is no reason to go digging up the past or anything else."

"People deserve answers," River said. "Sarah deserves answers. Michael is . . . was her dad."

He'd never been a dad to her and Sarah had always kind of low-key hated him for not running away with them. But what if he hadn't been able to? What if someone had killed him?

"Yeah, Grandma," Sarah said. "I want to know what happened to my dad."

Fiona sighed and shrugged. "I wish you luck, but I have a feeling you're going to be disappointed." She stood up and walked out then, leaving Sarah wondering what she meant.

That she wouldn't like what she found out about her dad, like he overdosed or something. Or that she might never find out what had happened to him.

Chapter 20

After the crazy week she'd had, Claire was supposed to be taking it easy this weekend. She wasn't on call, and Mallory had insisted that she not even look at any of her open cases. Not that she had many. Gold Creek wasn't as busy as other counties where Claire had worked.

Except for the past week and a half.

After that week, Claire shouldn't want to be back here at Gold Memorial Gardens and Funeral Services, but she found herself parking in the lot and walking underneath that portico to the lobby doors. Once she got there, she didn't know what to do. Did she just walk in?

It was a public business, but it was also a private home. And she wasn't here for the business part of it. She looked around on the brick exterior wall for a doorbell. And just as she found a ringer for after-hour delivery of packages, the door opened, which was good because she hadn't wanted to contemplate what those packages were.

Or whom?

Was Tyler here yet? Nana Blue had said she didn't have any

money to bury him, so Claire had given the older woman River's number and told her to ask for Noah Gold. Luke had told Claire why he'd been at the Buczynskis that day, to offer them a free funeral and burial plot. She knew why he had, that he wanted to do something for the kid because he felt like she did, that they'd failed him when he was alive.

If only they'd gotten to him a little sooner . . .

She shuddered to think of how close they must have been to his killer that night.

"You must feel about this place like I do," an older woman said as she stepped back and gestured for Claire to come in.

This place did bring back horrible memories for Claire. That awkward funeral of her mother's.

If not for Mrs. Sebastian holding her hand and Pastor Sebastian's kind words, she might not have made it through it. Even then she'd alternated between nearly crying and nearly laughing because mourning had seemed absurd to her.

Like being here was probably absurd, too.

"It creeps me out," the woman said, and she shuddered, too. She had long white hair and bright burgundy lipstick that matched the sweater she wore with leggings. "I know why my granddaughter, River, ran away from this place."

"*You* don't have to stay, Mother," another woman remarked as she walked down the stairs from the second story. Behind the petite blonde was River and Sarah and one of the male Golds but not Noah. "And don't be rude to our guests."

"I'm not a guest or a client," Claire said.

"This is Claire Underwood, the CPS investigator," River introduced her. "Claire, my grandmother opened the door for you, Mabel Hawthorne, and this is my mother, Fiona Gold."

Claire nodded at the woman. She'd met a lot of young mothers over the years, but Fiona certainly didn't look old enough to have a daughter River's age. But then River didn't look old enough to have a daughter Sarah's age. The family apparently had good genes.

"I thought that CPS investigation has been closed," Fiona said. "Didn't the boy's parents kill him?"

Claire shrugged. "That's the sheriff's investigation."

"Are you looking for him?" River asked.

Claire knew Luke and the woman were involved, but she wouldn't have come here to talk to him. She shook her head. "I just stopped in to check on Noah, to see if he's okay after the shooting."

Sarah smiled at her a little smugly, like she thought that Claire had a thing for Noah. And she didn't, or at least she didn't want to, which was why she'd stayed away as long as she had. But then she'd started worrying about him again.

River smiled, too. "He must be fine. Apparently, he called Luke at the crack of dawn to go fishing with him."

"Where do they go fishing?" Claire wondered, not that she intended to track him down, but she was curious. And concerned.

"They fish on this property somewhere," River said. "There are some ponds just past the marsh behind the grave digger's grave."

Of course that was where they would be, where Claire didn't want to go back. She turned to leave. "Please tell him I stopped by."

He knew where she lived, if he wanted to see her again. But even though he was feeling better, he'd chosen to go fishing instead. She'd been foolish to come here. Whatever interest she had in him wasn't reciprocated despite how he'd seemed almost as if he was going to kiss her that night he'd come to her bungalow. But he hadn't come back; he'd gone fishing instead. And he'd probably spent time out in the cemetery, too, despite being shot. He obviously cared more about the memorial gardens than anyone else, just like the grave digger had.

But that was good. She had no time for personal relationships. And she wasn't even entirely sure that she was staying in Gold Creek.

Maybe she would accept another transfer, somewhere without the memories this place held for her.

Noah walked around the edge of the ponds that had drained the water from the swamp. He knew there were ways to lower their levels. Switches for the pipes that drained from the swamp into the pond could be reversed. There was even a pump.

"I thought you wanted to come out here to fish," Luke called out to him as he watched him walk the perimeter.

"I do intend to fish," Noah said, just not for what his friend thought. "They made this pond decades ago when they drained part of the swamp to make room for more burial plots."

"So your family literally sold swamp land to some mourning family of the deceased?"

Noah grimaced but nodded. "It was once swampland." And he had to make sure that it didn't become it again. How low could he drain the ponds before the swamp overtook that part of the cemetery again?

At the edge of the swamp, between it and the ponds, he found a small shed with a metal roof and cement block walls. The door was rusted, and he had to fight the corroded hinges until he could wedge it open. The pump was inside. While he hadn't brought his fishing equipment, he had brought a toolbox. Luke must have thought it was a tackle box.

"What are you doing?" Luke said, and he peered into the shed over Noah's shoulder as he messed with the pump.

"I have to get this going," he said. It didn't take him long. He was as good with equipment as he was with plants, grass, and flowers. The pump rumbled as it ran, and water began to gurgle through the thick hoses.

"What the hell are you doing?" Luke asked.

"Check the pond, see how low it's getting," Noah said.

"This is a hell of a way to fish," Luke said.

"We're not fishing for fish," Noah said. There were fish in the pond, but that was because he'd added them years ago and kept stocking more.

He didn't want to lose them, so he didn't want to drain it too far down, just enough to see if his hunch was right.

Luke's forehead scrunched up as he stared at Noah, still confused or shocked.

Noah pushed past him to walk over to the pond again. As the water level dropped, it was as if something else began to rise. Something old and big and rusted and covered in muck and algae. His stomach churned with dread, and he was glad he hadn't eaten because he probably would have been sick. This was actually where the grave digger had been trying to lead him all these years. Not to his grave but the unmarked grave of others, of the runaways.

"What the hell is that?" Luke asked even though he knew. He recognized it. Despite the rust and corrosion caused from being submerged for sixteen years underwater, he recognized his brother's vehicle. That was why he hadn't been able to find the old Chevelle no matter how many databases he'd checked for the vehicle identification number. He hadn't even found it as scrapped or junked or for parts.

Because it had been here all this time.

Luke started walking toward the edge of the water, and his boots sank into the mud and muck from where it had already receded. Noah caught his arm.

"It's still deep," Noah said. And then he stepped back and

grabbed the rowboat he always left on the edge. The ponds were so big that they often fished from that. Noah grabbed the oars and tried to push the boat into the water but grimaced.

And Luke remembered his friend was still recovering from a gunshot wound. He shook off the shock gripping him and focused on the rowboat. Once he and Noah were inside, he started paddling them toward that vehicle. The windshield, although covered in mud and muck, looked intact, but the side windows were either down or busted out. Through one of them, Luke could see the skeleton lying across the front seat. Its body was encased in tatters of denim and flannel. And the head . . .

The skull had a big chunk missing while the rest of it looked shattered, like a spiderwebbed windshield. But that front glass wasn't broken. Just the man who'd once owned that vehicle.

"It's Michael," he whispered, his heart aching as he instinctively recognized his baby brother.

"How can you tell?" Noah asked.

"It's his vehicle."

"But the body . . ." Noah shuddered a bit, rocking the boat. "There's no way to tell who it is."

Luke would need DNA or dental records to confirm that it was Michael. But he doubted that the body found in his brother's vehicle belonged to someone else.

Michael being here all these years made sense. He'd loved River too much not to leave with her when she'd run away, pregnant with their child.

And this was why Luke had never been able to find him, because Michael had been here all these years.

Chapter 21

River wasn't sure why she'd been so insistent on driving Claire out to those ponds on the other side of the swamp. Maybe she was playing matchmaker between the CPS investigator and her brother Noah. Or maybe she'd just wanted to get away from her mom and grandma.

"You really didn't need to bring me out here," Claire said as River drove one of the business vans down a bumpy service road that wound around the swamp. "Noah must be doing fine, or he wouldn't be fishing. And he could have just checked in with me if he wanted to . . ."

There was something in the other woman's voice, something vulnerable, like maybe she didn't think Noah was interested in her. Or that anyone would be.

From what River remembered about her, tragedy had cut Claire Underwood's childhood short. But maybe something or someone else had.

"He's been taking it easier after the gunshot wound than after the head injury," River said. "Or maybe the week exhausted him. So I was surprised he was up so early and heading out to fish."

"You're worried about him, too?" Claire asked. "That's why you want to come out here."

"Or I just wanted to get away from my mom and grandma before they start fighting again."

Claire chuckled. "They are pretty intense."

"You have no idea. Or you probably do. You must meet all kinds of people with your job," River said. "I can't imagine how you handle it."

"I used to say it was easy because I'm dead inside—"

"Oh, that's sad," River said, the words slipping out before she could hold them back.

Claire chuckled. "I actually took some pride in it. It's better to not feel anything. It makes it easier to do the job when you can stay uninvolved."

"But you're not uninvolved now," River said. "You said that's what you used to say."

Claire pointed out the windshield. "Is that the pond? It looks like the water is dropping, and what is that?"

River pulled up behind Noah's truck and shut off the van. Then she stepped out and studied the rusted metal that seemed to be rising from the water, or that the water was receding from.

The Chevelle.

She gasped.

"What?" Claire asked. She'd stepped out, too, and come around the van. But she was staring at the two men in the rowboat rather than at the vehicle. "What's going on? What's he doing?"

"He's digging up the dead," River whispered, which was exactly what her mother hadn't wanted to happen. But Michael hadn't been buried in someone else's grave. He'd been submerged, hidden away, back behind the cemetery, behind the swamp. "For sixteen years I believed he didn't want to run away with me. That he changed his mind about loving me and raising Sarah with me."

Claire let out a soft gasp. "Michael."

Guilt overwhelmed River that she'd thought so badly of the boy who had once loved her. "He must have come here that night. He used to park out here on this service road and then walk around the swamp to the grave digger's grave."

"That's what the teenagers did," Claire remarked. "Probably what Peyton did." She moved closer to the water.

River followed her, the mud sucking on the soles of her shoes as she tried to move. River remembered Noah looking up burial dates from around the time that Peyton, Claire's friend, had disappeared like Michael had. Was he here, too?

Luke looked up from the boat and called out to them, "Stay back. I've called the state police."

"So he didn't just drive his car into the pond," Claire said. "Or Luke would have investigated it on his own."

"No, he didn't just drive in there," River said. But she didn't know for certain; she just had a feeling, the same one she'd had since she'd learned that Luke hadn't seen his brother since the night he'd left to run away with her. "Someone murdered him."

River was afraid to find out who might have done that, so afraid that she started shaking.

Claire Underwood reached out and put her arm around her shoulders. "I'm sorry, River. I'm very sorry."

River wasn't sure why she was sorry. While this was hard, it was better to know where Michael was, that he hadn't abandoned her and their baby. "Sarah," she whispered. "I have to tell Sarah."

Would it help her daughter to know the truth? But first they would have to learn what that truth was and who was responsible.

*   *   *

Claire was going to have to stop coming out to Gold Memorial Gardens. Every time she did, she either found a dead body or someone who was nearly dead, like Noah. He was alive now, but he looked like he'd seen a ghost; his face was pale except for the dark circles beneath his eyes.

He and Luke had rowed the boat out of the water and beached it in the mud on the edge of the pond. Their boots and the bottoms of their jeans were covered in mud. They and River and Claire stood behind the perimeter that the state police were setting up around the ponds.

"I'm sorry, Luke, I should have warned you," Noah said.

"How did you know the body was there?" Luke asked. Even though he'd turned over the investigation to the state police, who had just arrived, he was still asking questions.

Noah shrugged. "I didn't know for sure. But when River and I looked up burial dates around the disappearances of Michael and Peyton, we didn't find any that synched up perfectly timewise. So I was thinking about other places that someone could hide a body, and the ponds and swamp came to mind."

"Do you think there could be more than one body in there?" Claire asked.

"There was only one in the car," Luke said.

And River let out a little squeaky noise. She'd said earlier that she needed to tell her daughter, but she hadn't left yet. Maybe she was waiting for Claire to go back with her. Or for Luke.

The sheriff just kept staring at that car in the pond.

"But the state police will dredge the whole pond and the other one," Luke continued as if he hadn't heard the sound that River had made.

"They should check the swamp, too," Noah said.

"How many bodies do you think could be out here?" River asked the question now.

"When I checked CPS records for runaways, Michael and Peyton weren't the only ones who *ran away*," Claire said.

"So what are you saying? There's a serial killer in Gold Creek?" River asked. "I shouldn't have brought Sarah back here. I shouldn't have . . ." She started sobbing again. This time Noah reached for her, offering her the comfort that Claire had tried to give her earlier.

But it was hard for her; she wasn't a warm or affectionate person. She liked to stay uninvolved and removed, and she'd thought Noah was that way, too. But now he said to his sister, "Let's go back to the house. Let's get out of here."

"Claire rode with me," River said.

Claire's cell rang. Even though she wasn't on call this weekend, she still carried her work phone, and that was the one ringing. She picked it up. "Hello?"

"Miss Underwood, this is Mrs. Blue. I have a neighbor watching the little ones, and I'm at my daughter's house. I need to pick up some more clothes and things for the kids, but Buzz and Tammy are not letting me in."

"Buzz and Tammy should still be in jail," Claire said.

"No. They were released," Luke said.

Surprised that he'd overheard her one-sided conversation as much as by what he'd said, Claire looked at the sheriff. "Buzz and Tammy were released?"

He nodded.

"Their vehicles are here," Mrs. Blue said. "I don't want to just walk in. I don't think she'd hurt me, but . . ."

"Wait for me," Claire said. "I'll be right there."

"You can't go to the Buczynskis on your own," Noah said.

Luke shook his head, as if clearing it. "I can't do anything here. I'll go with you, Claire." He walked toward his vehicle without even looking at River. And he hadn't offered her any comfort at all, either. Was he so wrapped in his own misery that he hadn't seen how much she was hurting, too? Or was he hurting because she was hurting?

None of that was her business, though. So Claire just hurried after him and jumped in the passenger seat.

As he drove the sheriff's SUV toward the Buczynskis' house, Claire asked, "Why would they be released?"

"Because the doorbell footage confirmed they were both home the night Tyler died," he said. "Even if they went out a back door, there was no way for one of them to leave in a vehicle without the doorbell catching it backing out of the driveway."

"So they didn't kill him?"

Luke shook his head.

"And Michael didn't run away."

He shook his head again. "No, and the body in his car"—his voice cracked—"had a crushed skull."

"Like Tyler's," she said. "So there is a serial killer in Gold Creek?"

"And there might have been for years," Luke said. "My brother and I were separated when we were little. My mom ran off with him and I went to live with the Sebastians. I wanted him back. I wanted him to come live with us. When she died, we were finally reunited. I thought he would finally be safe, but I didn't keep him safe, Claire."

"I don't think anyone can keep anyone else safe," she said. "We're lucky if we can keep ourselves safe."

"But now I'm the sheriff," he said. "It's my job. And the same person who killed my brother might have killed Tyler, too."

"You'll figure out who it is," she assured him. But she didn't know that he would, that he could. This person had been killing for years and getting away with it. They were very smart.

Like maybe a doctor.

"We should get back to the Golds as soon as we're done with the Buczynskis," she said. And not because she'd left her car there. She wanted to make sure the teenagers in that house were safe.

"We're here," Luke said as he pulled into the Buczynskis' driveway. The minute he shut off the ignition, they heard the screaming. "Stay here," he told Claire.

But she got out of the SUV, too, and ran up to Mrs. Blue, who was standing on the front porch, her mouth open with her screams as tears trailed down her face. She must have gotten inside somehow because the door stood open. While Luke entered the house with his gun drawn, Claire closed her arms around the hysterical woman. Over her shoulder she could see inside the house, and the scene was so eerily familiar to her.

Tammy and Buzz sat on the living room couch with holes in both their heads, blood and brains spattered across the wall behind them.

Noah looked across the console at his younger sister who was driving her vehicle. His truck was blocked in back at the pond. But maybe he should have driven since she was so upset. "I'm sorry, River."

She drew in a breath and released it in a shaky sigh. "I'm glad you found him. It's better to know what happened to him."

"Yes, but . . ." It was damn sad. Another life cut too short like Tyler's. And that reminded Noah again of lying on that concrete floor in the maintenance building and watching his life pass before his eyes. It had been so quick even though he'd lived longer than Tyler and Michael Sebastian had. But Michael had a daughter and people who'd loved him.

"Do you really think they might find other bodies in the pond or swamp?" she asked.

He shrugged. "I hope not. But I can't say for sure." He had a feeling that Peyton Shusta might be in there. And maybe the other kids that Claire had found missing in CPS records. He glanced around them; she hadn't driven back to the house. "Where are you going?"

"I . . . I know I have to tell Sarah . . ."

"But you're not ready yet?"

She shook her head. "I feel like running away again like I did all those years ago. I couldn't wait to get out of this place when I was growing up."

"I know." And he felt that twinge of guilt again that he hadn't been there for her more, that he hadn't protected her better.

"I never intended to come back here."

"And then our father died."

"He was murdered," she said, as if he needed the reminder.

He wasn't going to forget that or all the other lives that had been lost because of greed and the power struggle.

"And with my mother as Luke's prime suspect, I thought I had to stay to protect her."

"She wasn't responsible," Noah said.

But River didn't nod in agreement. Instead she looked tense. "I don't really know my mother as well as I thought I did."

"She's surprised me, too," Noah admitted. She was just as money and power hungry as everyone had accused her of being, as everyone else was, but for him and River.

"I shouldn't have stayed," she said. "I shouldn't stay now. I should go back to the house and get Sarah and leave."

"Because there might be a serial killer?"

"Because that serial killer could be in the same house with us, Noah," she said. "And my daughter is there alone."

"She's not alone," he said. "She and Gigi are like conjoined twins. They're never apart. And Toby is always around them, too. They'll keep each other safe." He wasn't worried about Sarah. At the moment he was more worried about River.

She nodded. "That's true. That's true."

"But we should get back there," he said. "Just make sure that she hears it from you first."

She gasped. "You're right. I didn't think about that." She'd driven farther away from their home than either of them had realized, though. So by the time they got back to the house, Luke's SUV was also pulling into the parking lot.

Noah breathed a slight sigh of relief as he stepped out of River's vehicle as Claire and Luke stepped out of his. "I'm glad Buzz and Tammy didn't give you any trouble." And he touched his side where his gunshot wound was beginning to itch as it healed.

Luke shook his head. "Buzz and Tammy . . ."

"What?"

"They're gone," the sheriff said. "Murder-suicide."

Knowing that was how Claire's mom and stepdad died, he turned to her. She was deathly pale, almost as pale as the grave digger's ghost. He went to her and reached out, wanting to comfort her. But she stepped back and wrapped her arms around herself.

River was obviously not the only one who thought it had been a mistake coming back to Gold Creek. With as miserable as Claire looked, she probably thought it was as well. Seeing Tammy and Buzz like that had to have brought back the nightmare she'd wanted to put behind her all those years ago.

Noah had a horrible feeling that both Claire and River might decide to leave Gold Creek, and if they did, he doubted that they would ever return. And he would go back to being the loner he'd always been, like Lyle had been. When being alone had once brought him comfort and peace, now the thought filled him with dread.

Chapter 22

Sarah, Gigi, and Toby raced each other down the double staircase, Toby on one side, Gigi and Sarah on the other. "No fair!" Gigi shouted when her brother jumped over the railing and down nearly one of the levels.

"Let him break an ankle if he wants," Sarah told his sister. She didn't mind that they were moving fast. They were going to pick up Jackson, and she didn't want to keep him waiting. But before they could cross the lobby, the exterior doors opened and her mom, her uncle Luke, Uncle Noah, and Claire from CPS walked in.

The expression on Mom's face chilled Sarah. "What's wrong?" she asked, because she could tell that something was.

But her mom just stood there, staring at her with a weird, almost blank, expression on her face.

Sarah glanced at her uncles. "I thought you guys were fishing."

"Doesn't look like you caught anything," Toby said.

"They always throw them back," Gigi said.

Sarah turned back to her mom. "What's going on? Tell me."

River opened her mouth but just a little squeak came out.

Her uncle Luke looked as shell-shocked as her mom, and when Sarah turned to Uncle Noah, he turned to Claire. So she did, too.

"Your uncles found something in the pond," Claire said.

And Sarah appreciated that somebody was answering her.

"What?" Toby asked.

Claire didn't have to answer that question because, for Sarah, everything clicked into place like the last piece of a jigsaw puzzle. She knew why her mom and Uncle Luke looked like they did.

"My dad," Sarah said. "They found my dad."

"I'm sorry, Sarah," Uncle Noah said. And he glanced at her mom and Luke, too. He was clearly sorry for all of them. Uncle Noah was a good guy.

"So he is dead?" Gigi asked, and she sounded sick. But she slipped her hand into Sarah's and squeezed it.

Claire nodded.

And Gigi said, "I'm sorry, Sarah."

Tears stung her eyes like a strong wind, but Sarah blinked and cleared them. Then she released a breath so deep that her body felt limp when she let it go. "I'm glad," she said.

"What?" her uncle Luke asked, as if appalled.

And her mom's face flushed, too, as if she was embarrassed her daughter had said that.

"No. What I mean . . . he didn't desert us, Mom. He didn't choose to let us go without him."

"How do you know?" Toby asked. Then his face flushed. "I mean . . . he could have offed himself."

She shook her head. "No." She didn't know why she knew; maybe it was from the expression on her mom and Luke's faces. Maybe it was just her own gut instincts. "He was murdered."

Noah caught Claire as she tried sneaking out of the lobby. He understood her well because that had been his inclination, too. To get away from the people, at least the living ones, and go back to the dead. He followed her out the doors. "Why are you leaving?" he asked.

She tensed but didn't turn around. "I don't want to intrude."

"Why were you at the pond with River?" he asked. "Why did you come here today, Claire?"

She didn't answer him, but she didn't keep walking.

"Are you working Tyler's case yet?" he asked. "Or a new one?"

She turned around then to face him, and her face was slightly flushed. "I'm not working this weekend."

"You just went to the Buczynskis with Luke."

"Because Mrs. Blue called because she couldn't get in. But by the time we got there, she'd found an open back door. She was screaming." She shuddered.

He reached out again, and this time she didn't step back, she didn't step away from him. She let him close his arms around her. "That must have been horrible for you."

"I barely knew them," she said.

"But it had to remind you . . ."

"Of all the things I wish I could forget?" she asked, and she stepped back, out of his arms. "It bothers me. But maybe it bothers me more that it doesn't make sense. Luke cleared them in Tyler's murder. They couldn't have done it. So why kill themselves?"

"They're still facing drug charges, and you were going to take their younger kids away," he said. "Would that have been reason enough?"

She sighed. "For some people. Maybe. I've had suicide notes left for me before. But those cases were more extreme than this. The father or stepfather was up on criminal sexual contact charges or something . . ."

"You've had suicide notes left for you?"

She nodded.

"I don't know how you do your job," he said, and he looked longingly toward the cemetery. "I don't have to worry about losing my clients. They're already gone."

She smiled slightly. "That does make your job easier."

"Except when there are so many dead." Then he had so many graves to dig and sod to plant over them and flowers around them.

"Do you think Peyton could be in that pond?" she asked.

"Don't you?"

She nodded. "And maybe some of the others." She glanced at the house behind him. "You shouldn't stay here. You could be in danger."

"Is that why you came here today?" he asked. "To check on me?"

Her smile widened a bit. "Yes." But she sounded exasperated with herself for admitting it. Or maybe she was exasperated with him. "You could have wound up like the Buczynskis are now that day you went there." She shuddered, and Noah drew her back into his arms, holding her as she trembled.

He patted her back and said, "I'm fine."

"You were shot."

"According to my nephew, I was lucky. It was just a flesh wound."

She shuddered again and clutched him back, so tightly a twinge of pain passed through his side. But he ignored it.

"There was a lot of blood," she murmured.

He didn't know if she was talking about when he was shot or what she'd seen today. "I'm sorry, Claire." He was sorry that she'd had such a traumatic life and that she'd chosen such a difficult profession.

"So you two are together now?" a male voice remarked.

Claire tore herself from his arms and whirled around to where Wynn stood behind her under the portico. Even though

Noah had been facing that way, he hadn't noticed his nephew drive or walk up. Wynn was like his father with that creepy ability to just spring up out of nowhere.

"There's a lot going on right now," Noah said. "Luke and I just found a body in the pond behind the swamp and Claire and Luke found the Buczynskis dead."

Wynn gave an exaggerated shudder. "So our new sheriff is earning his keep. And it looks like we'll have more work for the family business. Father and Fiona will be thrilled."

"Don't you care?" Noah asked. "The body in the swamp, it is probably Sarah's father."

Wynn shrugged. "So what? She never knew him. And he was just some druggie like that kid who worked for you until you fired him. They weren't ever going to amount to anything anyways."

"So they didn't matter?" Claire asked. "Like the animals you killed?"

Wynn let out something that sounded like a growl. "For the hundredth time, I didn't kill those fucking animals." He gestured at Noah. "I thought he did. If it wasn't him, I don't know, maybe it was your ghoulish little friend Peyton."

"Ghoulish?" Claire asked. "You were the ones called the ghouls."

Wynn shook his head. "Not me and Taylor. That was Noah and River and the others. Taylor and I were popular." And from the way he said it, he took great pride in it.

"Where is Taylor?" Claire asked.

Wynn shrugged. "I don't know. I'm not my sister's keeper."

"What does she do?" Claire asked.

And Wynn shrugged again. "Collect her allowance from my father. I'm not sure she has a real job. We're not close anymore. We haven't been since . . ." He trailed off and tensed. "I guess we just grew apart. Some people got stuck here, like Noah and my father. While some people left, like River and myself and

Taylor." He yawned. "I had a long shift, and I'm going to bed now." He brushed past them and headed into the lobby.

"I should leave, too," Claire said.

"Stay," Noah urged her. He didn't want her to be alone after what she'd seen at the Buczynskis. He didn't want her alone with her terrible memories. And he didn't want to be alone, either.

Claire stayed. She didn't know why. But the thought of leaving, of going back to her empty little bungalow . . .

It had filled her with such dread. And she knew she would have just paced as she waited for answers. But no answers came. While Luke tried to get updates out of the state police, they'd shut him out of the investigation completely.

So Claire and Noah just walked around the cemetery, enjoying the sunshine and the beautiful gardens. "It really is so peaceful here," she said.

Noah grinned with obvious pride. "That's the goal. Your final resting place should be restful."

She smiled. "Your mission is accomplished, Mr. Gold."

His grin slipped away as they neared the grave digger's grave. Water was bubbling up out of the thick grass. "Damn it."

"What?"

"Those ponds were formed decades ago when the water was drained from this area. This part of the cemetery used to be part of the swamp."

"And now that the state police are draining the ponds, this area is going to get all wet again," she surmised.

"I'm going to have to figure out a way to keep this from getting too wet. Maybe get some loads of sand or pile up sandbags . . ."

"I know how important he is to you," she said. She could see it now, see the panic in him over the thought of the grave digger's grave getting disturbed.

"He saved my life," he reminded her.

Lyle McGinty hadn't been the monster that legend claimed he was, and neither was the modern-day grave digger. They were both men who loved nature and beauty and honoring the dead. And Claire felt a rush of warmth for both of them.

"If you have to work, I can leave," she said. And she knew that she should before she started feeling anything more than she already did.

He shook his head. "It won't take me long. I'll put my crew on it," he said. "I'd like for you to stay for dinner." He glanced at his watch. "It's closer than I realized."

The day had slipped away from her. After seeing what she had at the Buczynskis, she hadn't felt like eating. She wasn't sure that she did now. But yet she didn't want to leave. So she walked back to the house with him, quietly while he spoke on his cell to one of the groundskeepers. When they walked into the lobby, he stopped at the foot of the double staircase.

"The dining room is to the right off the second landing," he said. "I'm going to run into the office where Lawrence probably is and fill him in on the water situation."

"I can wait for you."

"Go up," he said. "River will probably already be in there, and Sarah, Toby, and Gigi, too."

She smiled as she thought of the kids. "Okay." But when she climbed the first set of stairs, she noticed someone continuing up another flight. How many stories was this house?

And was that . . .

Long black hair hung down the woman's narrow back; the hair was longer than Gigi's even. It had to be Taylor. Claire had asked Wynn about her earlier, and he'd had no answers for her.

Here was Claire's opportunity to ask Taylor about herself, and to hopefully get answers to the questions she'd had for so long about Peyton. So she followed her but moved as quietly as she could. Taylor didn't even stop on the third floor but continued up another narrow staircase to what must have been the attic.

The door at the top was locked because Taylor had to put a key in the knob and turn it before it opened. And when it opened, Claire rushed up after her. Taylor let out a slight scream when she saw her and tried to slam the door, but Claire was there too fast and pushed it open. She did so with such force that she stumbled into the room.

It was an attic. Bare wood rafters and walls, but there were dormer windows that illuminated the space and that horrific collection of dead animals that had once been out in the maintenance building. And Claire was the one who let out the scream now.

But Taylor had shut the door behind her, and with as far up in the house as they were, she wasn't sure that anyone would hear her and be able to rescue her in time. Because she was very afraid that she was in danger and that she'd found the true psychopath of the Gold family.

Chapter 23

Luke's heart literally ached. He hadn't been able to stay at the Golds, not with his brother's body having been there all these years without him knowing. He was also torn between River's emotional reaction and Sarah's matter-of-fact one. He understood both in a way. River had loved his brother. Sarah had never known him, and maybe she felt better knowing that Michael hadn't abandoned her and her mother.

Luke was also both upset and relieved that his brother was dead. Upset that a young life had been cut so short but relieved that Michael hadn't run away again. He was also furious with whoever had killed his brother.

While he knew he couldn't investigate Michael's death, he was frustrated that the state police were not going to keep him apprised of the investigation until they'd concluded it. It was as if they didn't trust him. Or maybe they considered him a suspect, too?

He wasn't a Gold. He would never intentionally hurt a member of his own family. But he felt like he had hurt Michael unintentionally. If he'd offered him and River his support instead of his condemnation and judgment, maybe neither of them would have tried to run away from Gold Creek. But he'd already been in the service then. He wouldn't have been able to offer them much support. And he'd thought, at the time, that he'd given his brother the right advice.

He released a deep groan of frustration and pushed open the driver door of his SUV. After leaving the Golds, he'd gone back into the office. But he should have come here first. His parents had also adopted his brother; Michael had been their son.

And maybe that was why he'd waited, why he hadn't wanted to deal with the reaction of anyone else who'd known his brother. He'd had to figure out and deal with his own reaction first.

He ached. That was all.

And that hollow ache made him feel so old that he slowly climbed the steps of the front porch. Before he could reach for the knob, it turned, and Jackson stood there. "Are you okay, Luke?"

"Sarah told you."

"Is she okay?" Jackson asked.

Luke sighed. "Yeah."

"She sounded okay, but I don't know . . . sometimes she acts like she can't be sad and depressed around me because . . ."

Because Jackson had been through so much more, had lost both his parents in equally senseless and tragic ways. That ache inside Luke eased a little as he reached out and hugged his godson. Jackson was taller than he was now, like his dad had been. When Jack died, Luke had lost his very best friend, but with Jackson, he still had a piece of him, the heart of him. What did Sarah have of her father besides the dimple in her chin? Michael hadn't raised her like her mother single-handedly had done. He hadn't even gotten to meet his baby girl. Tears stung his eyes, but Luke blinked them away and stepped back. Then he gestured toward the kitchen from which the usually delicious smells wafted. "Do they know?"

Jackson nodded.

"Are they okay?"

"Miss Mary cried. Pastor Sebastian is upset but trying to hide it, probably for her sake."

"Of course," Luke said. His dad was used to taking care of everyone else but himself.

"Luke?" his mother called out, her voice raspy and shaky. She stood in the doorway to the kitchen, her face pale. "Is it true? Is it Michael that you found?"

He nodded.

And she crumpled, sliding down the doorjamb. He rushed forward, but his dad was there, holding her up.

"Oh, poor Michael," his father said, tears glistening in his eyes. "Poor Michael . . ."

"He was just eighteen years old," Luke said. Just a couple of years older than Jackson. Luke had to make sure that his best friend's son didn't end up like his brother had. If Jack knew, he probably wouldn't have appointed Luke his son's guardian. Adele had considered changing it after Jack died because she hadn't believed Luke would last longer than she would. But death could happen anywhere.

Why was so much of it happening in Gold Creek? Was there really a serial killer living among them for all these years?

If Lawrence had been in his office, Noah might not have heard Claire's scream. But since he'd only been a few minutes behind her, he was still on the staircase, just getting ready to step off onto the second-story landing, when he heard her scream coming from above him. He scrambled up to the third floor and called out, "Claire!"

And she screamed again. And still it came from above him. The attic? He climbed those narrow, rickety steps up to the top of the house, but the door was locked.

"Open this!" he yelled to whoever had her inside the attic, because she was obviously being held or she would have opened it herself. Knowing that, remembering how Tyler's skull had been crushed and how Michael's must have been as well, urgency and fear surged through him. He thrust his shoulder against the door, but it held. Then he kicked the wood, the door and the frame where a dead bolt must be holding it shut. It shuddered but held. Despite the twinge in his side, he kicked it again, harder until the frame broke and the door opened.

Light, streaming in through the oval windows in the dormers, illuminated the dust dancing in the area over the matted fur of dead animals. Some of them were hanging from the rafters. Some were standing or lying on an old dining room table. Claire was at one end of that table while Noah's niece Taylor was at the other. Neither were in chairs; it was as if one had been chasing the other around it.

And since Claire was the one who'd screamed, he knew which one was in danger.

"What's going on?" he asked even though he could guess.

But Taylor was between him and Claire. She could get to Claire before he could since she was closer. And he wasn't sure if there were weapons on that table of dead animals. Bile rose up the back of his throat at the sight of all of them.

"Your girlfriend followed me up here," Taylor said. "She forced her way in. She's trespassing."

"So let me leave," Claire said.

"No, you can't tell anyone about this," Taylor said. "They won't understand."

"We already know about this," Noah said. "Claire saw it years ago when you had it out in the maintenance building."

Taylor shook her head. "No, that wasn't mine." She gestured at the animals. "This . . . isn't mine."

"Is it Wynn's?" Claire asked. "Does this belong to your brother?"

Taylor shook her head again, then turned toward Noah. Was she going to try to blame it on him like Wynn had when he'd first showed it to Claire when they were teenagers?

"Did you find him?" Taylor asked, and her voice sounded so soft, as if she was slipping away even though she was standing in the room with them. She was like the grave digger's ghost.

"Find who?" Noah asked. "I found Michael, or so we think."

"Could it have been him?" Taylor asked.

"Peyton? Is that who you're talking about?" Claire asked. "You knew Peyton?"

"I loved Peyton. I loved him so much," Taylor murmured. "And he just disappeared."

"Peyton was my friend, too," Claire said. "He was my fri—"

Taylor let out a loud laugh. "No, he wasn't." She snorted. "He was using you."

Claire shook her head. "No. We weren't ever together. We were just friends."

"He was going to do this to you," Taylor said, and she gestured toward an animal hanging from the ceiling. "You had nobody after your parents died. So nobody would miss you. He was going to kill you. You were going to be his first human kill."

Claire tensed. "What? No . . ."

"These belonged to Peyton," Taylor said. "It was his collection. And I'm keeping it for him. I thought he would come back someday." She turned toward Noah again. "But you found him."

Noah shook his head. "No. I'm pretty sure Luke and I found Michael. The body was in his car. It had to be him."

Taylor sucked in a breath and then smiled. "He'll come back

then. For these . . ." She gestured again at the dead animals. "And for me. He'll come back for me."

"What are you all doing up here?" a male voice asked.

And Noah whirled around to find that Lawrence had snuck up behind him. He wasn't alone, though. Sarah, Toby, and Gigi stood at the bottom of the stairs.

"Should I call Uncle Luke?" Sarah called out. "Is Claire okay? We heard her scream."

"Yes, call Luke," Noah said.

"No!" Lawrence snapped. "This is not a crime. Taylor found this stuff. It's not hers but it reminds her of someone. And her therapist said she could keep it."

"She won't let me get past her," Claire said.

So Noah's demented niece had been chasing her around that table, trying to carry out her boyfriend's plan for Claire? To kill her?

Lawrence pushed past Noah. "Taylor, sweetheart. Let's go down to your room. I don't think you took your medication today."

"Daddy?" Taylor asked, and she sounded like a little girl, but like one who was scared and lost.

"Yes, honey," Lawrence said, and he closed his arms around her. "Let's get you downstairs. I'll call Dr. Trent for you."

"Dr. Trent," she murmured, and nodded.

As she and Lawrence drew close to where Noah stood in the doorway, he could see that her dark eyes were glazed. She looked like she'd taken her medication, maybe too much, or she was just that out of it. He stepped aside and let them pass. The kids did the same on the third-floor landing. But once Lawrence and Taylor were out of sight, the teenagers ran up to the attic.

"This door has always been locked," Toby said as he came through first. Then he stopped at the sight before him and murmured, "Oh, soooo gross."

"Sooo gross," Gigi agreed. "This is like super sick. I can't believe it's been up here."

"Are you okay?" Sarah asked Claire the question Noah should have, but he was too damn stunned.

Claire kept staring at all those dead animals, like the teenagers were, but she nodded. "Yeah. I saw her heading up here, and I wanted to talk to her. And when I saw she had the door locked, I wondered . . ."

"If this was where that collection had gone that Wynn showed you years ago," Noah finished for her.

She met his gaze and nodded.

"Are you sure you're okay?" he asked. "Did she touch you?"

Claire shook her head. "I kept the table between us."

"Should I call Uncle Luke?" Sarah asked. "Do we report this to the police?"

"Yeah," Noah said. "It was an assault."

"She didn't touch me," Claire said.

"But she tried," Noah said. "She chased you around the table. You need to call him."

"No," Claire said. "He just found out his brother died. And then we found the Buczynskis. It's been a hell of a day for him. This can wait."

"That's why I didn't call him when I heard the scream," Sarah said. "I wanted to see if it was just Grandma Fiona and GG Mabel before I bothered him." She tipped her head back and stared up at those animals. "This is next-level bizarre, though."

"Psycho," Toby added. "Like where's the old lady in the rocking chair?"

Gigi shuddered and edged toward that open door. "I'm going to have nightmares about this."

Claire sighed. "Yes, you will. The first time I saw this I was your age."

"It's been here all that time?" Toby asked.

"No, it must have been moved from where I saw it."

"But into the house?" Noah asked, and shook his head. "How did nobody notice? Except Lawrence. He must have known."

"Well, we probably weren't alive then," Toby said. "No offense, Miss Underwood."

She chuckled. "No offense, Toby. And you're right. You weren't."

"My mom would have lived here yet then. She isn't much younger than you are." Sarah shuddered. "God, no wonder she hates this place."

"Do you?" Gigi asked. "Are you guys going to leave now?"

Sarah shook her head. "I don't think so. I don't know. Mom is pretty upset."

"Go, be with her," Claire urged. "And don't any of you worry about this. We will talk to Luke."

The kids stayed for a little while longer, poking around the attic and looking in horror and fascination at that grotesque collection. Noah didn't feel right leaving until they finally filed down the narrow stairs.

"Come on," he said to Claire. "Let's get you out of here."

She nodded and ducked around the broken doorframe to descend the stairs. But she didn't stop on the third floor or the second. She continued down to the lobby and kept walking.

"Claire, wait!"

She slowed her steps but didn't entirely stop until she got to the lobby doors to the outside. "I'm not hungry anymore," she said.

"I get that," he said, doubting that he would eat, either. "I just want to make sure that you're okay."

She sighed. "I'm creeped out, and I don't know what to think."

"My niece accused your friend of wanting to kill you," he said. And if the guy was dead in that pond with Michael Sebastian, Noah wasn't sorry that he was. But . . . "I wouldn't believe what she says unless someone else can confirm it. She seems really messed up. And I'm not sure how I never noticed that before."

She turned around then and smiled at him. "Your family is really messed up, Noah."

He nodded. "I'm sorry."

"Don't be," she said, and she stepped closer to him and touched his cheek. "It's not your fault any more than my messed-up family was mine or Tyler's was his or any of the other kids whose cases I've handled over the years. We don't choose our parents or grandparents or aunts, uncles . . ."

"Or nieces," Noah finished for her.

"Or nephews," Claire said. "I'm not sure what Wynn knows about all of this and how involved he is."

Wynn was a little older than Taylor and bigger and stronger. If one of them was a killer, it would make more sense that it was Wynn. And what about Peyton?

"Do you think Peyton is dead?" Noah asked. Or was he the one still killing? He disappeared before Michael and Tyler. But maybe he wasn't really gone.

She shrugged. "I don't know what to believe," she said. "I just need to be alone for a while."

He thought about asking if he could go home with her, to get away from the nightmare that life in this house had become. But River was here and Sarah and that macabre collection upstairs. And while some of his family was messed up, he didn't want to lose any of them, especially not the ones who weren't messed up.

He touched her face then, stroking his fingertips along her jaw. "Be careful," he implored her.

She nodded. "You too."

He wanted to kiss her, like he'd wanted to that day outside her house. But just like that day, he had that sensation that someone was watching them. And in this house, it could be anyone. So he trailed his fingers away from her jaw and stepped back.

She drew in a breath, then turned and walked away. He had to believe that she would be safer anywhere but here. This was where the danger was, where he and his family were.

Claire glanced back at the house as she climbed into her vehicle. But she couldn't see the doors under the portico. She didn't know if Noah was still standing there, watching her, or if he'd gone back upstairs to his family. She should have insisted he come home with her where he would be safe.

Nobody was safe in that house, not with those people. The collection wasn't in some outbuilding anymore; it had been moved inside, as if for preservation or protection and privacy. She couldn't remember if there were more animals than she remembered. And she had remembered it over the years, just as Gigi had said she would, in nightmares.

Maybe she shouldn't drive straight home. Maybe she should go over to the Sebastians and check on them and Luke. But when she pulled out of the wrought iron gates of Gold Memorial Gardens, she noticed a vehicle pulling out behind her.

It was one of those big white vans, one of the company vehicles. Was it Noah? Was he following her to make sure she made it safely home?

She would have seen him walk out with her, though. Or if he'd gone out another door, he would have had to run to get keys for a vehicle, then run to that vehicle in record time to catch up to her just as she drove out the gates. She didn't think it was possible, with his wound, for him to have moved that quickly.

No. Whoever was driving that van wasn't Noah. Who was following her, and what the hell did they want with her?

Was it Lawrence trying to cover up what his daughter had done? How sick she was?

And how did he intend to do that?

Did he intend to run Claire off the road?

With as fast as the van was coming at her, coming so close to the rear bumper of her small hybrid, that certainly seemed to be the case. The windows were tinted, even the windshield, so she couldn't see who was behind the wheel of the van.

Even as she pressed harder on her accelerator to create some distance between them, she grabbed her cell and punched in the contact for Luke. She should have let Sarah call him because now it might be too late.

Chapter 24

River didn't know why she walked into the dining room. She had no desire to eat. But she wanted to check on Sarah, to make sure she was really as okay as she'd seemed when she'd heard the news about her father. Michael was dead, had been dead all this time.

And River felt so damn guilty for how angry she'd been with him. She'd thought he hadn't shown that night, that he'd let down her and their daughter. But she was really the one who'd let him down. Instead of getting on the bus that night and heading across the country to her grandmother's, she should have reported him missing.

"Are you okay, honey?" Grandma Mabel asked as she walked into the room.

River nodded.

"I hope that wasn't you screaming," her mother said.

And River was surprised that her mother was looking at her as she said that and not at her grandmother. "Screaming? What?"

"I can't believe you're actually mourning that boy now," she said with a slight sneer.

River had once thought her mother was so beautiful, but Fiona didn't look as beautiful as she'd once been, and it had nothing to do with getting older. She was cold in a way that River had never noticed before. It was like she didn't really care about anything or anyone anymore, like she was dead inside . . . like Claire Underwood had claimed she was.

"Why shouldn't I mourn him, Mom?" she asked. "He didn't desert me and Sarah. He was at the cemetery, and somebody killed him. To stop me from leaving with him?"

Fiona narrowed her green eyes. "Are you accusing me of something, River?"

She didn't want to, for so many reasons. She sighed. Then she tried to focus on what else her mother had said. "Somebody screamed?"

"It was Claire again," Sarah said as she, Gigi, and Toby walked into the dining room. They looked around the circumference of the long table as if looking for someone.

Very few people were actually there. The people in the dining room were River, her grandmother and mother, and three of River's sisters-in-law. Where was everyone else?

"What happened to Claire?" River asked with concern.

Gigi shuddered. "She found something gross in the attic."

"Bats?" Mabel asked, and she shuddered in revulsion. "Are there bats in this house?"

Fiona looked at her and nodded. "Yeah, one old one that I'm looking at right now."

Mabel flipped off her daughter. And the teenagers all laughed.

River ignored their usual antics and asked her daughter, "What was it that Claire found?"

Even Sarah, who was always so tough, shuddered. "Some sick collection of dead animals."

"Dead animals?" Fiona asked. "Did the exterminator not take care of them?"

Sarah shook her head. "No. It's not like that. Taylor had them up there, and when Claire found them, Taylor wouldn't let her out of the attic. That was why she screamed."

Ellen, Taylor's mother, jumped up from the table. "She wouldn't hurt her. She wouldn't hurt anyone." But she didn't sound that convinced, and she rushed out of the room as if to check.

River stood up, too. She'd not been hungry, and now she just lost her appetite again. "I don't think we should stay here," she said.

"Mom?"

"I don't think it's safe for us." Or maybe for anyone in this house or in the cemetery.

"The state police are on this now," Sarah said. "And even though Uncle Luke isn't supposed to be involved, I think he will be. And Claire Underwood . . ."

"What about Claire?" River asked.

"She's determined to find out what really happened to Tyler and to her old friend Peyton and I think she will."

Claire did seem smart and determined, but whoever had killed Michael had gotten away with it for a long time. They would probably have no problem killing Claire if she got too close to figuring out the truth.

The second she'd slipped out the lobby doors, Noah had regretted letting Claire leave on her own. So he'd rushed to grab the keys to a van and race after her. But someone had already beat him to her. There was another Gold Memorial Gardens and Funeral Services van between Noah and Claire. Someone driving too fast and too close to the bumper of her small hybrid vehicle. But he wasn't the only one who noticed, because suddenly lights flashed and a siren blared as an SUV appeared beside him.

He pulled off to the side of the road. The van in front of him and Claire's little car pulled off as well while Luke parked in the road next to the van in the middle. The sheriff parked so close that the driver couldn't open the door. But he could jump out another one.

Noah hopped out of his, prepared to chase that driver if he tried to flee the scene.

But he didn't. Wynn just brazenly lowered his window and said, "Sheriff, I'm sorry I was speeding. But I need to get to the hospital."

Claire was out of her vehicle, too. "Why didn't you pass me then? Why did you keep following me, right on my bumper?"

Fury coursed through Noah. He was so damn sick of his family harassing the woman he cared about. "What the fuck is wrong with you?" he asked his nephew. "Why would you try to hurt her?"

"Hurt her?" Wynn asked, his eyes wide with feigned innocence. "I didn't touch her. She's paranoid."

"Driving so close to her? That was road rage, threatening behavior," the sheriff said. "I could take you in."

Wynn shook his head. "And say what to the hospital, to the people who need medical attention? You need to let me leave. I'm on call and need to get back to the ER."

Luke closed his eyes as if mentally debating what to do.

"Arrest him," Noah urged. "Or at least call the damn hospital and find out if he's telling the truth."

"Don't bother," Claire said. "Let him go."

"Why?" Noah asked.

She shrugged. "Because he doesn't matter."

Wynn sucked in a breath like she'd punched him. And Noah realized that nothing bothered a narcissist like his nephew more than not mattering.

"And whatever he thinks he's doing, trying to intimidate or scare me, it will only make me more determined to figure out what he's scared of me discovering what he doesn't want me to know." She stepped closer to the van. "Is it that that sick collection in the attic is yours? Or that you killed Peyton and then Michael? That you've twisted your sister's mind? What are you capable of, Wynn?"

"You're not just paranoid," Wynn said. "You're crazy. Dangerous."

"I should bring you in for questioning," Luke said.

"The hospital—"

"But," Luke continued as if Wynn hadn't tried to interrupt, "the state police are handling the investigation now. They might even bring in the FBI. So they'll look deeply into Wynn's past and his present. And I'm sure they will find reasons to question him."

Noah wasn't so sure. His family was clever and damn good at keeping secrets. He was a member of that family and there was so much even he hadn't known. But he didn't protest when Luke let his nephew drive off.

Instead he focused on Claire. "Are you okay?"

She nodded.

"She called me," Luke said, "when she saw the van following her."

"Did you tell him about Taylor?" he asked.

She nodded. "Luke stayed on the phone with me until he caught up to us. I didn't know you were back there, too."

Noah nodded. "I just had a weird feeling. And after what happened with Taylor, the stuff she said, I wanted to make sure you got safely home. I shouldn't have let you drive off alone."

"I'll be fine," she said. "I probably did overreact to his following me. He didn't touch my car or me. And neither did Taylor. I really have no reason to report them."

"I could arrest them both for attempted assault or harassment," Luke offered.

"Do it," Noah urged him.

"No," Claire said. "Let the state police handle this. And, Luke, I'm sorry about your brother."

He nodded.

"You should be with Sarah and River," Noah told his friend.

"Are they not okay?"

"I don't think anyone is okay in that house," Noah admitted.

"Maybe you most of all," Claire said. "I know you wanted to stay to protect your sister and the teenagers."

He nodded. He'd already failed to protect Tyler; he wanted to make sure the others were safe. But he also wanted to make sure Claire wasn't in any danger, either, especially if his family posed the threat.

"I'll make sure Claire gets back home safely," Luke offered. "You should stay with Sarah and River."

"You don't want to be with them?" Noah asked. Had he been wrong to think that Luke had feelings for River? Or was it because he had feelings that he didn't want to be around her right now while she was mourning her first love?

"I just . . ." Luke sighed. "I feel so damn bad about Michael. Maybe if I supported his relationship with River, he would still be alive. Sarah would have had a father and River . . ."

"You don't know that," Claire said. "If there's a serial killer in Gold Creek, they might not have any reason for picking the victims that they have."

"Do you think it's Peyton?" Noah asked her. "That he's still alive? That he intended to kill you?"

She wrapped her arms around herself then as if she was suddenly cold. "I . . . I don't know . . ."

"If he was going to kill you once, he might try again," Noah said. "That's why I wanted to make sure you got safely home."

"Nobody's tried to kill me," Claire said. "You're the one who's nearly died, Noah. I can get myself home. Luke, why don't you make sure Noah gets safely back and that River and Sarah are okay?"

Noah was impressed. Claire was tough and considerate. She

seemed to care more about others than she cared about herself. Would she give up her life for someone else?

He was afraid that she would do just that in order to protect a child because she had once been that kid who'd needed protection. But nobody had protected her when she'd needed it. He wanted to be the person she could count on, the one who was there for her. But he'd spent so much of his life hiding from the living, staying out in the cemetery with the dead instead, who expected nothing from him, that he wasn't sure how he could step up for her. How he could make her trust him. But it wasn't just her trust that he wanted.

Claire didn't go to her house after she left Luke and Noah on the side of the road. It wasn't just because she didn't want to be alone in her little bungalow; if that was the case, she would have invited Noah to come home with her.

But there was something else she wanted to do, something she wanted to look into on her own. So she drove back to the CPS office. It didn't matter that she wasn't on call this weekend; she was still working.

Still thinking about everything she'd learned, everything that had happened, everything she'd seen.

When she'd looked up those old records, she'd only read the notes in Peyton's file about his running away. She hadn't read the entire thing, because she'd figured she knew why he'd been with her at the Sebastians.

She'd trusted what he'd told her. But after years of doing CPS, Claire knew that even kids in trouble lied. Maybe that was why they lied—because they were in trouble already, and they didn't want it to get worse.

So who had lied? Peyton? Or Taylor?

That was what she needed to know.

So she read all the CPS investigator's notes on Peyton. And then she opened other files, like Michael's, and read them. And she looked at a few of the other missing kids whom the police had concluded were runaways.

She had a feeling that they wouldn't be missing much longer. With the state police draining the ponds and swamp, their bodies would be found where Michael's had been all these years.

They would have been murdered just like he had been, and Tyler Hicks had been. There had been other deaths, too, ones that made a hell of a lot more sense now to Claire than they had before.

Claire knew who the killer was.

But nobody was going to believe her unless she got proof or a confession.

Chapter 25

When Noah brought Luke up to the attic, they caught the kids inside it. And not just the kids who lived in the house, but also Jackson. "You said I could come over," the kid reminded his guardian.

"To comfort Sarah," Luke said, "not to mess with a potential crime scene."

"I don't think these animals were killed here," Toby said. "There's no blood and they look old."

"They would be old," Noah said. If they were the ones Wynn had shown Claire all those years ago. Either he or Luke should have gone home with her. Preferably him because he hated being back in the attic with all those poor dead animals.

"So was Taylor telling the truth?" Sarah asked. "Do you think these belong to that Peyton guy that Claire used to know?"

Noah shrugged. "I don't know. I don't really remember him." He turned toward Luke. "He was a foster with Claire at the Sebastians. What do they say about him?"

Luke shrugged. "I don't remember them ever talking about him."

"They don't ever talk about the *bad ones*," Jackson said with a gesture of air quotes. "Just the *good ones*, like Luke and Claire. The ones who do stuff for other people."

Claire and Luke were definitely the good ones; Noah couldn't argue with that. But *bad ones . . .*

Was that what someone had considered Tyler Hicks? A bad kid? And the others . . .

"You kids need to go back downstairs," Luke said. "I do think these animals should be taken in for evidence."

"Evidence of what?" Gigi asked.

"Of a psychopath serial killer," Sarah said.

"Come on, out," Luke said, gesturing them toward the door.

"It's not like we all haven't seen worse stuff than these animals," Sarah said. But she and the others finally walked out and down those stairs.

While Luke followed them to the doorway and listened, as if making sure they were gone, Noah took a closer look at the animals. And he noticed the holes in the hides, the slashes.

These weren't the carcasses of roadkill. These animals had been deliberately killed. "If that Peyton kid did this, he was dangerous. Why wouldn't your parents talk about him?"

"They feel bad for the kids they couldn't save," Luke said, "for the ones who ran away like Michael and this Peyton."

"But Michael didn't run away," Noah said. "And maybe Peyton didn't, either." But the people who'd been fostering them must have insisted that they had, so there hadn't really been any police investigation into their disappearances. Nobody would question the word of such well-respected people.

"Or maybe Peyton is the one who killed Michael," Luke said. "He disappeared first. And he could have killed Tyler, too."

"That's right," Noah said, his head beginning to pound as he thought of all that had happened that day. "Buzz and Tammy didn't kill him. So why did they kill each other?" And why did that seem so eerily similar to what had happened to Claire's parents?

Sure, murder-suicides happened a lot, but not in Gold Creek, and not with the same person finding the bodies.

Luke shrugged. "I don't know."

"You really think they killed each other?"

"Who else would have killed them?" Luke asked, and he touched his head as if it was pounding, too.

"I don't know, but I don't think it was Peyton Shusta. Taylor might have been able to hide these animals up here all these years, but she couldn't hide a person. A living person."

"What about Taylor?" Luke asked. "Could she be the one carrying out her dead boyfriend's plans?"

"She's still hung up on the guy," Noah said. "She didn't kill him."

"How is she hung up on such a bad guy?" Luke asked.

"Only the bad kids," Noah murmured.

"What?" Luke asked.

"I'm thinking about what Jackson just said," he admitted. "About the Sebastians."

"He said that my folks only talk about the good ones," Luke said, and some of the color drained from his face.

And Noah gently pointed out to Luke what had occurred to him. "But only the *bad kids*, and the *bad parents*, are the ones who have died."

The rest of the color drained from Luke's face, but he shook his head. "No."

His friend looked like a ghost now, like the grave digger. He was so damn pale and shaky. And even though he was denying it, he had to have the same suspicion that Noah had.

Claire stood on the front porch at the Sebastians', debating whether or not she should ring the bell or walk right in or turn around and run away, like they'd claimed so many other kids had run away. Luke's SUV wasn't in the driveway, and she wasn't sure if Jackson was there. If he was, she definitely didn't want to talk in front of him about the suspicions that were tearing her up inside.

But before she could decide what she was going to do, she heard a scraping noise and turned around to find Pastor Sebastian standing behind her. He carried a shovel.

"Uh, what are you doing?" she asked.

He shoved the blade into the dirt in the flower bed at the front of the porch. "I was going to dig up a mum and plant it in the cemetery."

"On my mother's grave?" she asked. "You're the one who put the flowers there the other day?"

The door behind her opened. "I heard voices," Mary said. "And I thought Jackson left with those Gold kids."

Jackson was gone. That was good. For Jackson.

For her, though . . .

She wasn't as sure. There was a recorder in her purse. She reached inside and clicked it on. But would anyone find it if she was right and hers was the next body that went missing?

"Come inside," Mary said, and she linked her arm with Claire's, pulling her into the house.

Behind Claire, heavy footsteps landed on the stairs, then padded across the porch. Then the door swung shut behind Pastor Sebastian. She turned back to see him standing there in the shadows. And she was reminded of the grave digger who'd been so tall and lean.

Was this whom the teenagers had seen over the years? The reason the legend had grown so big?

"You know," he said, his voice gruff.

"I know what?" she asked, trying to bluff. "A lot happened today."

"I know," Mary said. "Michael was found. Poor Luke was so upset."

"And the Buczynskis," Claire said. "They died, like my mom and stepdad did."

"Oh, that's tragic," Mary said. "Murder-suicide. It never makes sense to me."

Of course it wouldn't. "It doesn't," Claire agreed. "It doesn't make any sense."

"We knew Tammy," Mary said. "She stayed here with us for a few weeks, before you, when she and her mother were fighting. But she straightened out for a while."

"Until she met Buzz," the pastor said. "But even then, I thought there was hope for her."

Claire forced a sigh. "Unfortunately, there isn't now."

"Unfortunately for you, too," Pastor Sebastian said.

"What are you talking about, Peter?" Mary asked. "I don't understand."

"Our Claire was always a success story. Such a sweet girl and so very clever," he said, but with bitterness instead of pride. "I warned that boss of hers, Mallory, to keep an eye on her. To keep her in check. But Claire kept investigating, and she figured out something she shouldn't have, Mary."

Claire shook her head. "I don't know what you think I figured out."

"You can't lie, Claire," he said. "That's why I knew you were telling the truth about that creepy stepfather of yours. That's why I took care of him and your mother for you. And you felt so safe after that, I could see it on your face. You always felt safe here, like you were supposed to. But just now, when I saw your face, I can tell you don't feel safe anymore, Claire."

She was definitely not safe.

"Peter, I don't understand," Mary said.

"You're getting so forgetful, dear," he said. "You should go lie down, and I'll take care of Claire. And you'll forget all about this, just like you've forgotten so many things over the years."

So Mary hadn't known, or if she'd suspected, he must have gaslighted the hell out of her so that she didn't know what was real or not right now. She stared at Claire like she wasn't even sure she was there.

"I don't understand . . ." Mary murmured again, and tears welled in her eyes.

At least there was that, that one of them hadn't been evil. But the place Claire had always considered so safe had been the most dangerous place of all, anywhere near Pastor Sebastian.

"I saved your life, Claire," he said. "I saved you from that horrible man who married your stupid mother. And I saved you from that sick boy that was staying with us."

"Peyton . . ."

"He was going to hurt you," he said. "I heard him tell one of those Gold girls what he was going to do to you. He was evil. Pure evil. And now he's gone."

"And Tyler?" she asked. "He was a good kid. Why Tyler?"

A nerve twitched below his eye. "His mother, Tammy, she wasn't like you. She was a good liar. I believed her, that Tyler was just bad. That he was into drugs and dealing them to other kids, corrupting them, too."

"Her husband was the dealer," Claire said. "He was forcing Tyler to sell them for him. Tyler didn't want to." She hadn't talked to him, but from what Noah had told her, she believed that about him. "Tyler was a good kid. You killed a good kid."

"Are you going to call Michael a good kid, too?" he asked. "He got that poor Gold girl pregnant, and instead of growing up, he doubled down on the drugs and booze. River and Sarah were much better off without him."

"I wasn't," Luke said as he appeared suddenly at the back door of the kitchen.

Pastor Sebastian grabbed Claire and pressed a blade to her throat. He must have had it behind his back, because she hadn't seen it. But she felt it now, the sharp point digging into her skin, stinging as it drew blood.

Luke had arrived in time, but she still wasn't sure that he would be able to save her. Or if he would just wind up watching a man he loved murder someone.

Luke had seen some horrible things in his life, but this . . . he couldn't even wrap his mind around what he was seeing now. He was so stunned that he wasn't sure what to do.

Mary screamed, and Luke put one hand on her arm, pulling her out the door he'd left open behind him. "Peter!" she yelled. "Don't hurt her. Don't hurt Claire."

"I don't want to," Peter said.

"No, you don't want to hurt her," Luke said. "Let Claire go, and we'll talk about this, Dad."

Peter shook his head. "No. Like I told Claire, there are some people that it just doesn't pay to preach to. They either don't want to listen, or they're just too evil to save."

Was he talking about himself or Claire? But Claire was one of the good ones.

Why hadn't Luke seen what Jackson had? The judgment, the secrecy.

"You're not evil," Luke said even as disgust churned in his stomach like bile. "You're a good man."

Peter sighed. "I had good intentions. I want to protect the people I love. I protected Claire."

"And now you're hurting her," Luke said. "She's bleeding. You need to let her go."

But instead, the pastor pushed the blade a little deeper into her skin. And Luke raised the gun he'd been holding behind his back. "You need to drop the knife."

"You need to make a choice," Pastor Sebastian said. "You

need to decide which one of us has done more good. I saved people. Claire lets them go back to their abusive homes. That's why I had to kill the Buczynskis, too. They lied about Tyler. And they didn't deserve kids. It wasn't fair that people like Tammy and Claire's mother could have kids and my sweet Mary and I were never blessed with our own."

Luke had thought that he was their own. That they'd loved him like a son. But now he didn't know what was true besides the fact that Claire was in mortal danger.

"Put down the knife."

"No, Luke. You need to decide."

"I'm not the judge or the executioner," Luke said. "And you shouldn't have been, either."

"I have no problem killing."

And Luke knew that his time had run out. He had to pull the trigger and kill his father, or Claire was going to be killed right in front of him.

Chapter 26

Noah knew he had no choice. And he swung the shovel he'd picked up on his way in the front door. The knife dropped from the older man's hand, and then he dropped to the floor.

Mrs. Sebastian screamed. Luke let out a cry, too, before he holstered the weapon he'd nearly fired.

And Claire wobbled back. Noah caught her in his arms, then he spun her around and pressed his hand over the wound on her throat. "Call 9-1-1!" he yelled. The wound wasn't gushing, but he didn't know how deep it was.

While he'd knocked the old man out, he might not have acted fast enough. And neither had Luke.

"I'm okay," Claire said, as she covered his hand with hers. "I'm okay."

But she wasn't. Even if the physical wound wasn't that deep, she was still going to need stitches to close it. And the other wound, the emotional one—he wasn't sure that would ever heal.

She'd loved and trusted Pastor Sebastian just like Luke had, and he'd wound up being the most dangerous person in their lives. Noah understood how messed up it was when you discovered the people you love are evil. Luke hadn't wanted to believe what they'd figured out in the attic; that was why Noah had come back with him. And Luke had let him, because he hadn't been able to believe that Pastor Sebastian was a killer.

But then they'd heard him talking to Claire.

Luke had gone around to the back while Noah had grabbed the shovel and slipped inside the front door. Noah was supposed to have waited in the SUV until backup arrived.

But he hadn't wanted to lose Claire.

She would probably leave after this, though. And he wouldn't blame her if she did. There was nothing for her in Gold Creek but bad memories and tragedies.

And him . . .

If she wanted him . . .

River was stunned. Just like everyone else in Gold Creek, she had loved and respected the Sebastians. But no one had loved or respected them more than Luke had. Hours after the arrest of Pastor Sebastian, he finally walked into the lobby of the funeral home where she, Jackson, and Sarah waited for him. She jumped up and ran to him, closing her arms around his tense body. "I'm so sorry. I'm so, so sorry."

He pulled back, and tears streamed down his face. "I'm the one who's sorry," he said. "How did I not know? How did I put the people I love in danger?" He reached out then and grabbed Jackson's shoulder. "You were alone with him so much. Your dad trusted me."

"Because you're a good man, Luke," Jackson said. "And everybody thought that Pastor Sebastian was, too. You weren't the only person who was wrong about him."

"You weren't," River said, her voice cracking. "Everybody loved him, trusted him. You had no way of knowing."

He pressed his hand over his eyes, as if trying to stem the

tears that continued to fall. "But I lost my brother." He drew in a breath. "You lost the man you loved and Sarah, you lost your father."

Sarah squeezed in between Luke and River and hugged her uncle. "And none of that is your fault, Uncle Luke. None of this is your fault."

And finally the tears stopped, and the tension drained from Luke's body along with a ragged sigh.

"You couldn't have known," Sarah said. "Nobody knew."

"Claire figured it out," Luke said. "And even Noah did before I did."

"Well, they're freaks," Sarah said, but she laughed. "In a good way. Freaks like I am."

And then Luke laughed, too. "They're smart."

"They're cynical," Jackson said. "And I thought I was, too, but I had no idea, man. I had no idea." He sucked in a breath then. "Did Miss Mary know?"

Luke shrugged. "I don't think so. At least she wasn't in on it. She was horrified. And after . . . Well, she's at the hospital yet. They're going to keep her for seventy-two hours."

"And Claire?" River asked. "Is she okay? Noah said she was hurt." But he hadn't gone to the hospital with her. Instead he'd come back here, and he was out in the cemetery, despite how dark it was, walking.

"She's fine. Shook up, like me."

He was more than shook up; he was devastated.

"We're going up to fill in Toby and Gigi," Sarah said, as she grabbed Jackson's hand and tugged him toward the stairs.

Once they were out of view, River kissed Luke. "I am falling for you," she said. "I hope you know that. And I hope you're okay with that."

"Michael . . ."

"Michael is gone," she said. "And if he had lived, we probably wouldn't have lasted. We were kids. And he was a good friend to me when I needed one. But you and I, Luke, we have something that could last."

"Mutual tragedy."

She laughed. "That, too."

Then he kissed her back. "I'm falling for you, too, River."

Claire found him in the moonlight, standing near the grave digger's grave. Bags of sand were walled up behind it, as if holding back the swamp. And he stood over the grave as if to protect it as that man had once protected him.

She held a mum in her arms. And when he turned toward her, he pointed at it. "Did you bring that for your mother's grave?" he asked.

She shook her head and sat it down next to Lyle McGinty's headstone. "For him. And for you."

"For me?"

"You saved my life," she said.

"We've even, then," he said, his teeth gleaming in the moonlight as he grinned. "You saved my life, too."

She smiled back at him. "I can't believe you whacked him with that shovel."

"Well, he and I are even, too, now," he said. "Because I have a feeling that's what he whacked me with in the maintenance building."

"Fortunately, it didn't do the damage to your head that he did to the others." When they'd taken her recorder and her report, the state police had confirmed finding more bodies.

Noah pointed down at the grave. "I have a feeling that Lyle might have tried to save me more than once, that he might have been in the maintenance building that day. Is that weird?"

She smiled. "No. I could imagine him looking out for you the way you look out for this place that you both love."

"I think he was leading everyone to where those bodies

were," he said. "That's why people saw him out here so many times."

"People?"

"I have," Noah said. "I've seen him more than once. Did you ever?"

She tilted her head and remembered that night so long ago. "You know, I might have."

"So you don't think I'm crazy?" he asked.

"No, I think you're pretty great."

"I think you are, too," he said. "But I'm worried that you're not going to stick around Gold Creek, not after all that's happened."

"Bad stuff happens everywhere," Claire said. "But here . . ." She reached out and pressed her palm to his chest, over his madly pounding heart. "There's more good than bad."

He leaned down then, and finally he kissed her. And all the feelings Claire had denied so long came alive inside her. She closed her eyes and kissed him back.

After a long while, he lifted his head from hers. Claire stepped back, and as she opened her eyes, she noticed a light moving across the grass mixed in with the mist. It was the wavering light of a lantern.

"You see it, too," Noah murmured.

She nodded. Then she heard the scrape of a shovel.

"And you hear it?"

She nodded again.

And then a whistle rang out like the melody of a sweet song.

That wasn't part of the legend. Nobody had reported hearing that before. Even Noah looked surprised, but then he grinned.

The grave digger was happy.

Visit our website at
KensingtonBooks.com
to sign up for our newsletters, read
more from your favorite authors, see
books by series, view reading group
guides, and more!

Become a Part of Our
Between the Chapters Book Club
Community and Join the Conversation

Submit your book review for a chance to win exclusive
Between the Chapters swag you can't get anywhere else!
https://www.kensingtonbooks.com/pages/review/